# She felt no fear

Jenny realized she was not alone in the attic, but she knew the presence behind her was either the spirit of Patience Ellsworth or the living presence of the dead woman's nephew, Stephen.

Jenny turned. Stephen was standing at the top of the stairs. He looked so handsome in his uniform.

"How incredible, finding you here," he said.

"Why?"

"Because one of the things I remembered most poignantly was you standing in front of that very window, looking out. I stood behind you and wanted so much to touch you."

Very deliberately Jenny turned and faced the window. She heard his footsteps crossing the wooden floor.

Yes, this was how it was. He had been standing behind her that night, and she had wondered how it would feel to step backward into the circle of his arms. Stephen's arms came around her waist as she knew they would.

"Oh, Jenny," he said. "This is the first peace I've know_____ ____ ___ long time."

D1374094

## ABOUT THE AUTHOR

As the daughter of an army officer, Indiana-born Anne Henry moved frequently during her childhood. Now she makes her home in Oklahoma, where she edits alumni publications for the University of Oklahoma. Anne is the mother of three grown children.

## Books by Anne Henry

HARLEQUIN AMERICAN ROMANCE

Don't miss any of our special offers. Write to us at the following address for information on our newest releases.

Harlequin Reader Service
901 Fuhrmann Blvd., P.O. Box 1397, Buffalo, NY 14240
Canadian address: P.O. Box 603,
Fort Erie, Ont. L2A 5X3

# A Colonel for Jenny
## Anne Henry

# Harlequin Books

TORONTO • NEW YORK • LONDON
AMSTERDAM • PARIS • SYDNEY • HAMBURG
STOCKHOLM • ATHENS • TOKYO • MILAN

In memory of my brother Bill

Published June 1988

First printing April 1988

ISBN 0-373-16252-9

# Chapter One

Sleet. Not again, Jenny thought as the rain on her car window began turning to ice. One ice storm a winter was quite enough, and this would make three if the icy precipitation continued. She'd better make her visit to the new house a quick one, Jenny decided, and get home before driving became hazardous.

She turned her Chevy off Hefner Road onto Lakeside Drive. The traffic thinned, and she increased her speed. After a mile or so, she could see the distinctive dormer windows through leafless treetops.

Graystone. The bronze nameplate on the brick pillar was almost covered with winter-barren ivy vines. As many times as she had driven by the house over the years, she had never noticed the name before. A dignified name for a dignified home. Jenny approved.

The drive curved over a small hill before looping its way around an oval-shaped lawn edged with boxwood.

The sleet intensified just as Jenny got out of the car. She put her briefcase over her head and made a dash for the entryway of the stone house.

As she fumbled with the unfamiliar key and lock, tiny pieces of ice cut at her hands and legs. And to think the sun had been shining when she'd left for work this morning. That was Oklahoma's changeable weather for you. Will Rogers had once said that if you didn't like the weather in Oklahoma, you should wait a minute. Well, she didn't like this stuff one bit, but she had the feeling that waiting a minute wasn't going to change it.

The right side of the ornate double doors swung open, and Jenny hurried inside.

It wasn't much warmer in here than outside, but at least there was no sleet. Was that stuff predicted, Jenny wondered, as she rubbed her hands together and stamped her feet on the marble floor. She hadn't paid any attention to weather reports on last night's news—a mistake this time of year in Oklahoma—and she had no idea that a winter storm was on its way. If she'd known, she would have worn a warmer coat, as well as gloves and boots. And she might have waited until another day to visit this house, although she was terribly anxious to see the inside of the stately dwelling after so many years of admiring it at a distance.

When the new owner of the house engaged her services through his attorney, Jenny was delighted. She had been occupied with another job at the time, and although she had agreed to take the assignment, today was the first day she had met with the attorney, Frank Jolly.

Jolly—not an apt name for the rather dour little man who had escorted her into his paneled office earlier that afternoon.

"No one is living in the house," Mr. Jolly had informed her. "My client, Stephen Carmichael, took possession of the house in October but only stayed for a few weeks before leaving on an extended trip. He read an article about your service in the newspaper, and he asked that I engage you to research the house during his absence."

The attorney explained that the abstract on the house would be available to Jenny at his office. And based on her fine references, which he had thoroughly checked, Jolly was willing to allow her access to the interior of the house for any clues it offered, and had given her a set of keys.

"The utilities are off in the house," he said. "If you plan to spend much time there, let me know and I'll have them turned on."

Late as it was, Jenny decided to brave the rush-hour traffic and drive out to the house before she hurried home to prepare dinner for her sons. Dinner wouldn't take long. She had a casserole ready to put in the oven. And if she wasn't at home when Barry and Joe arrived, they'd make themselves comfortable. Of course, they'd probably eat the brownies she'd made for dessert, but in all their nineteen years, she'd never once known her twin sons to spoil their appetite for dinner.

Her legs and cheeks stung where the ice had bitten into her flesh, and her hands were red and raw. She really should keep a pair of gloves in her car.

She let out a low "Wow" as she received the full impact of Graystone's entry hall. She put her briefcase and purse down on a large glass-topped pedestal table that stood in the center of the spacious hall and turned slowly around to take it all in. Double branches of a free-standing staircase curved their way upward on either side of the room, crossing at a large landing that was dominated by a magnificent leaded-glass window, which matched the leaded-glass French doors below. From the landing, the upper branches of the staircase connected to opposite sides of the second floor's open gallery. The result was a graceful, curving X that was dramatic and beautiful.

And overhead, like a giant kaleidoscope, a round stained-glass skylight formed the ceiling above an immense brass and crystal chandelier.

The heavy mahogany woodwork in the hallway reminded her of that in the historic Skirvin Hotel in downtown Oklahoma City, but she'd wager that the skylight and the crossing staircase were unique in the city.

Jenny had never seen a room quite like it. She could hardly wait to see the skylight with sunshine pouring through it. The windows and the skylight were works of art, the staircase an architectural masterpiece.

The house was of the same vintage as those built by the oil barons in the Heritage Hills section during the glory days of Oklahoma City's colorful history. But this house had been set apart, built farther north on a tract of land that was now being surrounded by newer homes—some quite expensive but none with the charm of the old stone house built during the city's heyday.

The mansion had been occupied by the elderly Ellsworth sisters for as long as Jenny could remember. She had read stories about them in the newspapers. Former belles who never married, the sisters had stayed on with their widowed father until his death in the 1940s. Then they continued to live together at Graystone until Miss Patience died about ten years ago and Miss Grace followed just last year at age ninety-four.

Now Graystone had been purchased by someone named Carmichael. Stephen C. Carmichael, his attorney had signed on the agreement with Jenny. And like so many owners of old houses, Mr. Carmichael wanted to know Graystone's history. That's where Jenny came in as the founder and owner of Home Researchers, Inc. She filled in the blank spots.

The house was empty now. No doubt about that. It was dark and smelled closed up—musty. It had the heavy chill of a house unheated for a long time.

Jenny tried the light switch. Nothing, of course. Mr. Jolly had said the utilities were turned off.

Well, if she hurried, there was still enough light from the windows to get some idea of the Graystone layout.

She shivered against the chill and pulled her lightweight coat more tightly around her body. The sound of the sleet against the windows was ominous. Maybe she should call Barry and Joe and tell them to forgo their usual Wednesday night dinner with her and come another night instead.

She found a telephone extension in the study, but it was dead, either because of the storm or disconnected like the other utilities.

Jenny began a quick walk through the old house. She would come back another day to begin taking pictures and making sketches.

Concentrating on architectural detail, she noted fireplaces, door and window frames, stairway balustrades, ceiling moldings, searching for clues as to the house's designer.

Even in her haste, she could not help but notice the furnishings, which were predominantly heavy, period antiques. In spite of the drama of the architecture, the house had a bit of old-lady fussy about its furnishings and decoration. Jenny wondered if the house had been purchased furnished. She speculated that some of the Oriental art work and chests might have been added by the new owner.

The living room was overfurnished with stiff, formal pieces. At the windows were brocade draperies edged with a deep fringe.

The formal dining room had a mirrored ceiling, outlined by a deep, scalloped molding. The opposite ends of the room held matching marble fireplaces. The Hepplewhite chairs and table were worthy of a museum.

As Jenny walked through the house, admiring room after room, she wondered where Carmichael planned to kick off his shoes and put up his feet to read the newspaper. Where would he feel comfortable drinking beer and watching Monday night football? As a matter of fact, where was the television? The pair of wing chairs in the study had no ottomans. There was no rack for magazines. No letter trays or pencil holders cluttered the top of the desk. The attorney had indicated that Carmichael had not been very long in residence. Perhaps he hadn't had time to personalize the house and make it his own. Even the sitting area of the master bedroom looked uncomfortable. The high-backed love seat in front of the fireplace was not meant for lounging. If there was a television in this room, it was hidden away in a cupboard.

Over the mantel in the bedroom was a painting of an Oriental woman and a little girl, who was a miniature of the woman. Unlike other paintings in the house, it was not framed in heavy gilt. Its frame was brass, and contemporary in style. Jenny stared at the painting. The woman and child were exquisite. Had the woman been responsible for the Oriental touches in the house? Jenny wondered.

Nowhere in the house, however, was there any indication that a woman was in residence. Or a child.

The bed in the master bedroom was one of the few pieces of furniture in the entire house that looked as if it had been purchased with comfort in mind. It was low and king-size with an abundance of colorful pillows stacked up against its teak headboard. A large Charles Russel print of a cowboy being bucked from his horse hung over the bed in a stark wooden frame. A fantastic Navaho rug occupied the space beside the bed, and the stack of books on the bedside table included authors Stephen King, Ken Follet, Herman Wouk and James Joyce. At least in the bedroom, Stephen C. Carmichael had left his mark, Jenny decided as she went to look at the other rooms opening off the spacious upstairs gallery.

Another bedroom housed body-building equipment. The other three rooms were only partially furnished and appeared to be unoccupied.

Jenny looked out a second-floor window at the end of the hallway. Surely the boys wouldn't drive up from Norman in that sleet, and she'd best get herself on home before the streets became impassable.

She hurried back downstairs and picked up her briefcase and purse. Giving the hallway one last look, she went through a quick mental checklist. No lights to turn off. No heat to turn off. She hadn't opened any outside doors except this one. The ice bit at her legs as she locked the front door after her.

Jenny scooted under the steering wheel of her Chevy and headed down the driveway.

Damn, it was slick.

Her tires spun furiously as her car inched forward. She hoped the traction would be better out on the street where the traffic would have melted the ice—if she could get to the street.

She felt as though she were driving on a sheet of glass. The car refused to go up the slight incline into the curve of the drive. She backed up and got a running start. Still no luck. She backed up again, and this time she was more forceful with the accelerator.

The car began to slide sideways. Almost before Jenny realized what was happening, the rear tires had slid off the driveway. She spun them for a while, then got out and pulled over some of the small branches that littered the ground and put them under the rear tires to increase the traction. The high-heeled pumps she'd worn in honor of her visit to the attorney's office were hardly appropriate footwear for such activity, and her feet were wet and freezing. Her ungloved hands were numb with cold by the time she was ready to try the hill once again. She started the motor. "Come on, car. You can do it." The tires grabbed for a minute, and Jenny dared hope, but they began their futile spinning again, the car once again sliding backwards.

The sleeting rain was increasing, cutting visibility to next to nothing. The trees and the car were rapidly becoming encased in a coating of solid ice.

Jenny sat with her frozen hands on the steering wheel for a while, considering her options. If only Barry and Joe were here with her. A push from a couple of strong lads was all she needed. There were lots of houses in the area, but they were part of two yet-to-be-completed housing developments. None of the houses were occupied. She was at least three-quarters of a mile, maybe more, from anyplace that might offer help or a telephone. And she knew better than to take off walking in this storm, especially with high-heeled shoes and no gloves.

If only the telephone worked.

But it didn't.

She'd just have to go back inside and wait out the storm. When this horrible sleet stopped, she'd walk someplace and call for help.

The house was darker. Jenny opened her briefcase and got out a flashlight—one of the tools of her trade. She sometimes needed to check on construction details in unlit attics or cellars.

She headed for the kitchen in search of candles.

Old Mother Hubbard would have been right at home here, she thought ruefully as she looked in the cupboards and pantry. Only a few containers of food. Peas. Tomato sauce. Condiments. A tin of Boston brown bread. A jar of caviar.

She braved the steep basement stairs in search of a lantern. At the bottom she could see some unopened crates and stored lawn furniture, and with the outdoor furniture were some hurricane lamps. Jenny picked up two of them. She also discovered an almost-empty wine cellar. As she tucked one of the few remaining bottles under her arm, she hoped the Italian Burgundy wasn't rare or expensive enough to be missed.

She found a corkscrew in the kitchen. She took the jar of caviar, and in lieu of crackers she opened the can of brown bread. Then she found a wineglass, spoon, plate and cloth napkin.

She tried to make herself at home in the living room. The sofa wasn't worth sitting on, much less stretching out on.

The one in the study was made of leather. Better, but she was so cold.

"Oh, hell," she said out loud. "Forget good manners or propriety or whatever." Jenny decided there was only one place in the house where she could be comfortable and warm for the rest of the night. The bed.

It took her two trips to get the wine and food and the hurricane lamps upstairs. She stared at the empty fireplace. Might as well go all the way, she decided. There was no firewood in the bedroom, so she went back downstairs and looked in the study. No logs. Determined to make a little warmth for herself, Jenny unlocked the kitchen door and went out back to search for a woodpile. She found it behind the garage. Getting her beige coat filthy, she carried an armload of wood into the house and up the dark stairway. Then before she lost courage, she forced herself to brave the cold and ice for a second load. She felt as though she'd never be warm again. She'd probably have frostbitten toes if she didn't get out of these wet shoes and stockings soon.

She made one last trip to the kitchen for matches and newspapers to get the fire started. Her flashlight was a godsend. There was a box of kitchen matches in the pantry and a stack of newspapers under the sink.

Jenny was exhausted by the time she finally had a fire going in the fireplace and the hurricane lamps burning—one on the bedside table, one on the mantel beside the painting of the woman and child. The windows were completely covered with ice and still the sleet came, beating out its rapid tattoo against the glass. The entire city would be immobilized. Snow could be dealt with, but when the ice started, everything came to a standstill.

She replaced her wet footwear with a pair of socks from the bureau then looked around the room she was borrowing for the night as an uninvited guest. Stephen Carmichael's bedroom. Jenny tried to remember how long it had been since she'd last slept in a man's bedroom.

Three years. Lorenzo's.

Jenny shook her head. No more thoughts of Lorenzo. It was her New Year's resolution. It had also been her New Year's resolution last year. Having her boys leave home last fall for college hadn't helped. Actually she suffered as much now from the empty-nest syndrome and generalized loneliness than from painful memories of Lorenzo, but she was doing better. Yes, definitely better.

But even as she congratulated herself, she felt the old feeling pushing against her chest. Depression, creeping up on her and trying to suffocate her.

"Away," she said out loud. "No more. Having no man at all was better than having a jerk, and she was strong enough to cope with loneliness. She'd think about Stephen Carmichael instead. Yes. That would be nice. Carmichael was probably eighty and crochety, but tonight she'd make him young and charming. No—make that *youthful* and charming. She was very aware these days that some men were too young for her. A strange feeling. Maybe she wouldn't feel that way if her sons weren't grown. But she'd start to admire a man—*really* admire a man—and then think, *My god, he's only a few years older than my sons!*

So Mr. Carmichael couldn't be young. He'd have to be between thirty-five and fifty. Forty-three or four would be nice, and he would be gallant and kiss her hand.

No, on second thought, Lorenzo had done that. Her Mr. Carmichael wouldn't be a hand kisser. He would be a great cook and go downstairs to figure out miraculously a way to fix her a wonderfully filling gourmet meal with the peas and tomato sauce. He would set a table in front of the fire with crystal and silver, and he would tell her that green eyes were his favorite, that he

greatly admired women who made their own way in the
world. He would be sincere. Yes, that was the most important thing—that he be sincere.

"Since I'll be sleeping in your bed," she said aloud to
the imaginary Mr. Carmichael, "I think we should be on
a first-name basis. So, *Stephen*, if you don't mind, I'll
pour a glass of your wine and help myself to your caviar. I wish there was a picture of you. At least I'd like to
know what my host looks like."

Jenny pushed the settee closer to the fire. She pulled
the comforter from the bed and wrapped it around her
shivering body and tried to make herself comfortable
before continuing her one-sided dialogue.

"I think I'd like you to have some gray hair so I won't
have to worry if I've missed a few gray hairs in my last
plucking session. And you probably don't have a paunch
if you use that exercise equipment down the hall, so let's
give you a fantastic body. You're attractive, but not a
show stopper. Beautiful men are so conceited, and I hate
it when a man's better looking than I am. Also, you're a
decent sort of guy, in spite of all your money and big
house. And you definitely prefer mature women. No
way in a million years would you want to date a woman
half your age. Right? A man like you wants his women
friends to remember Audrey Hepburn and Gary
Cooper."

She poured herself a glass of wine, and since she'd
forgotten to bring a knife to slice the bread, she spooned
hunks of it out of the can and spread on the caviar. She
decided that caviar on canned bread wasn't so bad when
one was starving, but it just took the edge off her hunger. As an appetizer, it was fine, but now she was ready
for the main course and there was none.

Jenny thought of the wonderful chicken tetrazzini she had made for tonight's dinner. And the French bread was garlic buttered and wrapped in foil ready to pop into the oven. The greens were washed, stored in plastic bags and ready to be tossed in a salad. And those brownies! Jenny made the most fantastic brownies, even if she did say so herself. They were moist and nutty and iced with rich chocolate. "Chocolate." She said the word out loud. Even its sound was rich.

*Stop thinking about your stomach, Jenny,* she told herself. She could always go downstairs and open the can of peas, but canned peas hardly seemed worth the trouble considering how cold it was. Even with the fire, this room was far from cozy. She spooned some more caviar out of the jar.

The wine was good, *really* good after the inexpensive jug wine she usually bought for herself and the few guests she entertained in her apartment.

She refilled her glass and looked up at the woman in the painting. She seemed almost alive in the flickering candlelight, her dark eyes looking directly at Jenny. The portrait had been painted eight years ago, according to the date under the artist's signature. The little girl, standing beside the seated woman, looked about five or six.

"And who might you be, lovely lady?" Jenny asked. "I think if you were still in Stephen's life, there'd be some female belongings in this house. But if you'd left him, would he still have your picture in his bedroom? Perhaps, but not likely. Are you dead? I hope not. And what about your sweet little girl? She'd be a teenager by now. Is she with you? I feel a sadness about your picture being here in this room. It makes the house seem even lonelier—and our friend Stephen even more alone.

Even my little apartment seems empty with my boys away at college. Living in a big house like this all by myself would really depress me.''

The woman in the picture was more than beautiful, Jenny decided. More than exotic. She was one of the most fantastic-looking women Jenny had ever seen portrayed. Had the artist enhanced her appearance, or had the woman really looked like that? *Good grief, I'm jealous,* Jenny realized. Stephen had another woman's picture in his bedroom. Jenny smiled at herself. What a silly mood she was in.

She decided it was time to seek the warmth of the bed. The room was less cold now but still far from warm. She put her wine and food on the bedside table and propped herself up against the headboard with the comforter tucked around her body. She supposed caviar on canned brown bread would be considered awful by purists, especially since the bread had raisins and nuts in it, but the combination tasted better with each bite.

She wondered if there was a television hidden away behind the doors of the handsome Queen Anne highboy. Then she laughed at herself. It wouldn't work if there was. And there wasn't enough light to read one of Stephen's books. It was going to be a long evening, but if she could get warm enough, maybe she could catch up on her sleep.

''You have any suggestions for how to pass the time, Stephen?'' Jenny asked. ''A sing-along? Charades? Or shall we settle for wine and repartee?''

She took another sip of wine. Yes, she'd definitely get a good night's sleep tonight. Stephen wasn't drinking his fair share of this bottle.

''Do you have a lady friend other than the lady in the picture, Stephen?'' she said, continuing her one-sided conversation. "And what sort of man are you any-way?"

Jenny pondered this. She already knew some things about him. Stephen liked Western art, and perhaps also Oriental art. He had good taste in old homes, having chosen a very classy one to buy. There were no ashtrays in the bedroom, so he probably didn't smoke. His attorney was a partner in a prestigious law firm. His reading tastes were reflected in the books on the bedside table. He at least cared enough about physical fitness to buy exercise equipment. Not much to know about a man in whose bed she was going to spend the night.

The fire had finally taken some of the chill out of the room, and Jenny decided she wouldn't freeze if she got up and did a bit of sleuthing.

She carried one of the hurricane lamps into the dressing room-bath area off the master bedroom. The bathroom had an old-fashioned bathtub, but a large shower stall looked as though it was a recent addition. One of two closet alcoves was empty, the other was hung with only a dozen or so garments. Either Stephen hadn't finished moving in or he had another home somewhere else.

Staring at herself in the mirror, she saw a disheveled woman holding a candle-powered lamp. A mirror on the other side of the room reflected the back view of her and the image from the other mirror. In the flickering candlelight, the mirrors reflected themselves back and forth into infinity.

She leaned closer to the mirror, admiring the way she looked in the candlelight. Her brown hair looked almost black. Pinpoints of flame shone from her eyes. Her skin took on a golden glow. It was a softer, younger woman than the woman who usually looked back at her. There was an unhurried look about this woman. Yes, that was nice. Her son Joe used to accuse her of even hurrying down the hall to go to bed at night. "What's your rush, Mom?" he'd ask. But she always hurried. There was so much to do—especially in the years since Lewis had left them. With two boys to raise, she had been forced to shoulder a great deal of responsibility. She hurried to get things done, to earn money, to be a good mother, to be a good teacher, to get enough sleep to get through the next busy day.

But tonight, there was no place to hurry to and nothing that needed doing. Jenny realized with a start that she was enjoying herself. The thought made her giggle. How silly, but it was true. She was having a good time in Stephen's house.

Jenny lifted the lamp in tribute to her reflected self. "I hereby give you permission to drink the whole damned bottle and be as silly as you want. Who's to know? Right?"

Feeling a bit like a voyeur, she fingered the fabric of Stephen's two sport coats. One was cashmere, the other was Harris tweed. Three dress shirts of silky cotton and two pairs of slacks hung beside them. Jenny took a pair of gray flannel slacks and held them up in front of her. Long legs. There were a couple of pairs of jeans and a few plaid sports shirts. A pair of loafers, expensive dress shoes and well-worn athletic shoes sat in a row on the floor, but no cowboy boots. The man was probably a newcomer to Oklahoma, Jenny decided. Most men in the state owned some sort of cowboy boots whether they were five-hundred-dollar hippopotamus hide purchased at Tener's high-dollar Western wear store or fifty-dollar work boots purchased at Lambert's, a store that served the working cowboys who brought their livestock to the nearby stockyards.

Jenny was intrigued with the idea of meeting a man first through his personal possessions. She began to embellish on her mental image of Stephen Carmichael. Judging from his clothing, he was lean and somewhat above average in height. His shoes were about ten and a half or eleven—average.

A hair dryer on the lavatory vanity indicated a contemporary haircut. A tray held aftershave among the assorted toilet articles, but no cologne.

Jenny smelled the aftershave. Clean and pungent. Nice.

Stephen was apparently a lean, elegant man who kept himself in shape. A man who did not display many mementos from his past. A man of some means who had bought a beautiful old house. A man who lived alone.

The wine was making her feel light-headed. She giggled again. "I think I'll just go to bed now, Stephen. I'd like to feel all warm and snug in your bed."

She pulled back the covers to reveal burgundy-colored sheets trimmed with gray piping. How classy.

"How many women have slept in this bed, Stephen?" she asked as she crawled between the sheets. "Are you the sort of man who makes one woman happy or lots of women miserable?"

The sheets were cold. She curled her body and tucked her hands between her knees, waiting for her body heat to warm the bed.

Jenny felt very strange being here like this. There was something intimate about being in Stephen Carmichael's bed even if he weren't here with her.

Was she ever going to feel stupid if he did turn out to be eighty and crotchety.

She closed her eyes and planned their first meeting—hers and Stephen's. She would have Graystone's history ready, carefully prepared and presented in a leather-bound book. She hoped the house had an interesting history since she'd like Stephen to be impressed. He would ask her lots of questions and would be totally fascinated by the history she had compiled. Then he'd inquire if they could continue their discussion over dinner.

Jenny spent a long time mentally going through a list of all the restaurants in Oklahoma City, trying to decide which one she and Stephen would go to. Would it be elegant like the Eagle's Nest high above the city on the top floor of an office building or a more informal place such as Flip's where she and other teachers sometimes went for a T.G.I.F. beer or glass of wine. Jenny opted for the Eagle's Nest even though her one previous visit there had been with Lorenzo. She was over Lorenzo, and she decided that the owner of Graystone would prefer elegant over informal.

Then Jenny wiled away some pleasant minutes deciding what she would be wearing. Her wardrobe was schoolteacher meager, so she had no trouble recalling each outfit in her closet. She mentally tried on each garment and discarded it. Finally she decided on her blue suit. It had a wonderfully provocative slit in the skirt that she had basted closed when she wore the suit to the state teachers' convention. It looked nice with her white beaded sweater. She could take the jacket off in the restaurant and look dressier.

Then her hair. Jenny had been debating about having it cut. She'd always worn it shoulder length before but had been wondering of late if a short cut wouldn't be more youthful. She'd been worrying more about what looked youthful and what didn't. Maybe it came with having two sons in college. Maybe it was being less than two years short of the big four-zero.

Barry said she was a good-looking woman "for her age group." Jenny had thrown a pillow at him.

She used to take her looks for granted. She wasn't beautiful, but she was attractive enough for general purposes. Some people told her she had grown more attractive with age. It was hard for her to be objective, however. After her husband left, her self-esteem sank to zero, and she hadn't felt pretty or worthy in any way.

Then her brief fling with Lorenzo, the dashing Italian, had convinced her that she was a beautiful and desirable woman. But sincerity wasn't his long suit, and he left, too, and never came back.

Yet, here she was again weaving fantasies about another man. Hope does spring eternal apparently. Were other women like her, Jenny wondered. In spite of past pain, were all women searching for the perfect man—the sincere, loving man who would never hurt them.

She snuggled into Stephen's down pillow and pulled the comforter up around her shoulders. She was a little tipsy with the wine. Maybe even very tipsy. Her fantasies were becoming more involved, but sleep was very close.

She knew she would fall asleep in a pair of imaginary arms belonging to a fantasy man named Stephen. She hadn't allowed herself to do that for a long time. Usually, she would read or watch television until sleep came, avoiding those soft minutes between sleep and wakefulness when yearning rose in her breast and she was forced to admit she was tired of being alone, that she ached with loneliness.

She didn't feel alone now. She felt her lips curve in a smile. "Silly, silly Jenny," she said to herself. "You haven't changed much since you were a girl and believed that someday your prince would come."

Jenny's eyes were closed. The imaginary arms were there now. Strong arms. Loving arms.

She felt warm and safe and loved. It didn't seem silly at all. It could happen. Someday her prince *would* come, and he would be sincere.

Just as she went to sleep, the word slipped from her lips.

"Stephen."

STEPHEN CARMICHAEL opened the door to his Washington, D.C., apartment, dumped his suitcase in the entry hall and headed for the kitchen without bothering to turn on the lights in the living room. There was nothing in the room he wanted to see. Anything special that he owned, he had moved to the house in Oklahoma City. He regretted that now.

The apartment felt even less like a home than it had before, and the house he had inherited in Oklahoma seemed just a harebrained fantasy. God, had he gotten carried away on that one. The very word *home* filled him with such yearning, but he had discovered that a big house full of stuff did not make a home.

Stephen loosened his necktie as he scanned the inside of the refrigerator. Bachelor fare. Beer. Moldy cheese. A couple of shriveled apples. Ketchup. Eggs.

He opened a beer and pulled a loaf of bread out of the freezing compartment, then thawed a couple of slices in the microwave before spreading them with the remainder of a jar of dried-out peanut butter. He added a layer of butter to make it more palatable and wished for jelly.

He didn't bother to sit down, consuming the sandwich leaning against the counter. He swigged down the beer and tossed the can in the trash. At least he wouldn't starve before reporting to the general in the morning over breakfast.

A second beer in his hand, Stephen picked up the suitcase and made his way down the long hallway, past two closed doors, to the open door of his bedroom. The telltale square of lighter wallpaper revealed where a picture had recently hung over the bureau. Stephen had mixed feelings about it being gone.

He picked up a small framed photograph of a little girl from his bedside table. Mindy. She used to ride her tricycle up and down the hallway. She used to run its length to leap into his arms when he came home from a trip.

Automatically, Stephen began removing the brass from his uniform collar. Eagles, for over a year now. A full colonel. It hadn't been the thrill he had once thought it would be.

Later, his head propped up on two pillows, Stephen stared into the darkness, exhausted yet wide awake. An aura of melancholy hung about him still. He had thought that telling the lawyer to draw up the necessary papers might change things, that with the decision made, he would be able to get on with his life. But the old pull was still there. If only he really knew what had happened maybe he could let go.

And if he let go, what would happen? he wondered.

He didn't know, but for the first time in years, he had a sense that it might be something nice. Strange. Maybe it was the beer.

He pulled one of the pillows from behind his head and clutched it against his chest. Closing his eyes, he willed his body to relax. His mind drifted over the events of his journey, plans for the forthcoming week, the papers he would sign that were supposed to change his life. And he thought of the house in Oklahoma City.

Sleep was reaching out to him. He welcomed the soft, gray fog wrapping its arms about him. It felt like a caress.

# Chapter Two

"Where have you been?" Joe's voice asked as soon as Jenny picked up the telephone. "Barry and I were beginning to get worried. We figured you were stranded someplace by all the ice but wondered why you didn't call."

"I was looking over a new research job," Jenny explained. She tossed her purse onto the coffee table and sank into the lumpy sofa. "My car slid off the driveway, and I ended up staying in a mysterious old mansion for the night. The phone was even disconnected, and I couldn't call for help. But everything's fine now—or will be when I get some of my more burly students to push my car out of a ditch. I'm glad you two didn't try to drive up last night. Everything is still like a sheet of ice."

"In Norman, too. Classes were canceled, and kids are skating on the South Oval. We couldn't have come anyway. The truck's transmission is out. We aren't going anyplace anytime soon, I'm afraid. How's your bank account?"

"Virtually non-existent," Jenny said as she kicked off her shoes and started massaging some life back into her frozen toes. "I need to do this new job fast and replenish it. I wish there were two of me. How much does a transmission cost?''

"A couple hundred, I guess. Maybe we can find a mechanic who won't charge too much. Sorry, Mom, but the truck *is* on its second hundred thousand miles, and they don't last forever. Maybe Barry and I can earn enough this summer to trade it in for a newer one. But for now, we can get around the campus on foot, but I guess we won't be coming home until the truck is fixed. Why don't you come down here and see us as soon as this weather lets up? We can eat nachos at Brother's and listen to the jazz. And don't forget, we've got tickets to the OU-Oklahoma State basketball game. That will be a blast. You can meet Linda.''

"Who's Linda?''

"Barry's new lady love.''

"What happened to Debbie?''

"She transferred to SMU at semester. When he came back from semester break and discovered she'd moved out of her dorm room, his heart was broken.''

"Obviously. He must have grieved for days. How'd he meet Linda?''

"She'd moved into Debbie's room.''

"I see. Well, how's *your* love life?''

"Can't you hear the women beating on the door? It really gets to be a drag.''

"I know what you mean. I'm thinking of hiring a social secretary to screen all my calls. Speaking of social, where's your brother?''

"Down in the lounge. Hang on, I'll get him. He said he wanted to talk to you. Come see us. We need our mommie.''

Two hundred dollars, Jenny thought as she waited for Barry. And tuition was due the first of the month. Her sons' textbooks for the new semester had cost almost three hundred dollars and would have been more if they weren't sharing the same history and philosophy books. Joe needed new glasses, and she couldn't remember the last time either of them had had their teeth checked.

Lewis's child support payments had ended last December on the boys' eighteenth birthday. Jenny had written to Lewis and asked if he wouldn't help out with the boys' college expenses, but he had written back reminding her that his legal responsibility to his sons had ended and that he had "earned the right to greater financial freedom." Lewis now lived part of each year in Colorado. He invited the boys to come up and go skiing with him, but he hadn't offered to pay for their plane tickets.

At times like that, Jenny realized she hadn't completely worked through her bitterness. She hadn't been able to afford a vacation since her divorce eight years ago, other than camping with the boys by one of the state's lakes or overnight excursions with them to Dallas for a visit to the Six Flags Over Texas amusement park. Lewis skied in Colorado while she worked at two jobs and his sons needed new winter coats.

But bitterness no longer dominated her life as it once had. For several years after Lewis left, she had played the role of victim. As long as she was suffering, it proved what a heel the man was. Strange how important that had gotten to be—proving that Lewis was a heel.

But eventually Jenny wearied of proving the point over and over again. She grew tired of being a victim, tired of being unhappy. She had two wonderful sons. She had her job. If Lewis didn't want her, she wasn't going to let the fact ruin her life. Her mother was fond of saying that nothing was worth ruining your life over, and obviously her mother was right. It almost seemed as if one had a moral responsibility to make the most out of the gift of life and not always dwell on its shortcomings.

Barry's voice interrupted her thoughts. "All right, out with it," he said with no preliminaries. "Who did you spend last night with? And don't say you were at home. We called there until the wee, small hours. I hope he's rich and generous. If so, we'll overlook his mean disposition and underworld connections."

"What about his fascination with necks and his tendency to grow fangs when there's a full moon?"

"No problem, as long as he'll loan me his Ferrari."

"How did you do on your chemistry exam?"

"Did I miss a transition in this conversation? I don't remember talking about examinations."

"You didn't do well," Jenny said.

"I did fine. Well, at least I passed, which is more than half the class can say. And I'm learning a lot. I'm learning that I don't want to be a chemist."

"But you already knew that."

"Well, it's reassuring to have one's decisions reinforced by concrete evidence," Barry explained dramatically. "I am ever more certain that I will be an internationally known star of stage and screen."

"My son, the star," Jenny said, feeling herself smile. "How lovely."

"Don't get sarcastic. You will one day be known as 'Barry Bishop's mother.' I'll bet you didn't ask Joe about his calculus exam."

"I know without asking. He made an A. Right? But then, I imagine he studied. I'm thinking about donating you two to one of those studies on twins. Let the experts try to figure out how two brothers born eight minutes apart can be so different.''

"They only want identical twins. Joe and I don't qualify. Can I help it if he got the genes for studying and I got personality? We are what we are and have only our gene pool to blame.''

"Well, Mr. Personality, I suggest you work a little harder swimming across your gene pool and try studying for a change. It's amazing what a difference it makes in one's grades.''

"I stand chastised. I'd better go study.''

"I'll see you at the basketball game, if not sooner. I'm looking forward to meeting Linda.''

"You'll love her. She studies all the time. Send cookies. And money.''

"Cookies, I can manage. I love you both.''

Jenny hung up and leaned her head back against the sofa. It was so quiet in the apartment house without those two characters about. She missed them—a lot. But she'd better get used to it. Her sons would probably never again be back under her roof for any significant period of time. Gregarious Barry had spent most of his semester break visiting college friends in Houston, and both sons were already making plans for next summer. Joe, the more studious of the two, had applied for a summer undergraduate fellowship at a Kansas City research institute, which offered invaluable experience but only a small stipend. And Barry was hoping to get a position with the summer stock company on the OU campus. It paid next to nothing, but it would give him good experience both on stage and behind the scenes with production.

Jenny was proud of her boys. They were nice human beings and each quite handsome in his own way. Dark-haired Barry, with his flashing smile and trim physique, was—in his mother's opinion—show-biz attractive. Joe was heavier, sandy-haired and shy, but with an endearing grin that never failed to turn her heart over. Although the first eleven or twelve years of the boys' lives had been spent in constant combat, the fighting had miraculously ceased one day, and while they still had frequent arguments, they were now best friends. It had been their decision to room together at college. Jenny was pleased.

The boys were growing up and away from her. It took years for Jenny to adjust to their father's leaving, and she had been determined to do a better job adjusting to her sons' departure from her day-to-day life. But since September, it hadn't been easy coming home from work to an empty apartment. And with the boys' jobs and involvement in university life, they came home less on weekends now than in the fall, which was as it should be.

Even the elderly cat had died.

Home Research Inc. helped fill the void and helped Jenny supplement the income from her teaching at Memorial High School. Her small business had done well in its first two years. In fact, she'd cut back to three-quarter time at the high school last fall so she would have sufficient after-school hours for visits to libraries, newspaper morgues, the county court house and historical society archives.

Her job was to find out who designed and built the homes and if any noteworthy craftsmen had a part in the construction. She discovered the background of the original owners and subsequent owners. She searched for references to the property and its owners in the pages of old newspapers. She interviewed longtime residents of the area. She had been able to tell owners about murders, supposed hauntings, celebrities who had once visited in the house. One of Jenny's clients had been thrilled to learn that President Theodore Roosevelt's colorful daughter, Alice, had once stayed overnight in her home. The great tenor Caruso had stayed in another. And Clark Gable in yet another. One couple who had used Jenny's services was titillated with tales of a shocking murder in their attic—a murder as yet unsolved. When she unearthed an actual skeleton, an apparent murder victim, in a hidden room in the cellar of a 1910-vintage Classen Circle home, the resulting publicity in the newspapers and on television had brought her additional clients.

Each new job excited Jenny. Like this elegant new house. It wasn't as large as many of the city's vintage mansions, but she had always admired the lines of its roof, viewed through the trees. She had imagined the days long past when chauffeur-driven Lincoln and Packard town cars deposited their occupants at the mansion's front door for glittering balls or elegant after-concert suppers.

And her evenings over the next weeks wouldn't seem quite so lonely as she compiled her notes and wrote a history of Graystone.

She often wondered what she would have done if she hadn't happened upon this way to supplement her income from teaching school. She had tried to save money for the boys' college during the years she still received child support from Lewis, but there were braces, eye glasses, car payments, car repairs, car insurance. The boys had finally stopped outgrowing their shoes and jeans every other month, but each time Jenny got ahead of her bills, something happened to take her fledgling nest egg.

A few years ago, she had read in a magazine article about a woman who researched the history of old mansions in San Francisco. Jenny's college major was history, and she was well versed in research methodology. The idea intrigued her. Why wouldn't such a business work in Oklahoma City? The city had at least a hundred noteworthy vintage homes, maybe more. She placed a small ad in the newspaper and had her first job in a week.

And since that time, she had worked steadily at her second job. She always had the next job waiting for her before she finished the current one. She'd even had inquiries from home owners in Tulsa and Dallas, and although she had to turn them down for now, it gave her the courage to raise her prices. Maybe she would again. People seemed to want her service, and each project did take a tremendous amount of time. But she enjoyed it. With every job she did, she became more knowledgeable about sources, more efficient about the way she used her time. After the boys were safely out of college, she might try to make Home Researchers a full-time venture, but for now, she needed the security of a salaried job. Strange, Jenny thought as she looked around her far-from-wonderful apartment, how the business that seemed to offer the key to her future was learning about genteel old homes when she herself lived in an ordinary apartment complex.

Her apartment was architecturally unimaginative, and all of her furniture needed either upholstering or refinishing. The Persian rug—a garage sale find—was doing a good job concealing the worn carpet of her living room. And the few good antiques she had inherited from her grandmother offered the only touch of character to the living room and dining room.

Sometimes she wished there were more hours in the day so she could make more money and fix things up a bit—or afford to move someplace nicer. Jenny wondered if the day would ever come when necessities such as transmission repairs on the pickup truck wouldn't be a crisis.

But in spite of money problems, Jenny realized her life was better without Lewis. True, she and her sons were poor, but conflict was gone. Life was more pleasant without an unhappy man under the same roof.

Actually, Jenny had come to feel sorry for Lewis. He had given up his sons' respect for his new life-style. She hoped for his sake the trade had been worth it. She no longer wasted time hoping Lewis was miserable or remorseful, and she didn't miss him anymore. She had learned to accept the new terms of her life and its new responsibilities. She took a great deal of pride in managing as well as she had.

But at times, she felt defeated and tired. Sometimes she fantasized about winning the Publisher's Clearing House Sweepstakes and never having money worries again.

And she fantasized about not being alone. Her marriage was long over. Her parents had moved to the southern part of the state, near the small town of Madill where they had both been raised. And the mothering time of her life was winding down. Hard as it was to believe, her sons were nineteen years old. They weren't her little boys any longer.

STEPHEN CLEARED OFF his desk in preparation for his upcoming trip. He dictated one last letter and made two last phone calls. Then there was just one more item on his agenda. Stephen stared at the notation on his desk calendar, took a deep breath and pushed his chair back from his desk. He would not cancel the appointment this time. It had to be done.

It was a ten-minute walk through a half mile of Pentagon corridors from Stephen's office to the Judge Advocate offices. The sergeant at the front desk took his name and asked him to have a seat.

Stephen thumbed through a dated copy of the military newspaper, *Star and Stripes*, but was unable to concentrate and tossed it back on the coffee table. He rubbed his damp palms on his uniform trousers and tried to relax, but his head hurt and there was a heaviness in his chest.

This was the day he had dreaded would someday come. He felt such a strange mixture of relief, defeat, sadness, indecision. Yes, still indecision. It was as though the filing of a legal paper would change things rather than simply acknowledge in a legal sense what was already so.

The sergeant announced that Major Wadlow would see him now, and Stephen made his way down the hall to the major's office.

"Colonel Carmichael," the military lawyer said with a brisk handshake. "What can I do for you?"

"I guess I'm ready to file those papers you drew up."

Stephen had a list of questions to ask first, then others that occurred to him.

"Colonel, it seems that you still have a lot of uncertainty. Would you like to put this off for a time?"

"No. I've waited long enough. It's time to get on with my life."

The major put the papers in front of Stephen. The sergeant and another attorney came in to serve as witnesses.

Stephen picked up the pen. It was just a legal formality, he reminded himself. The signing did not make Jade dead any more than not signing it made her alive. It meant he was officially giving up the searching and the waiting. He would no longer be married to an absentee wife, no matter what the reason for her disappearance.

Stephen signed.

"I anticipate no problems with this," the major explained. "I'll notify you when the hearing will be held. You'll need to appear."

On his way out of the building, he stopped at a drinking fountain to gulp down some water. He felt ill.

He had set the legal wheels in motion to have his wife declared legally dead. He wondered if she was.

He could have obtained a divorce by reason of abandonment, but it would have created a complicated property situation, making it impossible for Stephen to have clear title to their condominium apartment and other joint property. The attorney had recommended the other course.

Stephen wondered if the legalities were in reality meaningless. Perhaps the ghosts of his past would always haunt him. If only he knew for sure what had happened to his wife and child, he could feel more certain about what he had just done.

DUE TO THE ICY conditions, school was called off on Thursday. Apartment-bound for the day, Jenny used her time to grade papers and catch up on business correspondence. It was hard to concentrate, however. She kept wandering around, looking out windows, opening cupboard doors and staring into the refrigerator. She had a chocolate attack and sinned terribly with the brownies she had made for the boys. They were best served warm with a little ice cream on top. Finally, guilt got the best of her, and she resolutely put the remaining brownies in the freezer out of harm's way.

Fellow teacher Barbara Whinnery gave her a ride to school on Friday morning. Jenny enjoyed telling her about her strange night in a mysterious mansion. Most of the ice was gone off the main thoroughfares by then, but driveways and side streets were still hazardous.

Saturday morning, three of Jenny's students, who were also friends of Joe and Barry, pushed her car back onto the driveway.

Jenny waved goodbye to the boys in their battered Blazer, took a deep breath of the still frigid air, and turned toward the house. Jenny checked her watch. She had an appointment to have her hair cut later in the morning but still had lots of time. She decided to take another look at the inside of the house.

The house wasn't cold. Mr. Jolly must have already had the utilities turned on for her. Jenny slipped off her coat and tossed it with her purse onto the living room sofa then came back to the entry hall to stare up at the magnificent round skylight.

She had been thinking of doing magazine pieces about some of the houses she worked on as an additional means of income. Graystone might be a perfect one to begin with. The skylight with the right photos would be a story unto itself if Carmichael would give her permission to photograph and write about it. Such an article also would be indirect publicity for Home Researchers Inc.

Yes, it was a fine old house—Jenny knew she would enjoy learning of its past. She was curious to know the names of the designer and the builder. Had the Ellsworth family been the original owners? What skeletons were in its closets? Had anyone famous ever visited the house?

And who was Stephen Carmichael?

Jenny smiled to herself. After all, she had slept in his bed. She really should find out if the gentleman was married or a womanizer or a confirmed bachelor.

Jenny's hand trailed on the smooth, curving banister as she followed it up the stairs. She walked along the open gallery, getting a closer look at the detail in the skylight's design. Mentally, she began writing the lead to a magazine article and framing the photographs she would take.

Before she went back downstairs, Jenny could not resist a visit to the master bedroom.

The comforter was carefully folded at the foot of the bed just as she had left it. But she thought she had smoothed the blanket and fluffed the pillows better than that. Jenny sat on the edge of the bed and smiled as she remembered the strange evening she'd spent there. Stephen C. would never know that a latter-day Goldilocks had been sleeping in his bed or what thoughts she had had about him, sight unseen. It had been a long time since any of her fantasies actually had recognizable faces. Not since Lorenzo, and he proved unworthy.

Almost without thinking, Jenny pulled off her boots and leaned against the headboard. Maybe she should call Mr. Jolly on Monday and ask if he'd heard anything from Stephen. She'd like to know when he was returning to Oklahoma City. Jenny put her hands behind her head and stretched her legs out in front of her. She felt right at home here in the bed.

Then Jenny noticed there were ashes in the fireplace. But she had cleaned out the fireplace yesterday morning. She looked around the room, a prickly sensation crossing the back of her neck as the tiny hairs there rose in warning. A newspaper was folded on the love seat. A set of keys was on the mantel. And the bathroom door was ajar.

At that instant, a reflected movement in the bathroom mirror caught her eye.

There was a naked man in the bathroom! *Completely* naked. He was splashing his face with aftershave.

Good God! Stephen Carmichael had returned.

Jenny froze.

He was going to turn his head and see her own reflection in that mirror any second now. A strange woman in his bed.

Ever so carefully, Jenny sat up, bent over to pick up her boots and rose, expecting his challenge at any moment. Her heart beating furiously, she tiptoed to the door.

Once out of the bedroom, she ran silently down the carpeted hallway and stairs. Just let her get out without him hearing her. He was *naked* in the bathroom!

She sat on the bottom step to pull on her boots, grabbed her coat from the living room sofa and was already at the front door before she remembered her purse. She glanced nervously upstairs, took a deep breath and soundlessly retraced her steps to retrieve it.

Once she was safely outside, her first impulse was to run as fast as she could, but she had to be careful of the ice on the driveway. At least the master bedroom was at the back of the house. He wouldn't be able to look out of the window and see her. If he could, he might wonder why the strange car had suddenly disappeared from his yard, but that wouldn't be as difficult to explain as a strange woman in his bed.

Jenny didn't take a breath until she had exited onto Lakeside Drive. *Never assume a house is unoccupied,* she instructed herself. *Please remember that in the future. Always ring the doorbell and call out even if it looks as if no one has been there in the last century.*

Jenny knew she'd never forget the shock of seeing that man's reflection in the mirror. Naked. What if she'd dozed off, and he had found her there? How in the world would she have explained? Or worse, what if he'd come strolling out of the bathroom naked while she had been stretched out on his bed?

Jenny replayed the scene, remembering this time not so much her horrified reaction as how the man had looked.

Nice, she realized. Stephen C. was lean. No paunch at all. His thighs and calves were well muscled. He had a puncture-wound scar on his hip just like the one Barry had gotten when he was nine years old from sitting on a board with a nail sticking through it.

Except for the scar, Jenny thought, her fantasy man had a good body, that was for sure. His hair was graying at the temples, and maybe a little thin on top, but his body had weathered well.

Jenny started to laugh. How about that! Stephen had nice buns.

## Chapter Three

"Stephen Carmichael is in town and would like to meet you," Frank Jolly's voice informed Jenny over the telephone Monday morning.

"Is that right?" she said too brightly. Yes, Stephen Carmichael was definitely in town, she thought.

The lawyer continued. "Could you possibly stop by his house today? I told him you taught school, and it would have to be late afternoon. Is four o'clock all right?"

Jenny agreed, then hung up and hurried back to her classroom. Third hour was about to begin. They had finished fighting the Civil War and were going to start Reconstruction today.

Reconstruction was Jenny's least favorite period of American history, but she found she didn't mind dealing with the carpetbaggers quite so much today. In fact her lecture was damned good. She really took those kids back to the post-Civil War South and made them feel how it was to return to burned-out farms, what it meant to be a newly freed slave, why the scalawags failed and the carpetbaggers emerged with power. Who was right or wrong was no longer an issue—only who won and who lost, and how the victor treated the vanquished. It

was one of those times when Jenny knew she had made
the right choice in becoming a teacher rather than an
accountant. And flitting about the corners of her mind
as she conducted her class were thoughts of that afternoon, of actually meeting Stephen Carmichael, of being
there with him in his house, of what in the world she was
going to wear.

"I'll have your exam papers back tomorrow," she told
her class at dismissal time. "Of the ones I've already
graded, some of you did well. Some of you still seem to
think Appomattox is a medical condition."

Jenny raced home after school to change clothes. Her
denim dress and flat shoes would never do for a face-to-
face meeting with Mr. C. It was foolish, she supposed,
but she wanted to look... How? Glamorous? Competent? Sexy? Professional?

All of the above, she decided. She wanted to look like
a glamorous, sexy, competent business woman. But as
she stared at the interior of her closet, she doubted if that
was possible. The clothes that greeted her were practical
and dated—schoolteacher clothes and weekend grub-
bies. A few dress-up outfits that saw little use.

She pulled out her perennial standby, a navy gabardine suit. No, today it seemed too matronly.

She checked out the green silk shirtwaist. Too long.

She held up her black two-piece knit. Better, but she'd
been putting off taking it to the cleaners until after the
first of the month.

Finally she decided on a straight black skirt and white
sweater worn with a colorful silk scarf, wide black belt
and gold hoop earrings. Jenny glanced at the clock on
her bedside table. This outfit would have to do. The next
ten minutes had to be devoted to makeup and hair.

After she'd freshened her makeup and fluffed her hair, Jenny surveyed the results in the mirror. Not great, but okay as a hurry-up job. Of course, it wasn't as though she was going out on a date with the man, she reminded herself. This meeting was strictly business. Except she'd seen the man naked.

Jenny gave herself a devilish grin in the mirror.

At precisely four o'clock, she rang the doorbell at Graystone. A fully clothed Stephen answered the door. He was wearing navy slacks and a pale yellow pullover. A white shirt showed at the V neck. He was not as tall as she had judged him to be from his reflected image in the bathroom mirror, and his hair was thinner. But somehow he was more attractive than she'd expected—not movie-star attractive but a nice-looking man to be sure.

"I'm Jenny Bishop," she said.

"Won't you come in? I'm Stephen Carmichael," he said offering her his hand.

"I'm happy to meet you," Jenny said with a smile, hoping she seemed more at ease than she felt. "And I'm pleased to be working on this assignment. Graystone is a lovely old home and deserves to have its history recorded."

He didn't smile, but his head nodded in agreement. "Yes, it is rather special, isn't it?" Stephen said.

Jenny looked up into the brilliant skylight, lit by the late-afternoon sun. "I've never seen anything like it," Jenny said, aware that his eyes were on her face. She wished she'd checked her mirror one last time. "Do you know anything about the skylight or the rest of the house? How did you learn of the house in the first place?"

"Let's sit down," he offered, "and I'll tell you what I know. I understand you've already visited the house.

My attorney explained that car abandoned in the yard was yours. I gather you got the problem taken care of."

Jenny wondered if he was always so serious. You'd think they were discussing nuclear disarmament.

"Yes, I've visited the house. Once. Just once. I slid on the ice and couldn't extract my car from your front yard. A few of my students came and got my car out for me Saturday morning. I'm glad Mr. Jolly explained about the car. I had no idea you were coming back so soon."

Jenny knew she was talking too fast and saying too much. *Calm down,* she told herself.

"My visit is rather spur-of-the-moment," he said, touching her elbow lightly and escorting her into the living room. The lamps were on, and a fire blazed in the fireplace. It looked considerably more hospitable than the last time she had seen the room, but the love seat didn't feel any more comfortable.

Stephen seated himself across from her in a wing chair. He made a striking figure sitting there in the high-backed chair, his handsome face serious.

"Actually, I inherited Graystone. My mother was an Ellsworth," he explained, "but I really know very little about the house."

"Oh, how was your mother related to Miss Grace and Miss Patience?"

"She was their younger sister, but she was estranged from her family most of her adult life. They had opposed her marriage to my father."

"Do you mind if I ask why?" Jenny asked, curious.

"Not at all. She was eighteen and had known him only for a few days," he explained. "My father was in Oklahoma City visiting his grandparents while on his way to a military base in North Carolina. My mother's father and her sisters claimed she was too young, and they felt that Marie would be marrying beneath herself because my father was just an Army enlisted man at the time. The country was at war, the future uncertain, especially for a soldier. I think another reason was that the Carmichael family was Irish. My father's grandparents had had a neighborhood grocery store in Oklahoma City since the turn of the century and still spoke with a brogue. My aunts were of the generation who considered the Irish lower-class and fit only to be laborers. My grandfather said he would disinherit my mother if she married my father, but she ran off with him to North Carolina. I was born there while he was in Europe during the war."

"And the family never forgave her?"

"No, and my mother never forgave my grandfather. Apparently he was quite authoritarian and did not tolerate disobedience in his children. She admitted to me once that part of the reason she wanted to get married was to get away from him."

"Had you ever visited the house before you inherited it?" Jenny asked.

"Only once. My mother brought me here when she came back for the old man's funeral. I was about seven or eight. I thought the aunts seemed ancient then. My mother was considerably younger than they were. Aunt Grace, it seemed, had never forgiven my mother for running off with a worthless Irishman. She insisted that their father had never gotten over the disappointment and humiliation of losing his youngest daughter and had grieved himself to death. Of course, the old man had managed to live until almost eighty, so I think Aunt Grace overstated the case a bit. I hadn't had any sort of contact with the old ladies for years and was shocked when Aunt Grace left the house to me. It seems I was her only living relative.''

"Maybe it was her attempt to rectify old grudges,'' Jenny speculated. She enjoyed watching Stephen as he talked. He had good, strong features—especially his mouth. A full mouth with well-defined lips and beautiful teeth. His jaw was rather square, but it only added to the strength of his face. His eyes were richly brown, his brow line bold. His nose might have been too large on other faces, but on Stephen's face, it was fine. His skin was tan and weathered, giving him an outdoor look but making it difficult for Jenny to estimate his age. Mid-forties, she finally decided.

"What are your plans for the house?'' she asked.

"I'm not sure," Stephen admitted. "At first I thought I'd sell it, but I was charmed when I saw the house again and started recalling all my mother's stories about growing up here. She was born upstairs, read Nancy Drew mysteries in the attic and raised rabbits out back. Anyway, I decided to keep the house for a while, at least until I have a better idea about my future needs. As I'm sure you've noticed, I moved in some of the things I've acquired during my travels, but I'm not too sure how they fit in with my aunts' somber furnishings. Any suggestions you have about livening up the place would be appreciated. And whether or not I keep the house, I'm glad its past will be reconstructed before the record dims any further.''

Yes, his mouth was definitely his best feature, Jenny decided. A wide, sensuous mouth. But didn't he ever smile?

"Then you aren't planning to live in the house anytime soon?'' Jenny asked.

"No, probably not. And I'm not sure I can afford the upkeep. I really don't know what to do with the old place. It's going to be sitting in a sea of newer homes. Maybe its day has passed."

He sounded sad. Was it just for the house, Jenny wondered, or was the man himself sad? She thought of the portrait of the woman and child upstairs in the bedroom. Were they why he was sad?

"Do you know if the Ellsworths were the original owners of the house?" Jenny asked.

Stephen shook his head no. "Come, let's take a tour," he suggested. "You probably already know more about the house than I do."

"No, not really," Jenny said. "However, I think it's the same vintage as the homes I've been researching south of here in the Heritage Hills area. Did your aunts leave any sort of family history—diaries, letters, anything that might offer some clues? Even old photograph albums sometimes help pin down dates of construction or the years a family occupied a residence."

"There are some boxes in the attic, but I have no idea what they contain. You're welcome to look through them."

"I have been known to discover family skeletons," she warned.

"So I've read." For an instant Jenny thought he was going to smile. His face relaxed a bit. "Well, have a go at it," he said. "I doubt if you'll find out anything colorful about those two old ladies, but I hope I'm wrong. I'd like to think they had more of a life than just two spinster sisters living in their father's house, never having any excitement or romance. I'd love to look through all that stuff myself, but I'm only here for a short time."

"It's a shame to have such a lovely home and not have the opportunity to enjoy it," Jenny said.

"Lovely homes don't make people happy," he said, rising from his chair. "Sometimes they distract them for a time, but I doubt if the percentage of happy people is any higher in mansions than it is in frame cottages."

"Perhaps," Jenny said as she followed him out of the living room. A strange man, she thought. And leaving again soon—not that it mattered. She could do her work whether the owner was here or not.

They discussed each room in turn. She asked his permission to write articles about some of her findings—especially if she was able to discover the history of the skylight. Stephen was agreeable.

"You're certainly hard working," he said. "Teaching, a business and free-lance writing."

"The writing is a new thought," Jenny explained. "And it takes two jobs to support two sons in college."

"Are you alone then?"

"I'm divorced," Jenny explained. Saying the words made her feel strangely vulnerable. Now he was supposed to say what his situation was. Widower. Divorced. He didn't wear a wedding band, but then many married men didn't. He hadn't mentioned a wife or a family. Surely if he was married, his wife would have some say in the disposition of Graystone. Yet he had asked Jenny to suggest ways to liven up the house, usually a wife's job.

But no words of explanation were forthcoming, and an awkward silence hung in the air. They were standing in the kitchen, and Jenny hastened to describe to him the way the room would have looked before being modernized. She was talking too fast again, she realized, and made a concerted effort to speak at a more normal rate.

"There would have been a galvanized steel sink with a pump beside it," she said, carefully measuring her words. "The cupboards would have been freestanding. A wood-burning stove would have had a flue to the outside. And unless I miss my guess, the pantry and breakfast room were carved out of the original room when huge kitchens went out of style."

She watched him looking around the room, visualizing how it might have been.

"Yes, now that you mention it, the room was bigger," he said. "A big round table stood in the corner. There was a large, black wood-burning stove over against that wall, and a stovepipe came out of the back of it. It was summer and very hot. The housekeeper got up early to do the baking. She made fresh doughnuts for me one morning. The windows were open, and the curtains were tied back to let the breeze in."

Jenny was silent while he remembered. A little boy in a big kitchen watching the housekeeper make doughnuts.

"A long time ago," he said. "Would you like some coffee before we go look upstairs?"

Jenny agreed and seated herself on the high stool while she watched him. He seemed at home in a kitchen. The coffee was freshly ground and smelled wonderful.

"Have you always lived in Oklahoma City?" he asked.

"Yes. My parents were both schoolteachers here. Where did you grow up?"

"Everywhere. Japan. Europe. Hawaii. All over the States. Military families have to be vagabonds. My mother never really adjusted to it, but I think she had too much pride to admit it."

When the coffee was ready, he poured it into two white mugs. Jenny added a generous amount of milk to hers.

She watched him put the mug to his lips. His face relaxed momentarily as he relished the first taste. He put both his hands around his warm mug and held it for a minute before putting it to his mouth again.

Jenny found herself staring at his hands. Their manliness was intriguing. Barry's and Joe's hands were as large, the skin on the back of theirs smooth and young, but Stephen's hands were veined, the skin coarse. A sprinkling of dark hairs grew across the back. He wore no rings.

"Is it too hot?" he asked her.

"What? Yes, I'm letting it cool." She took a sip. "It tastes good," she said.

"Am I keeping you too long?" he asked.

"No, not at all."

"Would you have dinner with me?"

Jenny met his gaze. Still no smile. Such a serious invitation. He could have been inviting her to a wake. Other men would have been smoother, suggesting they continue their discussion over drinks and dinner. There was nothing suave in Stephen's invitation. He simply blurted it out as if he had just thought of it.

She wanted to tease him, to tell him to loosen up, but she didn't. Maybe he had good reason to look the way he did. She thought of her promise to have the Civil War exams graded by tomorrow. Several hours of work awaited her, but she wanted to go to dinner with him. Maybe over dinner he would relax. Suddenly, she found that she wanted very much to see Stephen Carmichael smile. It seemed a whole lot more important than a few hours of lost sleep.

"Yes, I'd like that," she said. His eyes were dark and intense. Jenny looked down and took a sip of coffee.

Stephen's left hand was very near to hers. Jenny looked at his hand. Her fingertips tingled. Yes, she wanted to reach out and take his hand and tell him they would have a nice evening together, and she wished he would smile at her just once. Maybe it was the mother in her. She was a pro at kissing away hurts, discussing away hurt feelings, teasing away pouts and patting hands to remind sons that Mother was there and cared.

Or maybe being a mother had nothing to do with it at all.

"There's not much to see upstairs except a closer look at the skylight," Stephen said as he led the way upstairs, "but I'll show you those boxes in the attic."

"Did you notice that the marble in each one of the bedroom fireplaces is different?" Jenny asked. "That's very unusual. In the master bedroom, the marble had both black and red mottling. I think that's rather rare."

When they stopped in at the master bedroom, Jenny avoided looking at the bed. The door to the bathroom was closed. They stood side by side looking at the handsome fireplace. She ran her hand over the polished surface. The beautiful Oriental woman and her daughter looked down at them from the portrait over the mantel, and Jenny couldn't resist saying something.

"They're exquisite. Are they mother and daughter?"

"Yes, my wife and daughter."

Jenny caught her breath for an instant to deal with the swell of disappointment in her chest. Damn. He was married after all. She could have wept.

Maybe she shouldn't be going out to dinner with him. Maybe even if he hadn't said so, he really meant it to be business, but she had accepted it as a date. She should have asked about the picture first.

"I haven't lived with her in some time," he offered, his eyes never leaving the painting.

"And your daughter?"

"No, I haven't lived with either one of them in a long time."

But the word *divorce* was not mentioned. Jenny thought of her iron-clad rule. No Married Men. But she said nothing. He was leaving soon. The dinner could be what she made it. She would see that it was just a friendly occasion between two people who had entered into a business arrangement. And she would still try to make him smile.

The attic was chilly and musty but really quite wonderful. The dormer windows marched along one side of the slanted roof and gave light and character to the large room. It looked like a place where little girls would come to play dress-up with clothes that were surely stored in the large trunks, and little boys would push the same trunks into a corner and build a fort. She thought of Stephen's mother coming up here to read Nancy Drew mysteries and wondered which window she had curled up by.

"Children surely played up here," Jenny said walking over to a window and surveying the ground far below her. "It's a wonderful hideaway." She was aware of Stephen coming to stand behind her.

"I came up here some during my one visit, but it was so hot in the summertime. I remember there wasn't another building to be seen out this window, just trees and meadows. Now, the house is being surrounded."

"Is that why you don't want to live here?" Jenny asked.

"Perhaps a part of the reason."

He was standing very close, looking over her shoulder. She wondered if he was as aware of her as she was of him. Was she imagining things, or were they sharing the same mood. How alive she felt at this minute because a man she was attracted to was standing near. If she gave in to the attic's chill and shivered, he might put his arms around her to warm her, but Jenny willed the shiver away.

Through the barren treetops, she could see the cars hurrying back and forth on Lakeside Drive. And houses in all stages of completion spread out on either side of Graystone. Across the road, there was another housing development underway. All construction had come to a standstill, however. Builders had gone bankrupt right and left after the bottom fell out of oil prices, and the state's economy collapsed. But this was a lovely area with large trees and a lake nearby, and the houses would be finished someday. And then Graystone would stand like a lonely dinosaur, a relic from another age.

Where would Stephen Carmichael live if he wasn't living here? And where did his beautiful wife and daughter live?

"I found a restaurant during my last trip to Oklahoma," he was saying. "It's not too far north of here. I was curious because the name of the restaurant was the same as that of my house, only with the British spelling for *gray* with an *E* instead of an *A*. Greystone. It was lovely. Have you ever been there?"

Jenny shook her head no. She'd heard of it, but most of her eating out was done at Pizza Hut or Burger King.

"But first, I'd like to offer you some of my aunts' excellent sherry in front of my fire," he said. "It's the first time I've used the living room fireplace, and I'd hate to waste it.

Jenny nodded again. She could almost taste the sherry and feel the warmth of the fire.

But still they stood there, staring out at the leafless treetops and the end of an era. Finally, however, the chill in the huge room got the best of her, and an involuntary shiver shook her body.

"Come," he said. "Let's get you warm."

The sherry was old and probably very precious. He had her sit in the wing chair this time.

"How long will it take you to research the house and prepare your findings?" he asked.

"It varies, but I hope to have something for you in a few weeks," she said, thinking that the faster she worked, the sooner she'd get paid for the job, and she certainly needed the money. But when she was finished, she'd probably never see Stephen Carmichael again.

"What sources do you use?" he asked.

Jenny explained how she went about researching a house, and told him about some of the more interesting houses she'd done in the past.

"Now what about you?" she asked. "What sort of work do you do?"

"I'm career military. Like father, like son. I'm in Ordnance—weapons procurement. It used to fascinate me, but now..." he said with a small shrug. "Well, shall we go? Or would you like another glass of sherry?"

"I'm ready anytime," Jenny said. She went to freshen her makeup while he tended to the fire.

His rental car was in the carriage house, which had been turned into a garage behind the main house. No wonder she hadn't seen his car Saturday morning.

The restaurant was a short drive up Interstate 35. It was located on a wooded hill overlooking the highway just south of the city of Edmond. The building had once been a gracious home and provided a genteel setting for a restaurant. Their table was in a corner and secluded from its neighbors.

Stephen ordered a bottle of Chablis. Jenny thought guiltily about the pile of test papers on her coffee table at home. The sherry on her empty stomach had left her light-headed enough, and now wine. Maybe she could get up early in the morning and finish grading the tests, or perhaps the world would not come to an end if she was a day late. Some students would grumble, but just as many wouldn't care one way or the other.

They both ordered red snapper, the featured seafood for the evening. Jenny sipped her wine, planning her attack. It was time for him to relax, to smile.

"This is a lovely change from Burger King," Jenny said with her best smile. "Or Pizza Hut, another of my sons' favorite spots for gourmet dining."

"Tell me about your sons," Stephen said. Good for him, Jenny thought. That's what he was supposed to say.

Raising twin sons was one of her best topics. She started with the alligator in the bathtub.

"Not a big one, mind you," she explained, "but an alligator nonetheless. I pulled back the curtain and was about to step in for my shower, and there was this Creature from the Black Lagoon in my bathtub—all mouth and ugly teeth. Barry and Joe couldn't understand why I wouldn't let them keep him. I'd gone along with the gerbils, birds, guinea pigs, cats and dogs. What difference could one little alligator possibly make? And it was only for three months. They had assured the biology teacher that good ol' Mom wouldn't mind if they kept him over the summer vacation.''

Stephen actually smiled. Jenny felt as if she'd been given a prize. He was beautiful when he smiled.

"I told them that I drew the line with reptiles," Jenny continued, encouraged by his response. "I said that only warm-blooded creatures were allowed. Joe said, 'Does that mean the boa constrictor has to go too?' Then they pulled out a box from under the bed that the snake is supposed to be in, and guess what? It's empty. The damned snake had vanished!''

Stephen's smile had turned into a grin. Jenny felt herself sparkling. The feeling was wonderful.

She took a sip of her wine before continuing. "We looked *everywhere*!" she said. "All the while they kept telling me it was just a little guy, and he'd turn up. Now, to say I'm not a snake person is probably one of the greatest understatements of all times. Just the word *snake* makes my flesh crawl. So can you imagine what it was like then to live in that house after that? Every time I opened a drawer, I expected a snake to come hissing out at me. I was afraid to put on my clothes without checking the sleeves first. I was afraid to put my hand under the sink or crawl into bed at night. I kept wondering how fast snakes grow. I had visions of this thing living on flies and June bugs and getting bigger and bigger under the floor boards.''

Stephen was chuckling now. "Did you ever find it?''

"Oh, yes. Two months later, I'd almost forgotten about the damned thing by then. I mean, after all that time I thought he'd crawled off and died or gone off and found some little boys with a more understanding mother. Well, one day I was driving down May Avenue at rush hour with the boys fighting in the back seat as usual, when I noticed this thing on the floor sticking out from under the front seat. It looked like a large salami. When I was stopped at a traffic light and leaned over to get a closer look, the salami moved!''

"The snake, I take it," Stephen said. "I can hardly wait to hear what happened next."

"Yes, the salami was the snake. It had apparently gone from house to garage to car. Well, I got out of that car so fast and jerked those boys out of the back seat. The light changed and people were honking for me to go. A policeman came up and demanded that I move my car, but I told him I couldn't because there was a boa constrictor under the seat. By this time, the cars were backed up for blocks. The honking was deafening. People were out of their cars demanding what the hell was going on. Barry and Joe kept explaining that it wasn't a big snake. The policeman was getting red in the face and ordered me to move the car immediately. Then the boys started pointing. The snake had draped himself over the steering wheel. '*You* move the car,' I told the policeman.''

Stephen was laughing now. Jenny felt wonderful. The wine was French and superb. The restaurant was lovely, and she didn't have to eat hamburgers or pizza. She forgave her sons for bringing that snake home from school six years ago.

"Did you bring home snakes when you were a little boy?" she asked.

"No, I guess I didn't. What a boring kid I must have been. I think my mother worried about me because I always had my nose in a book. But we moved so much, and I didn't make friends easily. Maybe if I'd had a twin brother, things might have been livelier.''

"No question about it," she said. "Your mother missed a lot. If you were Grace's only living relative, I assume your mother is dead now. What about your Irish father?"

"He and his second wife live on an island in Virginia. Dad's retired now. They have a place on the beach, and I think they're happier than they've ever been in their lives."

Stephen described their beach-side home and their fishing boat in great detail and, Jenny thought, with a little bit of longing.

"How much longer will you stay in the military?" she asked.

"I don't know," Stephen said with a shrug.

"Where are you stationed right now?" Jenny persisted.

"Washington, D.C., but I travel a great deal. Sometimes I think I've missed a lot by not having had a real home. I guess that's why I decided to keep my aunts' house, but I'm having second thoughts about the wisdom of that decision."

"Real homes usually mean families," Jenny said softly. "But you seem to be avoiding that subject. Don't you want to talk about your wife and little girl?"

"No, not right now," he said with a small shake of his head. His gaze left her for a few seconds.

Jenny felt as though she had intruded into a private place.

"Please, tell me more about your sons," he said. "They're nineteen? What do they bring home from school now?"

"Barry brings home girls," she answered with more brightness than she felt. "Joe brings home specimens.

Dead birds. Boxes of bones. He's wants to major in zoology and perhaps go on to medical school.''

The entrées arrived, and their attention was diverted to the really fine meal. The fish was especially good.

Stephen told her about fishing with his father and his father's wife off the coast of Virginia. She told him about fishing with her parents at Lake Texoma, a vast lake on the Oklahoma-Texas border. "Catfish, mostly. The boys love it. My parents used to have a little fishing cabin down there, more of a shack really. It was about the only vacation we ever got to take, but it was great. My folks have moved to a little town not too far from the lake and fish almost every day now. Dad can fry catfish better than anyone alive.''

They ended the meal with a rich dessert and coffee flavored with amaretto.

"I feel like I've died and gone to heaven," Jenny said. "You can't imagine what a lovely treat this is for a struggling schoolteacher.''

"You can't imagine what a treat it is for me to spend the evening with someone as charming and natural as you are." He was getting serious again. The evening was over.

Stephen was quiet on the drive back to his house. The porch light illuminated Graystone's handsome front door. Stephen pulled up by her car in the driveway and turned sideways in his seat to face her.

"I'll say good-night now," he said, "and thank you." He reached over and took her hand from her lap and kissed it softly. "You're a very special woman, Jenny Bishop. I'm glad I got this opportunity to know you.''

Jenny wanted to ask when she would see him again, but she had no right. He was a married man.

"Good night, Stephen. It was a lovely evening, and I'm glad I was able to make you forget your sadness for a time."

STEPHEN STOOD in front of the house and watched as she completed the circle of Graystone's drive and drove away, then he pulled the rented car around to the garage and let himself into his empty house.

He sat for a time in the living room, staring at the embers. The room felt empty now without her. How Jenny had filled it with her beauty and soft voice and charming ways. He sat there in the chair where she had been sitting and relived the evening. Yes, she had made him forget his sadness for a time. Lovely Jenny had made him laugh. He wished he could meet her sons. They must be great kids. He wondered what it would be like to fall in love with their mother.

Could he do that—love again?

Legally, he would soon be free to do just that. The hearing was Friday, and the attorney assured him it would just be a formality. But it took more than a court decree to erase a commitment he had felt so strongly for so many years.

Stephen knew he had to leave the next day to visit a California munitions factory, and he had to be back in the Pentagon on Thursday. But perhaps he could return on the weekend, he mused. Military transports flew from Washington to Oklahoma City's Tinker Air Force Base with great frequency, and it was never any problem for him to catch a ride. And he could see Jenny Bishop again. He wanted that very much, he realized, and the knowledge surprised him. But what if she didn't want to see him again? She had already figured out he was dragging around a lot of emotional baggage from a previous marriage. His was not a normal situation. Not normal at all. If Jenny had any sense at all, she'd turn and run at the sight of him.

Stephen's sigh was audible in the quiet room. He rose from the chair she had been sitting in, and with heavy steps he took himself up the stairway to bed.

He lay in the darkness, unable to stop thinking about Jenny. In the attic, he'd had to clench his fists to keep from touching her. In the car as he told her good-night, he had been overwhelmed with a desire to kiss her. He had thought about kissing her several times during the evening, but to be there alone with her in that dark car was almost more than he could bear.

Now he couldn't bear it. Her presence was there with him in the bed. He could sense how it would be if she were beside him and he could reach over and pull her to him. Her hair would smell so clean. And how sweet her body would feel next to his.

"Oh, yes, sweet Jenny," he said into the darkness.

## Chapter Four

The test papers were waiting on Jenny's coffee table when she let herself into her apartment. With a tinge of guilt, she ignored them and went down the hall to her bedroom.

The clothes she had elected not to wear were still scattered across the bed. Mechanically she began to put them on hangers and hang them in the closet. Then she stood in the center of the room and looked around. What now?

A bath. A nice hot bath to help her sleep. She turned on the bathroom heater and the water. She even remembered to add the bath oil before the tub was full.

While the water ran, she took off her skirt and sweater and hung them over the back of a chair. She didn't feel like hanging up any more clothes. She peeled off her underwear and hurried into the bathroom.

And there she was reflected in the mirror, a thirty-eight-year-old naked woman. Somehow, her body seemed more important to her tonight than it had last night, and she scrutinized it carefully. Her waistline was still intact, but there were little horizontal creases above her navel that only went away if she sucked in her tummy very hard. She knew that no matter how faithfully she did her exercises and no matter how flat she managed to get her stomach, those creases would never go away—nor would the stretch marks of pregnancy across her upper thighs and lower abdomen. Funny, she usually didn't even notice the stretch marks. They had faded over the years to thin, silvery lines. But tonight she was aware of them and the fact that her breasts weren't as high and firm as they once had been. But then she had nursed a set of twins and gotten older. Centerfold material she was not, but she wouldn't like the kind of man who insisted on a centerfold body.

What would Stephen Carmichael think of her body, Jenny wondered. In spite of its imperfections, it wasn't a bad body—actually she was rather proud of it. She hadn't gotten fat or lumpy, and her thighs were firm. She had a good shape, and Stephen wasn't perfect himself. Maybe even the centerfold guys and gals had to suck in their tummies and wear makeup on stretch marks before they had their pictures taken. With that comforting thought, she lowered her body into the bathtub for a nice long soak.

*Stop thinking of that man,* she told herself as the warmth relaxed her. *Cleanse your mind, woman. You've had other crushes before and gotten over them. No married man is worth the pain.*

But he was separated, apparently. She tried to decide how much difference that made.

For years Jenny had promised herself that she would find the right man or live alone. She wasn't sure about many things in life, but she was certain that she never wanted to go through the pain of divorce again if she could help it. She supposed one never really got over the wounds from something like that.

Of course, it was easy with the wisdom of hindsight to say that she never should have married Lewis Bishop in the first place. He was too old for her and had been married twice before. And Lewis was a modern-day Gypsy, following drilling rigs around Oklahoma, Texas, Kansas and Louisiana on a constant quest for new reserves of oil or natural gas.

But Lewis was the handsomest man Jenny had ever seen outside of the movies and had a grin that could charm the fuzz off a peach.

Jenny had been a senior in high school. She had been friends with Lewis's kid sister, and he had drifted back to his folks' house while he was between jobs and paychecks.

Running off to marry him seemed exciting and romantic at the time. And she was certain marriage would magically turn him into a responsible human being.

However, Lewis turned out to be exactly the same kind of husband as he had been a boyfriend. When he was around, everything was grand. They laughed and went dancing, only now they didn't have to say good-night and could go home together and make love until the wee hours of the morning.

But Lewis often disappeared without warning, and Jenny wouldn't hear from him for days, even weeks. Sometimes he brought home his paycheck; other times Jenny never saw a dime. Her parents helped out some, and she worked part-time and went to college for a while but the birth of twin boys put an end to that arrangement.

For a while, Lewis came home almost every night, but home was a pretty grim place in those days. The little apartment was full of baby beds, high chairs, diapers drying. The babies had colic, and one or both of them seemed to be crying almost all the time. The apartment smelled of soiled diapers and spit-up. Lewis came home less and less, and Jenny was too tired to protest, too tired to care.

When the babies were four months old, her parents insisted Jenny enroll in night classes. They came two evenings a week to look after their twin grandchildren while Jenny got out of the house and inched her way a little closer toward a college degree.

Those first years after her babies were born were a crazy time, a nightmare in some respects, but in other ways surprisingly happy. Barry and Joe turned into fat, funny little creatures who brought joy to Jenny's heart and to their adoring grandparents. And as the boys got a little older, there were even good times with Lewis. He would come home, promise to do better, bounce his sons on his knee, hand over a paycheck or two, then vanish again. Jenny swore from time to time she was going to kick him out for good, but the truth of the matter was she still loved her husband, worthless though he might be. She missed him when he was gone, and his grin still melted her heart. But Jenny didn't believe any of his promises anymore, and she had learned not to count on him for anything. With that lesson in mind, she made her plans. Somehow, she would earn her degree and get her teaching certification. She'd raise her boys as best she could, and when Lewis came home, she'd be there for him. While she never completely lost hope that someday her husband would grow up, Jenny quit waiting for it to happen.

And she wasn't terribly surprised when he went to live in Aspen with a twenty-year-old ski instructor from Sweden named Olga. But it hurt. God, how it hurt. Jenny had looked the other way all those years because she thought that deep down inside, Lewis really loved her. How could she have been so wrong? How could she ever trust her emotions again?

She hadn't for several years. Then she had dated from time to time, wondered if she was in love a few times but always decided she wasn't. But she found satisfaction in being a good teacher, a good mother, a good daughter, and she was damned lucky to have such a wonderful family.

*Damned lucky,* Jenny reminded herself as she got out of the tub. She wiped the steam from the mirror and stared at herself again. But her boys were all but grown. Her parents had moved away to fish during their golden years. And while teaching was a good career, it didn't fill her heart.

"Enough," she said to her reflected image. "Go to bed and go to sleep. It's midnight, and the alarm will go off tomorrow at six-thirty just as it always does."

In bed, however, Jenny's mind kept wandering to forbidden places. After a time, she went into the living room and finished grading the Civil War.

When she fell back into bed at two-thirty, she thought briefly about what a bear she was going to be in class tomorrow. Poor kids. She hardly thought about Stephen at all as she finally drifted off to sleep.

A FEW YEARS OLDER than Jenny, Barbara Whinnery was new that year at Memorial, having transferred there from a central city high school that had been closed. She taught English down the hall from Jenny's history class, and the two had gravitated toward each other as the only two "mature" single women on the faculty. They were in the process of becoming good friends.

After a particularly long teachers' meeting on Tuesday afternoon, the two women decided they'd earned a glass of wine.

"We might as well," Jenny agreed when Barbara suggested it. "The afternoon is shot. I think we've earned a little libation."

"That Mr. Peabody is such a jerk," Barbara said, once they were seated in a booth at a nearby bar. "He was just exercising his authority because the boss is out of town. As if purple hair and outrageous clothes couldn't wait until Monday when Mr. Jacobson gets back. As if hair and clothes mattered as long as we make sure the students' bodies aren't indecently exposed and that the messages on T-shirts aren't too obscene. Telling the kids they can't do their own thing just causes resentment."

"I agree," Jenny said, "but a group of teachers side with him. They bring this up and argue about it every year, but don't worry. When it comes to a vote next week, reason will prevail. Now, let's forget we teach school for a while."

"Something on your mind?" Barbara asked, dipping her chip into the salsa. "A man? Kids?"

Jenny relaxed into a corner of the booth. A fire burned in the huge fireplace. It was a cheerful place to be on a cold evening and put off for a little longer going home to her lonely apartment. "Both I guess," she admitted. "Kids first. Don't you dread the empty nest? Your last two won't be around much longer."

"Yes and no," Barbara said, munching thoughtfully on a chip. "I've been mother and father to my three ever since their dad went down in Vietnam. Missy was born after Ben's death. Gregory can't remember him. Libby was a preschooler when he left the last time."

Barbara waited while the waitress served their drinks. She took a sip of her Bloody Mary before continuing.

"It hasn't been easy, either. The kids haven't been perfect, and neither have I. If both sets of grandparents hadn't helped out financially, I don't know what I would have done. As it was, a broken retainer was a disaster. I have to make prom dresses, and hand-me-downs are the norm. We've lived on the brink financially since day one. Our house is too small. Disarray and sibling rivalry became a way of life. But before much longer, things are going to change. Libby goes to college next year, Greg the year after. I know I'll miss my kids, but surely the trade-off in privacy, quiet and an orderly life will compensate a little. I spend as much time fantasizing about having hot water for my bath as I do about men. It would be nice to be responsible only for myself, go to sleep when I want to and not forever have to stay awake until the last kid is in. And now I have a feeling you're going to tell me that solitude is not so glorious."

"It's awfully quiet," Jenny admitted. "I turn on the television more for company than for entertainment."

"Lonely, huh?"

"Yeah. At times." Jenny took a sip of her wine. Yes, she was lonely, and she didn't like it.

"Now, the conversation will quite normally take a turn to men, the not-so-surefire cure for loneliness," Barbara announced.

"How come you haven't hooked up with someone after all this time?" Jenny asked.

"Well, for a couple of years my husband was listed as missing in action. That made me neither fish nor fowl, neither widow nor wife. Even now, after all these years, his folks, my folks, even the kids are waiting around for a miracle—like in those Rambo movies. But Ben's not coming home. After he was finally declared dead, I started going out some. My kids would throw up or pee all over my gentlemen callers. Baby-sitters would cancel or call to report a catastrophe at the most inopportune moment, if you know what I mean. And a woman with three small children is not the most sought-after commodity in the world."

"But now your time has arrived, right?" Jenny asked hopefully. "You seem to be spending much of it with our young biology teacher. I've noticed that he sure hangs around you a lot. And I suspect he inspired that foxy new haircut of yours. Anything I should know about?"

"Oh, Chuck's okay," Barbara said, then covered her cheeks with her hands. "Look there, you've gone and made me blush." She picked up her wineglass and took a couple of sips to regain her composure. "Okay, Chuck is adorable. And I've been flattered by the attention, but you said the key word...*young*. I can't get involved with anyone that young."

"Ten years younger isn't so bad," Jenny said. "I've seen articles in magazines about how it's fashionable for men to go out with older women. Maybe it's because so many of the current film queens are older, or maybe men are just getting smarter, but anyway our time is supposed to be coming. So rejoice." Both women solemnly raised their glasses in tribute to older women.

"But how did I get to be an *older* woman?" Barbara asked. "It got here a whole lot sooner than I planned on. I never had a chance to enjoy being young."

"I know what you mean," Jenny admitted. "I think the message is to make the most of the years before *older* becomes *old*. It's important to make the most of the good years we have left."

"Well," Barbara said with a sigh, "at least you're still on the good side of forty. I've moved into matronhood, or some people might say I'm into dirty old womanhood. Chuck's not just ten years younger than me. It's more like twelve. But what bothers me the most is that he's never been married, never had kids. Chuck would like a child of his own, and I'm not the woman to give him one. I don't have the intestinal fortitude for another baby. No way. I keep telling him so, but he won't listen. He tells me about all these happy women with their midlife babies, but honestly Jenny, the time for babies is over in my life. Three is enough. I don't want to be the world's oldest kindergarten home-room mother. You wouldn't have another child at my age, would you?"

"Oh, I don't know," Jenny speculated. "One last baby might be kind of fun. I was only nineteen when my boys were born. Lewis was off working on oil rigs and was hardly ever home. Life was so hectic, I didn't have a chance to relax and enjoy their babyhood years. With twins, when you finish feeding one, it's time to feed the other one. When one cries, the other one cries. When one gets sick, the other gets sick. I couldn't afford disposable diapers—and they weren't very good back then anyway. I washed diapers in the bathtub half the time and hung them to dry on lamp shades, over chair backs, over doors, anyplace. It was grim. I think it might be fun to be a doting, rocking, calm nonimpoverished mother, but I'd better hurry before nature closes the factory."

"Oh, Jenny, your body still thinks it's twenty-five. I don't know how you do it."

"Well, obviously, you've still got what it takes if a young, sexy-looking guy like Chuck Ballard is hanging around."

"He's looking for a mother, remember, for his kid-to-be and for himself. He's just going through a stage and wants to be rocked and pampered. So do I. It'll never work. Do you really like my haircut?"

Jenny smiled. "It's dynamite."

And it was. Previously, Barbara had worn her dark brown hair in a no-nonsense ponytail. Now it was short and curled softly around her face. It was youthful looking and framed a pretty face with large brown eyes the same deep shade as her hair. And Barbara had started wearing eye shadow and blusher instead of just lipstick. She looked as though she liked herself better these days. Chuck Ballard had done that much for her, even if nothing else ever came of his courting Barbara.

Jenny just hoped no one's heart got broken—most of all Barbara's. She deserved someone wonderful and kind after all her years of struggle.

"Okay," Barbara said. "What about you? Who is he?"

Jenny sighed. "A melancholy Army colonel with a scar on his hip."

THE OKLAHOMA UNIVERSITY SOONERS were playing their cross-state rival, the Oklahoma State Cowboys. Jenny was crammed between her sons in the student section of the basketball arena on the OU campus. "You're sure they won't make me move to general admission?"

Barry and Joe assured her that no one would check and that none of the students were sitting in their right seats either. The band struck up the OU fight song, and the crowd rose to their feet. The pom-pom squad did an energetic routine to the music, while those in the stands clapped in time. The OU colors were red and white, and red was certainly the color of choice today. Jenny had never seen so many red shirts and red baseball caps.

Jenny felt quite proud to be standing between her two sons. Barry was dressed in a red pullover sweater, white shirt and jeans, of course. Joe had on a red-and-white striped rugby shirt with his jeans. Joe had inherited his father's sandy hair and stocky build. Barry, who had Jenny's dark hair, was more slender than his brother. Each boy was handsome in his own way. Barry with his movie-star smile and thick, curly hair attracted the most attention. Joe's good looks were more subtle, his smile a little shy.

Both boys had played basketball in junior and senior high school. Barry had been a razzle-dazzle guard, Joe a solid center. Jenny had never missed a game. She wished she could go to their intramural games now, but she didn't have time for frequent jaunts to Norman, and besides girlfriends went to intramural games, not mothers.

Barry handed Jenny a copy of the student newspapers. She had noticed that everyone in the student section seemed to be holding one. "What's this for?" she asked.

"You'll see," Joe assured her.

The announcer began introducing the Cowboys. The OU students held up their newspapers in front of their faces as though they were reading them, and following the announcement of each Cowboy player's name, called out "Who cares?" from behind their papers. Jenny joined in. "Who cares?" she yelled and giggled.

"But that's so rude," she said when the introductions of the visiting team were over.

"So that's polite?" Barry asked as he pointed to the Cowboy mascot Pistol Pete taking shots at the OU team with his cap-loaded six shooters.

The OU mascot, Top Daug, came running up behind Pistol Pete and lifted his leg doggie fashion. The student section roared its approval.

The basketball game was a back-and-forth affair with much cheering and band playing. The OU fans thought the officials were picking on their team, and much verbal abuse was offered in their direction. The students on several occasions offered a collective obscene gesture for the officials' benefit.

"Is this why I'm sending you guys to college—so you can learn such behavior?" Jenny said in mock horror.

"It's called assertiveness training," Barry insisted.

Jenny had a wonderful time. She would have had even if the Sooners hadn't won. She liked basketball, and she liked being with her boys.

"Strange as it seems, I really do miss you guys," she said, linking arms with them as they headed for her car in the parking lot.

"You want us to come home more often?" Joe asked, his tone full of concern.

"Oh, heavens no. You guys are in college now and belong here. If I get too lonesome, I'll get another cat. Besides I'm busy with a new house job. Just yesterday, I discovered that a famous French architect was brought to Oklahoma City in 1901 to build a house for the beloved bride of an aging cattle baron. It's really quite fascinating, and the house is lovely."

"Is that the house that belongs to your new boyfriend, Count Dracula?" Barry asked, reaching over to pull her collar away from her neck. "What *are* those marks on your throat, Mommie dear?"

"Has Mom got *another* new boyfriend?" Joe asked his brother. "Is it the guy she spent the night with during the ice storm?"

"Yeah, he's going to let me drive his Ferrari," Barry said.

"You guys better cut it out if you want those cookies I brought you."

"Are they chocolate chip?" Joe asked.

Jenny nodded.

"Double recipe?" Barry wanted to know.

"Of course. With pecans."

They decided to stop teasing.

Barry drove and soon stopped Jenny's car in front of a high-rise residence hall. "Is this where Linda lives?" Jenny asked.

"No. Paula lives here," Barry said.

"Paula? My goodness, Linda certainly didn't last long," Jenny said.

"Oh, I'm still going with Linda," Barry said casually. "In fact, I'm crazy about Linda. When we're both household words, we're going to have the biggest Hollywood wedding ever. I'm not sure whether we'll marry each other or other people, but we've agreed to share a wedding."

Jenny couldn't believe her eyes when Joe got out of the car and went up the front walk. "Joe has a girlfriend?" she asked Barry.

Barry grinned and nodded.

"What's she like?" Jenny said. Joe had never had a date, much less a girlfriend. Barry was the son who had gone steady with an uninterrupted succession of girls since the seventh grade.

"Oh, she's the studious type," Barry said. "A real Miss Jane straight off the *Beverly Hillbillies*. You know the type, mousy hair, glasses that are held together with a safety pin and always sliding down on her nose. She's also planning to major in zoology. She and Joe met at a Bird Watchers Club meeting. Don't look at me like that. I didn't make it up. They both belong to this club whose members get up at dawn every Saturday morning and go trekking across the countryside looking for cedar waxwings and tufted titmouses. Or would it be tit-mice?''

Jenny never knew if Barry was kidding or being serious.

Joe came out the front door of the dorm with one of the prettiest young women imaginable. She was tall, slender, with glorious red hair, a complexion like ripe apricots and glasses held together with a tiny safety pin. Barry grinned mischievously at his mother. Miss Jane, indeed, Jenny thought.

"I'm so glad to meet you, Mrs. Bishop," Paula said, pushing her glasses back on her nose. "Joe has assured me that you are the most fantastic mom on the face of the earth."

Then she leaned over and kissed Joe's cheek. Joe glanced at his mom and blushed.

Jenny worked very hard not to smile. She didn't dare look at Barry.

Barry's girlfriend, Linda, was a vivacious, raven-haired beauty. "Barry's the only boy I know who carries his mom's picture around in his billfold," she said with a smile that belonged on the cover of a movie magazine.

Linda scooted closer to Barry, and his arm went automatically around her shoulder.

They went to Othello's, the boys' favorite pizza restaurant. And the pizza was fantastic. So were the kids.

Joe and Paula were so full of new love, they couldn't stop brushing against each other and holding hands under the table. Paula kept pushing her glasses up on her nose. The glasses magnified her already large blue eyes and somehow only added to her unconscious charm.

And it was impossible not to like Linda. Jenny decided she would make a good talk-show hostess. She kept everyone involved in the conversation. She asked Jenny about teaching school and how it was to have twin boys. She got Paula to tell about her part-time job in the embryology lab. She insisted Barry give them a sample of his audition as disc jockey for the student radio station.

Linda even got Joe to admit he had made the highest grade in class on the American history test.

Every so often, Linda would turn to Barry and say in an exaggerated Oklahoma drawl, "You doin' all right, sugar?"

Barry would assure her he was doing just fine, then look over at his mother and wink. He liked Linda a lot, Jenny decided, but the two weren't in love. Both Linda and Barry were having too much fun being young and ambitious to fall in love.

But Paula and Joe seemed different. What Jenny saw between the two serious young people couldn't be dismissed as adolescent infatuation. The touching, the looks, the hand holding, the stolen kisses—how poignantly sweet it all was. Joe was so vulnerable and so inexperienced, the type of young person who falls long and hard when love comes along. Jenny had feared for him, but Paula seemed every bit as smitten with Joe as he was with her.

As she drove back to the city, Jenny found herself feeling melancholy. She was no longer first in her boys' lives. Of course, that was exactly as it should be. They were nineteen years old, and it was time for Joe and Barry to pull away from her, but she couldn't help feeling sad.

She understood that her sadness would be greatly tempered if she were not alone herself. People had a greater chance for happiness if they had a "significant other" in their lives. It had always been that way, and it always would be.

And she thought of Stephen Carmichael.

She wondered if she could be happy with him and if she would she ever have the chance to find out.

## Chapter Five

The two women carried their cafeteria trays back to Barbara's classroom. Usually Jenny and Barbara had lunch in the teachers' lounge, but Barbara was avoiding Chuck Ballard—again.

"And we can talk in here," Barbara said. "Maybe I'm getting a little paranoid, but it seems to me some of our colleagues are overinterested in the extracurricular lives of the school's resident widow and the resident bachelor. Chuck and I ran into Marion Fox and her husband the other night at the Neil Diamond concert, and she might as well have posted it on the office bulletin board the next day. I'm sure everyone in the whole school knows by now that Chuck and I went out together."

"If you don't want to be seen in public with someone, you shouldn't go to public places with that someone," Jenny said, trying to decide what the meatloaf was made of. Or was it a vegetable loaf? "As Shakespeare once said, 'The lady doth protest too much, me thinks.' Maybe you're more committed to this relationship than you realize and want to go public with it."

"Don't you go and get literary on me. *I'm* the English teacher here. And speaking about not denying one's true feelings, have you heard anything from the mystery man?'' Barbara asked.

Jenny shook her head. ''No, I haven't heard from him, and I have no 'true feelings' for the man. Good grief, Barbara, I saw him only once—well, twice if you consider stark naked as 'seeing'—and there's really no need for me to see him again. I can turn in my report on the house to his attorney when I finish it, and the attorney can pay me. I may never see Mr. Carmichael again. It's probably just as well.''

''Oh, come on. What's this 'just as well' stuff? Is that rationalizing, or is that rationalizing?''

''Okay, so I found the man intriguing,'' Jenny admitted. She decided not to finish the ''meat'' loaf and poked at her piece of cake with her fork. Jenny hadn't planned to eat it but changed her mind. She took a bite before continuing. Then another. ''But obviously Mr. Carmichael was not smitten by yours truly since almost two weeks have gone by without so much as a 'How're you doing on the house?' or a 'When can I see you again?' query from the man. I haven't the faintest idea in the world where he is. And as I keep pointing out to you, the man, by his own admission, has a wife and daughter. And smart gals avoid married men, remember?''

''Some marriage,'' Barbara scoffed, ''if he and his wife don't even live together. And you said yourself there is nothing in that house to indicate the woman even exists, except for a painting.''

''Maybe she hasn't moved in yet,'' Jenny said.

''Or maybe she's dead, or they're divorced. Is that cake any good? Please tell me it's dry and tasteless.''

''It's fantastic. It's the best spice cake I've ever tasted. The icing has cream cheese in it. If men are widowed or divorced, they say so. I can't imagine a man having an ex-wife's picture hanging in his bedroom. And if she's dead, wouldn't he have the little girl?''

Barbara ran a finger over the icing on her piece of cake and licked it. "My goodness, for someone who thinks it would be just as well never to see the man again, you have really been thinking a lot about his marital state.''

"Well, you're the pot calling the kettle black," Jenny accused. "All this talk about not wanting to have anything to do with the boy biology teacher, and just look at you. You've lost weight, cut off your ponytail and now, Barbara Whinnery, you've covered up the gray and are wearing *eye shadow*. What happened to the natural woman stuff?''

The two women glared at each other for a minute then burst out laughing. "Would you listen to us?" Jenny said. "We don't fool each other one bit.''

"No, honey, we sure don't," Barbara said between munches on a carrot stick. "You've got a crush a mile long and two miles wide on a man who's probably got a crazy wife stashed away in the attic like Heathcliff in *Wuthering Heights*. And I've gone goggle-eyed over a blond, curly headed Oedipus who's searching for a mother figure and who wants to impregnate said mother figure.''

Jenny regarded her friend with a shake of her head. "I don't know what I'd do without you, Barbara. It's impossible to take life too seriously with you around. Except you're wrong about the attic. I've been in the attic of that old house, and *she* doesn't live there. I suppose you're not going to eat your cake and make me feel even more guilty about those calories I consumed than I already do.''

"Here, you want my piece?" Barbara said with a superior tone. "For the first time in twenty years, I weigh the same as I did when I got married. I love this body so much that I'm not about to feed it cake or ever let it get pregnant again. I figure it's paid its dues and has earned some respect. Is there an attic over the carriage house? Maybe he stashed her there."

"I'm not sure, and no, I don't want your cake. I hope you have a serious attack of low blood sugar before the day is out just to pay you back for being so self-righteous. So, what are you going to do about Chuck? You say no, no, no, but your new body, hairdo and makeup say yes, yes, yes."

Barbara patted her short, reddish curls. "Can't I just have a fling with the boy—you know one last affair before senility sets in?"

"It's okay by me, but can Chuck handle it? The poor boy thinks he's dead serious about all this. If you're really certain about there being no future in the relationship, maybe you should end it now before it gets any harder for him."

"Yeah, he told me he thinks all the time about how wonderful it will be when we're married and his baby is growing inside of me. He wants to buy me a maternity dress."

"A maternity dress?" Jenny started to laugh. "To wear now?"

"Yeah. He says I can grow into it."

"You're kidding!" Jenny's shoulders shook with laughter. "Why don't you wear it to the Honor Society banquet and give Marion Fox a real treat?"

The door to the classroom opened. Barbara covered her mouth to hold back the laughter.

"Am I interrupting something?" Chuck Ballard said, sticking his blond head in the door.

Both women stopped laughing momentarily, looked at each other and started again.

"Come on in, Chuck," Jenny managed to say. "We saved you a piece of cake."

"No, thank you. I had some, and it was dry and tasteless. I just wanted to tell you, Barbara, that the Biology Club meeting's been postponed. I can come over and help Greg with his transmission after school. You look beautiful. See you later."

Both women stared at the closed door with its picture of Shakespeare in a Michael Jackson T-shirt.

"I wish he weren't so damned nice," Barbara groaned. "I wish he were a fat, ugly nerd. And that hair! Blond curls like a pretty cherub. My Gregory had blond curls like that when he was a baby. Oh, Jenny, what am I going to do?"

"Well, it looks like you're going to eat that cake for starters."

"Yeah, I guess I am. And I don't even like it."

"I know," Jenny said. "It's dry and tasteless."

THE PHONE WAS RINGING. Jenny hurried to unlock the door and rushed in to pick it up. She recognized Stephen's voice immediately. And immediately a warm flush radiated through her body. He had called—finally.

"Where are you?" she asked.

"Washington. On my way to Guam. The plane will have a short fueling stop at Tinker Field. Can you meet me for a cup of coffee."

"Yes. When?"

"In about three and a half hours. There's a drugstore right across the street from the main entrance to the base."

"Yes. I know where you mean."

"I won't have long."

"I understand."

Jenny walked around the apartment aimlessly for a time then remembered she had planned to work on her Graystone report this afternoon. She fixed herself a cup of tea and spread her folders out on the kitchen table and got out a fresh, yellow legal pad.

But after shuffling papers around for a while, she gave up trying to get her thoughts organized. Her mind would focus on only one thing—she was going to see Stephen again. Finally, she went for a walk to escape from the slow-moving hands on the clock.

The air was brisk. Her feet would have preferred to skip.

She stopped telling herself to beware. The man had a right to speak his piece before she judged him.

She waited in her car in front of the drugstore watching for him in her rearview mirror. It was dark, but the streetlights were bright. She recognized his reflected image jogging across the street and got out to wait for him beside the car. He was wearing fatigues, boots and an olive drab jacket with eagles on the shoulders. A cap was jammed in his jacket pocket.

He stopped a few steps away from her. "You look lovely. I've thought about that a lot—how lovely you are. How much I enjoyed being with you. How much I wanted to see you again."

"I'd given up on hearing from you," she said.

"I wanted to call but felt like I had no right."

"How do you feel now?"

"Longing for the future but bound by the past. Still. Letting go of an obsession isn't easy, but I'm working on it. Can you take me on faith for now, Jenny?"

"Are you married?"

"No. As of yesterday, my wife is legally dead."

She could see the pain in his face. Her eyes misted over as she opened her arms to him.

They clung to each other for a time in front of the Rexall drugstore. The roar of low-flying planes landing and taking off filled the air about them. A siren sounded in the distance. His arms were strong and made her feel safe.

By unspoken agreement, they took a walk instead of spending their few minutes together in the drugstore over coffee. Arm in arm, they walked a few blocks into the modest residential area behind the strip of stores. Jenny asked no more questions. Stephen offered no more answers. The time for talking would come later, but they had made a beginning.

REMEMBERING how chilly it had been in Graystone's attic, Jenny took a small electric space heater and an extension cord with her when she went to search for clues in the trunks and boxes there. And she had a thermos of coffee, a sandwich, an apple and a tablet for notes. It was Saturday morning, and Jenny was prepared to spend the day.

She was excited at the prospect. Jenny loved opening old things: old trunks, boxes, books, diaries, letters, newspapers. She even liked looking in the pockets of old garments. Historical research for her was like a wonderful game, a treasure hunt with information as the prize. The wonderful window into the past that research opened could reveal sadness or joy, defeat or triumph, goodness or evil, brilliance or stupidity. It was endlessly fascinating to Jenny. Through her research, Jenny had met villains and heroes, saints and criminals, the famous and just plain folks. She came west with them in the covered wagons and settled Oklahoma Territory.

And now, there in the attic of Graystone, she could once again journey in her own private time machine and spend a day reconstructing the lives of the people who had lived in this fine old house. It was evident that Miss Grace and Miss Patience had been pack rats, and that fact certainly was going to make Jenny's job easier, allowing her to glean information from family records, school report cards, deeds, military records, diaries, letters and albums.

Jotting down notes as she went, she looked through the albums first. While many of the pictures were rather formal studio-type photographs of various family members on the occasion of weddings, confirmations and graduations, there were others taken more informally at Christmas, birthdays and other celebrations.

After she finished with the albums, Jenny tackled Patience's eighteen diaries and a box of old letters, all of which Jenny had found in a black leather trunk with brass trim. The leather had grown stiff and split in many places. The trim was dented and tarnished, but the lock was still in good condition. She tried to unlock the trunk with a nail file, but finally gave up and pried it open with a screw driver. Inside was a gold mine. The letters were mostly business letters and polite social notes, but the diaries were detailed and personal, covering a period of seventy-two years. It was a good thing she had allowed all weekend for the job. Tomorrow, she would bring two sandwiches.

By Sunday evening, Jenny had pieced together much of the story of Graystone with complete details since the early childhood of the two older Ellsworth sisters, thanks to Patience's wonderful diaries.

Their father, Cassius Ellsworth, had not married until he was in his late thirties and brought his young bride to be the mistress of Graystone and bear his children. He was past forty by the time their two older daughters were born and almost sixty before Stephen's mother, Marie, was born. The girls' mother died while Marie was a baby.

Cassius was a politically powerful man who served many years in the state senate and raised his daughters with a strong hand. The older girls finished high school and Patience had a year of study at the teachers' college in Edmond before she ran off and married a cowboy who worked on the family's Logan County ranch.

Cassius followed the young couple all the way to Port Arthur, Texas, brought Patience home and had the marriage annulled. "I would have stayed with my beloved Jubal," Patience wrote, "if he had only stood up to Papa. But Papa convinced him that a girl like me would not be happy married to a man who could never give her a proper home and that if he really loved me, he'd send me back home. I begged Jubal not to listen, that Papa didn't know about happiness, that he preferred power over happiness. I told Jubal that I'd rather wear rags and live in a shack with him than be a grand lady in a mansion. But Jubal let Papa scare him away. He turned his back and left me."

Patience never forgave her father, or Jubal or herself. In later years she wrote again of that fateful day and said, "If only I'd run after Jubal and said, 'Jubal Muldowney, you'll have to pick me up and throw me bodily out of your life if you don't want me.' If I'd done those things then maybe I'd not have lived all these years alone, a childless spinster. I waited for Jubal to be a hero when maybe I needed to be more of a woman.''

Her sister Grace had been engaged at age thirty-three to a Methodist minister who was killed while serving as a chaplain in France during the Second World War.

''Foolish Grace,'' Patience had written, ''now that he's dead, she's decided that she really loved the Reverend J. Carter Upthegrove. She's chosen to forget about his pompous ways and how she wept in her pillow and swore that she wasn't going to marry the man no matter what Papa said. Now that her fiancée has died, Grace can become a tragic figure and wear her unmarried state with respectability.''

When Marie fell in love with the grocer's grandson, a self-righteous Grace and an elderly but still indomitable Cassius locked her in her bedroom. Patience, then almost forty, sold her jewelry, picked the lock on the door and gave the money to Marie. In the middle of the night, she kissed her younger sister goodbye and told her to go to her young Irishman and not ever to look back. ''One sister should be happy,'' Patience had told Marie in parting.

The light was growing dim in the attic when Jenny put the last diary back into the trunk and closed the lid. She felt that she had made a friend. She looked around the room and could feel Patience Ellsworth's presence there. Jenny just knew that some days Patience would have come up here to be alone and sit by one of the dormer windows and write in her diary. How sad that Stephen never got to know his Aunt Patience. But at least now Jenny could explain to him that one aunt had not stood in the way of his parents' marriage.

She walked over to the nearest window and stood there for a time, staring out into the twilight, visualizing the countryside as Patience would have seen it before modern-day developers subdivided it.

*"I waited for Jubal to be a hero when maybe I should have been more of a woman."* Poor Patience, having to live with a lifetime of regret. Love didn't come along every day, and when it did come, the circumstances and the people were usually not perfect, but it was still worth the risk.

When Jenny realized she was not alone in the attic, she felt no fear. She knew the presence behind her was either the spirit of Patience Ellsworth or the living presence of her nephew Stephen.

Jenny turned. Stephen was standing at the top of the stairs. He looked so handsome in uniform.

"How incredible, finding you here," he said.

"Why?"

"Because one of the things I remembered most poignantly was you standing in front of that very window, looking out. I stood behind you and wanted so much to touch you."

Very deliberately Jenny turned and faced the window. She heard his footsteps crossing the wooden floor.

Yes, this was how it was. He had been standing behind her that night, and she had wondered how it would feel to step backward into the circle of his arms.

She thought of Patience, who had to live with regret, and took the step backward. Stephen's arms came around her waist as she knew they would. She folded her arms across his; her head went back against his shoulder. His face was touching her hair. He sighed. His body relaxed.

"Oh, Jenny," he said. "This is the first peace I've known in such a long time."

Jenny knew she could turn in his arms, that they could kiss and that kissing could lead to something else. But she understood what he was feeling. Peace—like a boat that finally finds safe harbor after surviving storm-tossed seas. Tears came to her eyes that he would think of her in such a way.

So they stood for a long time in the quiet of an attic in an old house, not speaking, only touching, needing nothing more.

The feel of him against her back was solid and warm and real. His heart beat firmly in his chest. His breath was soft against her cheek. The hair on the back of his hands was coarse.

"Your hair smells like springtime," he said. "I like the smell of you and the feel of you and the look of you, Jenny Bishop. And I like *you*. You made me laugh. Do you have any idea how long it's been since I've laughed? I've thought a hundred times of you pulling back the shower curtain and finding an alligator in your bathtub."

Jenny chuckled to herself, remembering.

"And now, my dear lady," he whispered in her ear, "I think I'd best feed you. Your stomach is rumbling under my hands."

Jenny turned in his arms and leaned into their circle. "Now that you mention it, I'm starved. I forgot my sandwiches today, and I kept thinking I'd run to get something, but I got so engrossed with your Aunt Patience's diaries that I couldn't put them down."

"I want you to tell me all about them over a wonderful dinner with fabulous wine."

Jenny started laughing. "I can just see the two of us walking into a restaurant. You look like Clark Gable in a World War II movie. And I look like—well, I look like I've been in a dusty attic all day."

"My keen military mind tells me we have two choices. I can change into jeans, or we can take you home to change into something that looks like Greer Garson in a World War II movie."

"Would you give me a cup of coffee while I make up my mind?" Jenny asked. "This calls for some thought. I don't get an invitation to go out with a handsome man in uniform just everyday. But on the other hand, my wardrobe is sadly lacking in Greer Garson dresses."

Jenny unplugged the heater and gathered up her things. She felt as if she could fly down the stairs. Or to the moon. He said her hair smelled like springtime.

But the rest of her didn't. Suddenly she wanted a bath and to look pretty. She wanted to sit across a restaurant table from Stephen and relish his uniformed handsomeness. She wanted to make him laugh and for them to lift their glasses together and drink the wine of life.

"I don't need the coffee after all," she said at the bottom of the stairs. "I just made up my mind. I want you in uniform. Give me an hour, then pick me up at my apartment."

She wrote down the address for him. He took her hand and held it. His expression sobered. "I hate to let you out of my sight. You won't vanish, will you?"

"You asked that so seriously," Jenny said. "What makes you think I'd vanish?"

AS SHE DROVE HOME, Jenny tried to concentrate on what she could possibly wear. What she needed now was a fairy godmother.

It was hard to think about clothes, though, with the fresh memory of Stephen's arms around her body occupying her mind. Had he closed his eyes when he put his face against her hair, Jenny wondered. My God, he looked wonderful. And felt wonderful.

She wanted to wear something ethereal, she decided, something soft and billowy like Greer would have worn racing across the moors to meet a uniformed Clark before he went flying off to battle the Huns.

But once home, facing the clothes that resided in her closet, Jenny had to give up on finding something billowy. Her best bet was the black knit, freshly back from the cleaners.

Jenny took a wonderful shower. Her mind was so full of Stephen and the evening ahead, she didn't even sing. She couldn't remember the words to any songs. "Isn't skin fun?" she said out loud as she soaped herself. The lather floated across the silkiness of her body. It felt wonderful.

She patted her skin with bath powder and put on her best lingerie without allowing herself to deal with why she felt the need to put on lacy blue panties and bra—the only matching lingerie she owned. Maybe it just made her feel pretty.

She put on her makeup with great care then bent over from the waist to fluff her shorter hair. When she stood, she tossed her head back and stared at the results— wonderful exploding hair. She didn't look like Mrs. Bishop, the history teacher.

Jenny raced about picking up her apartment, running a dust cloth over the top of the television set and the coffee table. Clean-but-lived-in was the best look she could achieve. Graystone it was not.

When he knocked, she threw the door open.

"Were you standing there waiting for me to knock?" Stephen asked.

"Practically. I've been ready for hours. I look great, don't I?" Jenny twirled around for his inspection.

"You'll do," he said, but his eyes said more. "Well, so this is the home of the struggling schoolteacher who moonlights to pay the bills," Stephen said as he gazed about the room.

"It's not much, but it's home. And if you think it looks lived in now, you should have seen it before my sons went to college. Joe and Barry are adorable, but they're also world-class slobs. I feel my future daughter-in-laws will hate me, but I've tried, really I have. My sons just seem to have been born with a congenital defect that makes it virtually impossible for them to place a garment on a clothes hanger or in a hamper. Now, are you going to tell me about your daughter, or will it spoil the mood?"

Stephen's expression closed. He looked toward the window.

"Forget it," Jenny said. "We'll deal with that another time, I guess. I want to be outrageously happy tonight. What about you?"

"Yes, I'll vote for that," he said, smiling. "Outrageously will do just fine."

They went to a new restaurant. The Gypsy Camp. Jenny had read about it in the paper. "It's Hungarian," she explained, "and supposed to have wonderful music and food and a real live Gypsy fortune-teller. Do you want to see into the future?"

Again that closed look crossed his face. "I'm not sure," he said. "But I'm sure that the restaurant lady will have wonderful futures for us. She's paid to make people feel good, and I want to feel good tonight, even if it's a lie.''

The restaurant was opulent with fringed swags, brass samovars and ornate furnishings. A strolling violinist in an embroidered vest was filling the room with rhapsodies.

Stephen cut an impressive figure in his uniform, and the maître d' showed them to a secluded table in a corner of the room. Jenny felt a little foolish at how proud she felt to be walking across the restaurant with such an impressive man.

The wine steward helped them select a Hungarian Tokay, promising that it would be fabulous. The waiter suggested the chicken paprika.

The wine was incredible. The meal memorable. The music was happy and sad at the same time and so beautiful it made Jenny want to cry.

"I know the silver eagles on your shoulder mean you're a full colonel," Jenny said, "but explain the rest of the brass to me."

"My branch is the Ordnance Corps," he explained, pointing to the flaming cannon-ball insignia on the right lapel of his jacket. "The Ordnance Corps is a small part of the Army," he explained, "but quite important. We design, develop, procure, store, maintain and issue weapons. The patch on my left shoulder says I'm under the command of the Military District of Washington."

"And the ribbons on your chest?"

"They denote various military campaigns and awards for service. Everyone who's been around long enough gets some."

"Three rows of them?" she asked.

Stephen shrugged. "I served in Vietnam. I'm good at my job. I imagine you are, too, but they don't give teachers medals. Maybe they should. Now, you promised to tell me what you found in my attic."

Jenny excitedly told the story she had pieced together from his Aunt Patience's diaries.

" 'One sister should be happy,' she told your mother. Was your mother happy?"

Stephen nodded. "Sometimes. Dad was in the military and gone a great deal, and she didn't do very well at those times. She developed a drinking problem while he was in Korea, but when they were together, there was love."

"I'm glad," Jenny said and lifted her glass. "Here's to happiness and love."

Stephen lifted his glass, "And here's to Jenny."

At the end of their meal, they had a thick, sweet coffee. Jenny had forgotten about the promised fortuneteller, but suddenly there she was, a beautiful woman of indeterminate years with a heavy accent.

She took Stephen's palm and studied it at length. "You are a strong person, and loyal. You will not live to be old, but neither will you die young, and you will be healthy until you die. You have reached a time of change in your life, I think, but the past is still very much with you."

Stephen's eyes widened, and he withdrew his hand. The woman reached for Jenny's.

"Ah, but you are easy. A mother's hand. You have two children and perhaps there will be another. Even though you are hard working and practical about money, I see that you are a romantic by nature but are afraid sometimes of your own emotions."

Stephen gave the woman some money and thanked her. "Well, what do you think?" she asked.

"That she's very intuitive."

"I'm part Gypsy," Jenny announced.

"Oh? Can you read palms?"

Jenny reached for his hand and turned it over. "You must always be careful where you sit down, but perhaps you already know this. Yes, I see an accident, an embarrassing accident many years ago. You sat on a board with a nail protruding from it. It left you permanently scarred."

Stephen's mouth fell open.

Jenny tried so hard not to laugh. She really did. For a minute she was able to run her finger along the lines of his hand, telling him about the wise woman from Oklahoma who would leave an imprint on his life. But finally she couldn't hold it back. She started giggling, then laughing.

"How do you know that?" he asked. "I know it wasn't in that diary. That happened long after I'd visited my aunts. In fact, it was after my mother had died."

Jenny put her fingertips to her temple and closed her eyes. "It's a gift I have. It comes and goes."

No matter how much wine he poured into her glass, she wouldn't tell him how she knew about his scar. Maybe she never would, Jenny decided. Being a woman of mystery was kind of fun.

Finally, however, the wine bottle was empty. The evening was drawing to a close, and Jenny realized she had just as many unanswered questions as before. Were the wounds of Stephen's past still too raw and painful for him to talk about them?

The beautiful woman in the portrait at Graystone was legally dead. What exactly did that mean, Jenny wondered. And did Stephen still love her?

# Chapter Six

What now, Jenny wondered, as they walked across the restaurant parking lot. Thoughts of intimacy had certainly crossed her mind, but she pushed them aside. She wasn't ready for such a quantum leap into this relationship yet. There were just too many unanswered questions.

In fact, Jenny felt her mood shift from desire to anger. Why in the hell didn't the man just explain about his wife? And he owed Jenny some sort of statement of intent before they went any further.

Oh, hell, Jenny thought angrily. She was tired of going around in circles. Why didn't he just explain to her what was going on? She was a big girl. She could take it—probably.

Once they were both seated in the car, Stephen turned sideways in his seat and touched her hair. "Such soft hair," he said. "It feels like silk."

The streetlight across from the parking lot cast shadowed light on his face, accentuating its planes. It was the face of a good and gentle man who was struggling with a mantle of sadness.

Jenny touched the line of his jaw. "I don't want you to be sad," she said softly, more to herself than to him.

And suddenly she was in his arms. But hadn't she known he would kiss her? It was as though the whole evening had been arranged so they could get to this instant, to the time of touching and kissing.

His mouth was devouring hers. And Jenny found herself kissing him back just as physically. *Oh, yes,* she thought. This was what she wanted, to feel his strong arms around her, to feel the texture of his tongue as it moved against hers. How glorious that felt. His breathing was ragged. Or was it hers?

The brass buttons of his uniform and the medals on his chest dug into her flesh as they struggled against each other to kiss deeper, to give more of themselves. His hands were in her hair, on her face. *My God,* Jenny kept thinking, words beating through her brain like an insistant drum beat. *My God, my God.*

They parted long enough for her to say the words out loud, for him to say her name.

Then they lost themselves once again in the kissing. Jenny realized that the taste of tears was mixed in with the taste of their mouths, their lips. His tears or hers? She didn't know, but she understood them. The swell of emotion rose in her breast. Emotion surrounded them, brought out of individual pain and longing to this time of sharing.

And along with the emotion was a feeling of incredulity. Jenny couldn't believe that she was really here in this car, kissing this beautiful, sad, uniformed man of mystery. She was an impoverished schoolteacher hovering on the brink of forty, not a candidate for high drama and world-class passion.

Jenny had no way of knowing if she was involved in a fleeting moment or an enduring love, but she couldn't deal with what it all meant. The moment itself was what mattered to her now. She wanted the moment and its kiss to go on forever, this one long kiss and a hundred smaller ones that blended together, ebbing and flowing, cresting and falling, in imitation of another more intimate act that their bodies cried out for. No longer did she wonder if she was ready to become that involved with this man. She wanted all from him that there was to be given.

"I want you," he was saying. "I want you more than I can ever say."

"No," Jenny heard herself answering in spite of her body's urging. "It's too soon. There are too many things I don't understand."

He drew back for an instant, adjusting to the fact that the kissing was to be all there was. Then he pulled her close and kissed her again, but the urgency had lessened. The kissing was gentler, sweeter.

"You're right," he said finally. "I want to do this right, Jenny. I want to come to you unfettered and sure of what I'm offering you, but God, it's difficult. Right now, there's a part of me that says, 'Damn the torpedoes, full steam ahead.' "

"That sounds like Navy talk," Jenny said as she touched his beautiful mouth with her fingertips. How could lips be firm and soft at the same time? "Don't you mean, 'Praise the Lord and pass the ammunition'?"

He laughed. "Yeah. I guess I do. You're really something, pretty lady. I don't think I've ever enjoyed being with anyone the way I have with you. And I think we just took the act of kissing to a higher plane."

"Yes. To outer space." Jenny sighed, as she adjusted her clothing and smoothed her hair. "Kind of shakes one up, doesn't it? You okay now?"

"Depends on what you mean by okay," he said. "If you mean put back like I was before, I don't think that's possible. But I think the danger has passed."

"What now, Colonel Carmichael?"

"Can you trust me a bit longer?"

Jenny turned away from him. Tears came to her eyes, but this time, the tears were not born of desire. She was afraid. What if she lost him?

STEPHEN LET HIMSELF into his house, his overgrand house, that he had no business keeping. It had no place in his life. When he inherited the house, the dream of Jade and Mindy was beginning to fade, but Graystone revived it.

Stephen's immediate reaction was that he would have to sell the house, but he had found himself caught up in Graystone's charm. He had thought of installing Jade and Mindy in its tasteful, elegant rooms and decided to make the old house his home. Instead of flying over Oklahoma on his cross-country trips, he would stop and stay a few days each time in *his* house. And if he ever succeeded in reuniting his little family, he would take early retirement and live permanently in the house. He would plant a garden and keep a horse for Mindy. He'd get a job teaching school or perhaps working with his hands, and they would live a normal sort of life. Stephen had stopped just short of having one of the bedrooms turned into a room for Mindy but had looked at furniture. Mindy would be almost fourteen, and the decorator at the furniture store had shown him pictures of appropriate rooms for teenage girls.

He let himself believe that inheriting Graystone was some sort of omen. He now had a home; therefore, he would soon have his family back. So he had kept the

house for the dream, for the hope that the next clue
would lead him to Jade and Mindy. It was his way of
denying what he knew in his heart was true. Two months
ago, on the seventh anniversary of their disappearance,
he took a long hard look at his life and realized it was
time to let the dream die. Past time. The dream had become an obsession. That was the day he first went to visit
the attorney in the judge advocate's office to discover
what his legal options were.

But maybe the house had been an omen of sorts after
all, a prophetic sign that his life would change. Perhaps
destiny intended that he keep the house because it would
lead him to lovely Jenny, who was so unlike Jade they
could have grown up on different planets. He had wor-
shiped Jade. Stephen's feelings for Jenny were more human.

How complicated his life had become. How impossibly complicated. He thought of the report that had come
hours after the hearing in which the wife he had searched
for during seven long years had been declared legally
dead, and he cursed the fates that kept him on a string,
helpless and afraid. God, would it ever end?

Stephen knew he couldn't sleep, and he didn't want to
relive the evening in bed. In bed, his physical desire for
Jenny would overtake his thoughts, and he needed to
think, not lose himself in his longing.

He started a fire in the living room fireplace, poured
himself a glass of brandy from the liquor cabinet and
seated himself in the wing chair. The aunts had apparently gone in for the best in their alcoholic beverages.
Maybe when you got to be as old as they had been, that
became the only possible indulgence. He wished he had
known them better, but Aunt Grace never forgave his
father for marrying his mother, and she blamed Carl for

Marie's tragic death. Grace had finally broken the silence early last year, writing to Stephen and asking him to come and see her. By then her sisters and her father were long dead, and Stephen was her only living relative.

He had called Grace the night her letter arrived, and they had set a date for his visit. He would come to see her the following month, stopping over on one of his cross-country trips.

But Grace had died shortly afterward. Stephen was glad they had at least had that phone call. He still made his planned stopover in Oklahoma City, but instead of a visit, he attended Grace's funeral.

Inheriting the house had come as a shock to Stephen. After years of estrangement, he assumed Grace would leave it to one of her charities. The charities received the Ellsworth money, but Stephen inherited the house in accordance with an agreement Grace had signed with her sister before Patience's death.

But men such as he had no permanent home. And even if Jade had reentered his life, she probably wouldn't have wanted an ordinary life in an ordinary, middle-America city.

For such a long time, he had been obsessed with the idea of finding Jade again, but now he found himself taking a figurative step backward and reexamining his feelings for his wife. He had been in awe of her beauty and poise. He had been overwhelmed that such a woman had allowed him to touch her, to make love to her and eventually to marry her. He remembered how foolishly grateful he had felt that she would allow her sleek, flawless body to become pregnant with his child. He revered her like one might revere a priceless work of art, but not like a normal man would treasure the love and companionship of a worthy woman.

Stephen went to the handsome liquor cabinet and poured himself a second brandy. Yes, he felt different about Jade, about the rest of his life, about the house and its place in his life. The house was a dinosaur anyway, he supposed. No one could afford to live in a house like this. It didn't look as if it belonged anymore, standing as it did in a sea of all those housing-development homes.

Stephen was proud of his military career. He had served his country well, but often wondered if it was what he wanted to do for the rest of his working life. Perhaps the time had come for a mid-life career change.

For as long as he could remember, Stephen had always known he would have a career in the Army. He had grown up on Army posts surrounded by things military. He admired his military father more than any other man alive. It was only after his mother died, and he saw his father's regret at having invested all his time and passion in a military career and not in his marriage that Stephen had any doubts about the life he had chosen for himself.

But by that time, Stephen was the fair-haired boy of the Ordnance Corps and becoming ever more important, ever more indispensable. What a trap being indispensable had become. How weary he was of being the only one with the whole picture, tired of carrying the weight on his shoulders, of worrying how best to deploy munitions in each of a hundred different possible projections. What if there was an outbreak in Berlin? Another invasion of South Korea? Terrorist attacks in New York? He even had projected the deployment of munitions if there was a USA-Soviet dispute over the Aleutian Islands.

Stephen and his staff had designed deployment plans for each contingency. He was in constant contact with arsenals—both known and top secret—where the Army stored its weapons and ammunition around the country and the world. He had contingency plans on top of contingency plans for each projected incident, from minor to global war. He visited each munitions manufacturer regularly to oversee quality. He was ever aware of the movement of Soviet troops, of activity on the Arab-Israel border, of every revolt, revolution, insurrection that might result in military action by the United States.

And the older he got, the more Stephen yearned for a life of his own, a life where he worried about the leak in the roof instead of how many Soviet divisions there were in Eastern Europe.

After Jade and Mindy disappeared, he tormented himself for so long with accusations that he had failed his family with his overblown sense of patriotic duty. He longed for a second chance. Being important no longer mattered to him, but could he turn his back on national defense? His country needed him. No other individual, military or civilian, had his comprehensive overview of munitions procurement and distribution. No one else had his special set of talents, knowledge and almost photographic memory. No one else understood quite so well all the variables.

It had all started so innocently.

When Stephen was twelve, an uncle had introduced him to the sport of target shooting. Most target shooters were also hunters, but Stephen didn't really like to hunt. He liked to score bull's-eyes.

It could have just been a kid's phase someplace in between electric trains and cars, but Stephen had been really good, a natural. So he kept up the shooting even after cars and dating became a part of his life, going eventually to state and national meets, acquiring national rankings and championships.

And as a natural offshoot of the sport, Stephen acquired more knowledge of the small weapons themselves. He loaded his own ammunition and even learned to make rifles.

Stephen fulfilled his boyhood dream and went to West Point where his prowess with rifles and pistols had not gone unnoticed, nor had his expertise in the science of small-arms weaponry and ammunition. And his penchant for the science of logistics earned him a year of graduate study at Ohio State University if he would select Ordnance as his branch of service.

Since that time, Stephen's career had been a steady series of promotions and ever-increasing responsibility. He was now the foremost military expert on small arms and small arms ammunition in the country.

Stephen had been shocked when his father took early retirement after Marie's death. Carl was away at the time, and Marie had fallen down the stairs. She had been drinking.

Everyone had expected Carl Carmichael to be the up-from-the-ranks general of his generation, but he resigned his commission and went to live on the beach of Virginia's Chincoteague Island. After only two years, he remarried. His second wife, Peg, captained a small chartered boat for deep-sea fishermen. Carl became her first mate.

After years of regretting his father's decision to turn his back on military service, Stephen found that he envied him for his new life. And he had finally forgiven Carl for not spending the rest of his life grieving over Marie and accepted his right to be happy with his new wife.

Yet Stephen himself was not able to come to terms with his own past. For seven years he had grieved and agonized. For seven years he had searched.

Ah, Stephen Carmichael, he told himself, you have no right to drag Jenny into your hopelessly muddled life. Would the day ever come when he could truly be free of the memory of Jade? And would the feeling of loss ever soften enough for him to live a normal sort of life with a normal sort of woman?

Except Jenny was far more than normal. She was warm and funny and vulnerable. Yes, she was everything that Jade was not. He had known that even before he kissed her.

What a wonderful evening he and Jenny had shared. Had the wine really been that good, the food really that special, or had being with her made it so? Stephen had gone past enjoying himself. He'd actually had fun. It had been a long time since he'd had fun.

How in the hell had Jenny known about that scar on his hip? Stephen laughed out loud in the quiet room remembering the mischievous twinkle in Jenny's eyes as she "read" his palm. A Gypsy indeed! More like an imp. And a duchess, a teacher, a sister, a friend and the most passionate woman he had ever kissed.

He was a widower now, Stephen reminded himself. A judge in Washington had declared Jade legally dead. It was perfectly all right for him to be courting another woman.

Except there was one last stone to be overturned.

HER VOICE was the first thing Stephen heard in the morning. Stephen groped around a bit when the phone rang, wondering who the hell it could be, then realizing it was who he hoped it would be.

"You're still asleep at seven o'clock in the morning," Jenny's voice said accusingly from the telephone receiver. "I thought military men got up at dawn."

Stephen felt himself smiling. He rearranged himself under the covers and tucked the phone to his ear. "And don't deny it," she was saying. "You sound like you have cotton in your mouth."

"While you yourself sound nauseatingly chipper. I thought you said you're weren't a morning person," he said, thinking how good it was to wake up to her voice, how very good. The only thing better would be if she were here beside him.

"Well, maybe it was magical powers of chicken paprika, but I woke up this morning feeling just fine. And it's really a beautiful day. Have you looked outside? After a week of overcast gloominess, the sunshine seems like such a gift. Of course, it's still cold, but I like the cold when it's not windy. I know that I'm babbling, but I really do feel rather full of myself. How would you like me to stop by on my way to school and bring you the world's best doughnuts from my favorite bakery?"

"I'll put on the coffee," he said, feeling a surge of pure happiness at the thought of seeing Jenny.

"I can't stay long," Jenny said. "I have to be at school by eight."

"Then stop talking and hurry over."

Stephen fairly leaped out of bed, ran downstairs to put on the coffee, then dashed through the shower and pulled on jeans and a sweatshirt. He met her at the door carrying his shoes.

They stood looking at each other across the threshold. Jenny was smiling shyly. The morning sun made golden highlights on her rich brown hair. Her eyes were brilliant, her cheeks rosy from the cold. He drank in the sight of her and actually felt his knees go a little weak. This was a woman to love and cherish.

"Hi," she said, her breath making vapor in the cold air. "May I come in? It's chilly out here, and you're going to get frostbite of the toes."

"You can come in only if you promise to kiss me." His tone was teasing. Stephen hadn't realized he could talk like that, not *serious* Stephen who was as meticulous in his speech as he was in his work habits. *That* Stephen never teased, never joked. God, he never even enjoyed himself, or maybe in a contrite, sick way he did, getting caught up in the tragic drama of his circumstances. But this morning Stephen felt very young and carefree because this doughnut-bearing woman had arrived at his door.

Jenny stepped inside, pushed the door closed behind her, put her sack of doughnuts on the table and was in his arms in about two and a half seconds.

Stephen dropped his shoes on the floor and surrounded her with his embrace. God, she was magic—not the same kind of magic he had felt with Jade. No this was entirely different. With his wife, he felt as though he must touch her with great care, the way one would handle the most fragile of porcelain vases. Jade's body had been petite and delicate, Stephen always felt she would break if he squeezed her too hard. But Jenny was firm and strong. Tentatively, he hugged her harder. No, this woman would not break. So eagerly she met his embrace, his kisses. With Jenny, he would have to hold nothing back.

"When can I make love to you?" he whispered into her hair.

"I don't know," Jenny said, then he felt her body change and draw away. Damn, he thought. He'd spoiled the moment. But he did want her so much.

She picked up the doughnut sack. "Let's have breakfast," she said. "I have to leave in a little bit."

He poured their coffee. Jenny sat on the high kitchen stool. He leaned against the counter.

Jenny looked miserable as she stared down at her cup, her high spirits gone. She wasn't eating her doughnut. "That picture upstairs..." She hesitated, took a deep breath and began again. "I've learned some hard lessons, Stephen, and while my heart and body cry out to trust you, my instincts say 'beware.'"

Jenny stopped and took another breath. Stephen waited for her to continue. He couldn't avoid this conversation any longer even though he still didn't know what he should tell her.

"I do believe that people should enter into a relationship with open hearts," she said. "Is that too much to ask? All you've told me is that your wife is 'legally' dead. Nothing more. What are you *not* telling me? And if you're wondering why my voice is quivering and my hands are shaking, it's because I'm so damned afraid that this little speech will drive you away from me. But you understand why I had to say it?"

Stephen nodded.

"Is she really dead?" Jenny asked.

"I don't know," Stephen said. Just saying the words made him feel empty inside. Could he make Jenny understand how it was not to know, how unresolved his life had been? "But according to a judge in Washington, D.C., I'm a widower, Jenny."

Stephen turned and looked out the window over the sink, knowing it would be easier to explain if he wasn't looking at Jenny's face. It was all so painful, even after all this time.

"I came home from a trip seven years ago," he began, "and my wife and daughter were gone. There was no note, no clue of any sort about what might have happened to them, and I've spent the past seven years trying to find out. I have literally searched the globe until I don't know where else to look. My only dream for those long, joyless years has been to find them. The law says that after seven years, I don't have to wait any longer. I just wish I knew what happened to them. It's the not knowing that eats at me. And now, ironically, I have a lead. Although it's probably nothing, I must check it out just so I know I've done everything I could."

Stephen turned to face her. "I want to close this one last door and court you properly. I'd forgotten how it felt not to be sad. You did that for me, Jenny. You can't imagine how grateful I am to you for that. Before I met you, I only had one goal in life, and that was to find my wife and daughter. And now I have a new goal. I want to get on with my life. I want to stop being sad and learn acceptance."

"You loved her very much?" Jenny asked.

Stephen hurt for her. He shouldn't have done this to her. "Yes, she and my daughter were my life. I can't lie to you about that."

Jenny picked up her purse, but Stephen grabbed her wrist. "No, don't leave like this."

"I have to." She was crying. She fought him briefly as he pulled her to him. Then she relaxed and laid her head against his shoulder. He stroked her back while she choked back her silent sobs.

"Your hair really does smell like springtime, you know, like new life, all clean and sweet, like violets and lilacs freshly opened to the sun." And Jade's hair had smelled of the heavy scents of summer, Stephen thought, of gardenias and jasmine. But he didn't want to compare the two of them anymore. Both women were unique and special. And he loved them both, God help him. He loved them both. But his love for Jade was a love of something past.

"Was she as beautiful as her picture?" Jenny asked into his shoulder.

"Yes. She was very beautiful." Stephen closed his eyes remembering. Jade was the most flawlessly beautiful woman imaginable. He wanted to tell Jenny that there were all sorts of beauty, that her own was more comfortable and believable. But he knew the words would sound condescending and didn't say them.

"May I see you after school?" he asked still stroking her back. "I need to drive down to Fort Sill this afternoon. Come with me. We can stay overnight. The old post is quite fascinating. And there's a little range of mountains . . ."

"I know," Jenny's muffled voice said. "The Wichitas. The boys and I used to camp down there."

"We can explore a bit tomorrow," he said eagerly. "We can have separate rooms or whatever will make you comfortable, but I'd really like to be with you."

She didn't answer for a long time. He could sense her indecision. "Please," he said. "I want you to."

She pulled away from him and returned to her perch on the kitchen stool.

"I know I'm crazy, but yes, I'll go," she said.

"Good. I'm glad. Now, eat your doughnut," he said.

"I don't want it."

"You'll be faint with hunger, and your students will take advantage of you. Please, I'll worry about you if you don't eat."

"You'll worry about me?" she said. She looked up at him. "Gee, that's kind of nice. I'm so used to worrying about my kids and my parents and my students."

She smiled a funny little crooked smile at him. Stephen smiled back. He wondered if his smile covered his confusion. The past seven years had been sad, but in a sense they had been easy. His emotional responses to life had been preordained. He hadn't needed to concern himself with plans for the future, with falling in love, with being responsible to another human being. Obsession had provided a cop-out for life. His obsession had been his constant companion for so long, he wondered if he would miss it, if he could function without it. Maybe he would crumble and fall apart and be worthless without his obsession to shore him up and make him strong and single-minded of purpose.

Perhaps he didn't deserve a lovely woman like Jenny. What if he couldn't get his act together and ended up making her unhappy? What if he called out in the night to Jade? God knows, it had happened often enough in the past. Would he ever be free of her memory?

But at the same time all these misgivings were tumbling about in his mind, at quite another level he was planning their excursion. They would visit the historic sites and poke around the mountains. He wished it wasn't the end of February. He'd like to have a picnic.

# Chapter Seven

Since Vietnam, Stephen had been permanently based at the Pentagon in Washington, D.C., with fully half of his time spent traveling around on temporary assignments to consult with suppliers and inspect corps facilities. He was in New York when he first saw Jade, eating at his favorite Chinese restaurant, Sung Tieng's, on Bleeker Street in the Village. He looked across the tiny restaurant, and there she was, the most exquisitely beautiful woman he had ever seen in his life. Her long hair hung in a heavy curtain to her waist. It was the smoothest, shiniest hair Stephen had ever seen, and so black, it shone blue. Her skin was so smooth and perfect that it belied reality. Her features were a delicate blending of the best of Occidental and Oriental blood. She turned and looked over her shoulder at him, allowing her gaze to rest momentarily on his face.

Stephen felt as though he had been run over by a Mack truck. He was helpless to do anything but sit and stare at her. Long after she had returned her attention to her companions, Stephen sat staring at her profile, her gesturing hands, her incredible hair, her booted feet.

Still in uniform, Stephen had just come in by train from a routine inspection of Picatinny Arsenal in New

Jersey and was due at the Watervliet Arsenal in upstate New York the following day. He was allowing himself a couple days in New York to go to a play and enjoy his favorite restaurants.

But now his meal was all but forgotten because of the Oriental woman sitting across the restaurant. She was with a slender, graying man wearing a suit and tie and an older Oriental woman. They were speaking French. Stephen didn't have to hear them to know; he could tell by their mannerisms, by the way they pursed their lips. Once during their dinner, the beautiful young woman glanced at Stephen, their eyes meeting only fleetingly. His stomach contracted.

He watched with sinking desperation as the three finished their meal. Soon they would be leaving. What was he to do? He couldn't let that woman just leave and melt away in the city never to be seen again. But he couldn't go over to the table and announce that he was desperate to meet her, to see her again, to touch her perfect hair and skin.

He called the waitress over and asked if she knew the young woman at the other table. The tiny Chinese waitress shook her head no.

"Did she give her order in Chinese?" Stephen asked.

The waitress nodded yes.

"Does the man she's with speak Chinese?"

The waitress shook her head. "No think so," she said, "but the other lady does."

"Would you please go tell the beautiful lady in Chinese that I admire her greatly and would like to have the honor of meeting her? Tell her I have never admired anyone so greatly in my entire life."

The waitress giggled behind her hand and nodded. Stephen watched as she delivered the message. The older woman at the table glanced in Stephen's direction, her expression full of displeasure. The younger woman looked past the waitress. Her cool, almond-shaped eyes fell on Stephen, lingering this time.

The older woman waved the waitress away. A little later when she excused herself to go to the rest room, the younger woman called the waitress back to the table and spoke briefly in Chinese, and the tiny waitress once more giggled and covered her mouth before hurrying off to the kitchen. Stephen wanted to follow her, to find out what the beautiful woman had told her. He tried to make eye contact with the woman again, but she refused to look his way, and shortly she and her companions left the restaurant. Stephen wanted to run after her. How could he just sit there and let her go? Before he walked out the door, however, she looked back over her shoulder at him and nodded ever so slightly.

The waitress eventually made her way back to Stephen's table. She informed him that the young lady had said the food was very good, and she would eat here again tomorrow night.

Stephen was at the restaurant by six o'clock the following evening. She did not come until nine.

She walked over to his table and extended to him a slender hand. "My name is Jade," she said with a British accent. Stephen was smitten.

As FATE WOULD HAVE IT, Jade also lived in Washington, D.C., assigned to the diplomatic staff of the embassy for the People's Republic of China.

Jade's parents had escaped from her father's native country with their two infant daughters in the early 1950s and gone to live in England. Jade's maternal grandmother was English, and her mother had been raised in London. The family lived with her in London. Jade had been raised in a household where English, Chinese and French were spoken almost interchangeably, and she had been sent to school in Switzerland, where she'd mastered German and studied Russian.

Jade's professor father had never adjusted to life in England and decided there was less idealistic distance between himself and the new Communist masters of his homeland than he had previously thought. When he elected to return to China, Jade's mother refused to go with him. Jade's two younger sisters stayed in England, but Jade cast her lot with her beloved father and returned with him to his native Peking, where she continued her study of Russian and German at Peking University and eventually became an official government interpreter.

When Stephen saw her in the restaurant, she had come to New York to do some translating for the Chinese delegation at the United Nations.

She wasn't supposed to get involved socially with Americans. Her and Stephen's phone calls, letters, meetings were all clandestine, but that only served to heighten the intensity of their relationship.

From the first, the relationship had been a strange one. Stephen knew it was abnormal, that it was more obsession than love. He was intensely jealous of everything in Jade's life that had nothing to do with him. If she hadn't agreed to defect and marry him, Stephen often wondered what would have happened to him. He couldn't eat or sleep. Only years of finely honed professionalism kept him effective at his job, but it was agony each time he had to wrench his thoughts away from Jade and return to the world of ordnance.

But apparently total adoration by the American Army officer appealed to Jade. For reasons that were never quite clear to Stephen, she applied for political asylum and they were married. He knew she didn't love him in the way he loved her. Sometimes it was almost as if she tolerated him. But she allowed him to make love to her lovely ivory body with its small, high breasts and waist so tiny he could span it with his hands. In spite of her cool passivity, or maybe because of it, she excited him more than any woman had before.

Jade became somewhat of a celebrity in Washington. The story of her defection and her subsequent marriage made all the newspapers and television news programs, and because of her extreme beauty, the media's fascination with her continued. She was frequently asked to comment on news stories that came out of China. She became a U.S. government interpreter but never received security clearance to work on classified documents, so she turned to the world of finance and did free-lance interpreting for banking institutions and stock brokerages. Eventually, she worked part-time at a bank and could have worked full-time if she had chosen, but she was a mother by that time, saying that she preferred to spend her time with her daughter.

Fatherhood was a revelation for Stephen. He had not understood before how potent a parent's love for a child could be. It was frightening. It gave him so many more things to be afraid of: fever, speeding cars, large dogs, kidnappers. And those Russian divisions in Eastern Europe took on an even more ominous note. It was his daughter's future they were threatening.

Mindy looked a great deal like her mother although her features were less Oriental. Her hair, while blue black, had a slight wave to it, and her eyes were hazel rather than brown. But she was her mother's daughter, no doubt about it. And even as a small child, she had a presence about her. She looked like a doll, but she carried herself like a princess, except when she was around her father. Stephen never felt more blessed than when his daughter squealed her delight at his homecomings. She would open her plump little-girl arms, and Stephen would sweep her into his arms, burying his face in her sweet little neck. Jade would smile a little half smile and wait until Mindy was ready to share her daddy with her mother, then the three of them would embrace as a family. Stephen would put his cheek against his wife's smooth hair and inhale the gardenia scent of her perfume. He would feel her delicate body beneath his hands, and a surge of desire would sweep through him.

Even now, all these years later, Stephen could remember how it was and feel regret that it was no more.

AFTER JENNY HAD RUSHED OFF to school, Stephen spent the next several hours chopping down a dead elm tree and cutting it into logs. He found the physical activity quite pleasing and enjoyed making the chips fly and the stack of logs grow as the hours wore on. Finally, however, he went inside to shower and eat, then change into his uniform.

At three o'clock, he met Jenny at her apartment as arranged. She was wearing the same soft green knit dress she had been wearing that morning. "Are your jeans in the bag?" he asked, indicating the small overnight bag on the sofa. He wanted to kiss her, but there was a reserve about her that told him intimacy would not be welcome at this point. But then he had told her he would do whatever made her comfortable. They would be friendly companions on this overnight excursion and nothing more. He'd have to sit on his hands to keep from touching her, but he would honor her unspoken request.

"Your dress is the same beautiful color as your eyes," he said in an attempt to relax her a bit. "And I like the way it kind of clings when you walk."

She made a face. "It makes me look fat," she said.

"Take my word for it," he said emphatically. "You don't look fat. Are you ready to go?"

"Yes, just as soon as I pour coffee into the thermos. It's already made."

While Jenny was in the kitchen, Stephen walked down the hallway to study the framed photographs randomly hung along its length. A couple were family-gathering pictures including Jenny with an older couple—her parents probably—and her sons. But most of the pictures were just of her sons—school pictures, pictures of Little League and high school sports. They were handsome boys. One looked like his mother. Stephen wondered if the other boy resembled his father. She hadn't talked about her ex-husband, or any other men, except to say she'd learned "hard lessons." He suspected she hadn't had the cherishing from her men that she deserved. If ever he had the chance, Stephen promised himself, he would fuss over her. Yes, he would cherish her greatly.

What would her boys think of him, he wondered. But they really weren't boys anymore. They were young men. Would they be jealous of their mother's suitor? They would probably feel protective, but they were at that age when sons grow away from mothers and make permanent commitments of their own. Jenny was no longer a day-to-day part of their lives, and it was time for Jenny to find someone to fill her empty home. As lovely as she was, that would happen soon, he suspected. She was bound to be lonely, and if he didn't become the man in her life, someone else would. The thought of some other man touching her and holding her and cherishing her hit Stephen in the gut like a fist.

Yet this morning he had just told her about Jade. He could appreciate how that must have made her feel. How unfair all this was to Jenny.

She offered to drive since she knew the way. Stephen readily agreed and found he liked being the passenger in a car driven by a beautiful woman. He enjoyed watching her mannerisms, her hands on the wheel.

They got away from Oklahoma City before the rush-hour traffic began and were soon heading west on Interstate 40.

Oklahoma City was located in the center of the state on what geographically was known as the "cross timbers." East of the city, Jenny explained, the state was rolling and wooded. West was the beginning of the prairie, or "short-grass country" as the locals called it.

As Stephen watched the countryside roll past them, he realized such country was spectacular only in its openness and simplicity. This time of year the landscape was a study in browns, varying from beige to russet, with an occasional field of winter wheat standing out like a bright green jewel. The soil and cattle were a reddish brown as was the muddy water of the farm ponds, while the winter-dead grass was pale and almost yellow. They passed through the small town of Blanchard whose one wide, curbless street had mostly pickup trucks, with only a few cars, parked along its sides and down its center.

He poured them coffee in styrofoam cups. How very fine it was traveling new roads with Jenny at his side, he thought as he sipped his coffee.

Fewer than twenty buildings composed the hamlet of Middleburg. There was a combination store, service station and post office, a scattering of houses and a large consolidated school.

They turned south at Chickasha, a settled-looking town with a courthouse and war memorial statue.

Then there was little but rolling prairie between them and their destination. Jenny put on her history teacher's hat and told Stephen about the Indian wars, the land runs. "Fort Sill was built in the 1830s in an effort to control the southwestern tribes. The less warlike tribes from along the eastern seaboard were being uprooted and resettled into the eastern part of the state—or Indian Territory as it was known at the time. The eastern tribes were farmers and able to adapt to a settled way of life, while the Plains people were nomadic hunters, and civilization meant an end to their way of life. Cities and railroads and fences were being built, dooming the Indian and his buffalo."

Stephen asked her questions, and she seemed to enjoy sharing the colorful history of her home state. "You're a good teacher, aren't you?" he asked.

"Yes, I think I am. I like teaching. Of course, half the battle with teaching is getting along with the kids, but I do that pretty well, too. Being a mother has helped immensely, and I can still remember what it was like to be that age. I don't know why so many adults forget that they were once young and suffered all the same growing pains."

"Sometimes I think I'd like to teach," Stephen admitted. "I had so much math at West Point and in graduate school; I could do that—teach math."

"But why would you want to? It sounds to me like you're pretty committed to a military career."

"Yeah," he admitted. "I guess I am."

Jenny pointed off to the right. "Mount Scott," she said.

"That's a mountain?"

Jenny laughed. "The highest in the state, and we're damned lucky to have it. The Wichitas are just a few remnants of an early geological era. Actually, the surrounding countryside is so flat that when you stand on top of Mount Scott, you feel like you're on top of the world. The view is really quite spectacular."

"Is there a road?"

"Yes, it was built during the Depression as part of a government work project for the unemployed."

"You know the state pretty well, don't you?" Stephen asked.

"Oklahoma's my home. I've lived here all my life," Jenny said with a shrug. "And I love history. I teach American and Oklahoma history."

"I've been Army all my life and never had a home," Stephen said. "It must be a nice feeling."

"You have a home now," Jenny said. "Graystone is a very beautiful home."

"I inherited a house," he corrected. "I have no home. Homes require a commitment."

"Like relationships," Jenny said softly.

They were quiet as the small mountain range grew more distinct on the horizon. Jenny drove first into the outskirts of the nearby city of Lawton, where Stephen directed her to stop at the Holiday Inn. She waited in the car while he went inside. When he came back to the car, he had keys—one with 204, and one with 205.

Jenny accepted the one to 204. "Thank you," she said without looking at him.

Then they backtracked out to the entrance of the military post. The military policeman at the gate gave Stephen directions to the headquarters building. They arrived in front of the huge building in time to stand beside the car and watch the flag being taken down. An honor guard of soldiers marched smartly out to the flag pole. A cannon was fired, and all the vehicles in the vicinity came to a halt, uniformed occupants getting out and standing at attention beside their cars. Like Stephen, they saluted the flag. A bugler played taps, and with practiced ceremony, the soldiers brought down the flag and folded it before turning and marching smartly back the way they had come.

"That was impressive," Jenny said. "Do they do that every day?"

"Yes, it is nice, isn't it? A patriotic closure on the day. I've always been proud the military has clung to the old traditions. And now, I must apologize for leaving you, but if I don't hurry, I'm going to miss my appointment. I called to tell him I'd be late, but I don't want him to give up on me. I'll try not to be too long."

"No problem," Jenny said. "I'll just walk over and look at the artillery-weapons display by that old guardhouse. If I'm not here when you come out, I'll be over there."

Stephen reached out and buttoned her coat. Jenny grinned. "Thanks, Daddy."

He hurried inside the impressive building, feeling somewhat dishonest. He knew Jenny assumed he was on some sort of official business when it couldn't have been more personal.

Stephen was directed to a fifth-floor office, where he was greeted by an officer with Oriental features and coloring. The brass on the lieutenant colonel's shoulder showed him to be an intelligence officer, one of those individuals whose job it was to know the enemy.

Stephen introduced himself and they shook hands. "David Cheng," the man said by way of introduction.

Stephen apologized for being late as the man led him into an inner office and closed the door. "I still can't believe I have a carpeted office in Oklahoma," Cheng said almost apologetically with a decided Bostonian clip to his voice. "But I haven't been out in the field for three years now. I've been put out to pasture with a desk job."

"I would think that greatly enhances your chances of living to a ripe old age," Stephen said.

"Yeah. But sometimes the boredom gets me down. Now, tell me how you found out about me."

Stephen explained that his own top-secret security clearance had given him access to certain computerized files. He told of the countless hours he spent searching the computer record of intelligence reports for some mention of a certain Chinese woman who knew five languages including Russian.

"Usually I spend my computer time looking for information about the research, advancement and distribution of weapons by foreign powers. Intelligence supplies information about foreign powers to the Ordnance Corps that helps us plan our own arsenal needs. But I've also used the computerized record to search for a woman. I tracked down dozens of leads over the past seven years, and I don't really expect this one to go anyplace."

The lieutenant colonel lit a cigarette and leaned back in his chair while Stephen asked him about one particular undercover mission that had taken Cheng into Communist China several years before. "An intelligence officer in the Pentagon who had helped me some in the past came across your report and sent it over to me."

"It was pretty routine," Cheng explained. "We were doing surveillance of some visiting Soviets in Peking. They were acting like a business delegation, but we thought otherwise."

Cheng glanced at his watch, and Stephen realized he was keeping the officer far too long. He reached in his jacket pocket and pulled out a photograph. How many times had he gone through this little charade, he wondered. This is the end, the very end, he promised himself. He would get this over with and then court Jenny. He would put in the few more years necessary until he could take early retirement, then become a normal husband in a normal town. It was time to train someone else to worry about the Soviets.

Cheng was looking at the photograph and nodding. Why, Stephen wondered. Had he actually seen Jade and Mindy?

He grabbed the sides of his chair. Surely not. No one had ever recognized the picture before.

"I can't be sure about the little girl," Cheng was saying. "I didn't pay all that much attention to her. But the woman, you don't forget a looker like that. Yeah, that's her, but you understand, Colonel Carmichael, it's been almost five years ago. That's a pretty cold lead. I was in the big square in the center of the city, standing by the this big monument to the 'people's heroes.' I heard that woman in the picture talking to a girl. French with a British accent from a Chinese woman. You don't hear that too often. When she saw me, she switched to Chinese. It didn't seem significant at the time, but we're trained to report *everything* we observe when we're working out in the field. Is she really your wife?"

Stephen nodded.

"That must be tough," the man said.

Stephen's hand shook as he replaced the photograph. His throat felt dry, and his heart beat so hard in his chest it hurt. Somehow he managed to shake hands with the man and make his exit.

He had to compose himself. He couldn't return to Jenny just yet. He stopped at a lounge area and put a couple of quarters in the Coke machine. He needed bourbon, but a soft drink would have to do. He took a couple of swallows then walked over to the fifth-floor window and looked out.

Jenny was where she said she would be, walking along the footpath that wound through a display of artillery pieces from Revolutionary War cannons to present-day missiles. From this perspective, she was just a tiny lone figure, her shoulders hunched over, her hands deep in her coat pockets. She was cold. Stephen shivered for her. He wanted to go to her and put his arms around her to warm her and in doing so derive some warmth himself.

A five-year-old lead. What in the hell did it mean? He tried to digest it. It was hard for him to believe this was really happening.

Would it be dishonest of him to continue this excursion with Jenny, he wondered. He wasn't even sure he could. He felt drained.

Stephen tried to sort through his mind how things had changed. He had never believed his wife and daughter were dead, just gone. What he didn't know was if Jade had left him of her own free will or had been forced to leave. Except why would they bother making her and her American child return to China? It made no sense, but he had hoped against hope that that was the case, and that he would somehow mastermind a rescue and bring his daughter at least back to America.

But on the other hand, Jade could have simply decided to leave him. Maybe there was nothing political about her disappearance. Spouses did that sometimes, choosing the simplicity of a disappearance over the complication of custody disputes and visitation rights. This would be especially true if Jade had decided to return to Communist China, for she knew Stephen would have fought for his daughter with every resource he had.

It was the not knowing that had driven him crazy. His life had been in limbo for seven lonely years, and now, he had his first concrete lead, just when he had separated himself legally from Jade and cleared the way for the rest of his life.

If it weren't for Mindy, Stephen realized he would have called off the search years ago. But how could a father turn his back on his daughter? Did Mindy ever think of her father? Did she miss him still or was he just a vague memory? If given the opportunity, would she come back to him? Each year that had gone by made that less likely. Jade had loved their daughter, too, and Jade had had seven years to mold her into the sort of child she wanted her to be. The Chinese were masters at that. A Chinese daughter would not only mind her mother, she would be fiercely loyal to the woman who had been her only parent for most of her life. Or was he rationalizing away his parental responsibility, Stephen wondered, because of that woman down there, battling the wind as she crossed the street and headed for the car?

Would it be so terrible of him to have this one evening and tomorrow with her before he went off one last time to search for his wife and child. He wouldn't try to make love to Jenny, he promised himself. She was probably right about waiting anyway. It would be best for him to come to her unencumbered by the past. She deserved a new life with a man who would be there for her only, who would respect and love her.

This was no casual thing that had erupted between them. Of course, he realized, it was one thing to tell himself that he wouldn't make love to her while standing five floors above the reality of her. It would be far more difficult when she was close enough to touch.

They went to the officers' club for cocktails and dinner. A placard in the entryway announced there would be live music at nine. Jenny went into the rest room to freshen her makeup, then they were shown to a table overlooking the deserted terrace. Stephen could imagine summertime dances on the terrace with uniformed officers and ladies in pretty dresses, with Japanese lanterns strung among the trees. Military life, at established posts such as Fort Sill, was social and orderly. A good life, actually. Families lived in gracious old houses on tree-lined streets. He assumed that after a time, however, most military folks started wanting a real home.

Or was he thinking that way only because his career had been even more nomadic than most, and a home had become increasingly important to him.

All around him, people were gathering for Friday night socializing. Officers and their ladies. He had even missed that sort of normal Army experience. Being assigned to Washington, D.C., was not the same as living on a military base. Stephen found himself wondering if living someplace like Fort Sill would have made a difference, if Jade had had women friends and had done "couples" kinds of things with her husband and lived more like other Army wives. If they had brought Mindy to a club like this for Easter-egg hunts and Christmas parties, would Jade have felt more at home in this country? But suddenly Stephen was quite weary with rehashing the past. It was futile, and he couldn't rewrite history.

He and Jenny sat across the table from each other, sipping their drinks, and discussed the pros and cons of military life. She told him about her own upbringing as the daughter of two schoolteachers. "Apple pie normal," she said. "My folks are the salt of the earth. They're retired now and have a garden and chickens and seem quite content, although Dad has heart trouble and Mom arthritis. I don't get to see them as often as I did when they lived in the city, but then I don't see my boys very much now either. Nothing stays the same. Life is lived in phases."

Stephen agreed. He was at the starting line of the next phase of his own life.

After dinner, they went upstairs to the ballroom where a combo was playing. Stephen ordered two brandy alexanders, then asked Jenny to dance.

She was stiff at first, but slowly he felt her body relax, and she let the music take her. Gradually, the distance between their bodies melted, and she leaned into his arms.

The music was dreamy, and they danced well together, effortlessly. She was the right height for him, and their bodies fit together nicely.

She tucked her face against his neck. He could feel her warm breath. His hand was at the small of her back, at that very sexy place just where the swell of her buttocks began. He increased his pressure there, pulling her even closer to his body. She did not resist.

In spite of the crowded dance floor, Stephen felt as though he and this lovely woman were separated from the other dancers. He felt suspended between the past and the present, enclosed with Jenny in their own safe little cocoon where neither the world nor his worries could penetrate its invisible walls. Only the music could, and it was nice—incredibly nice.

Time grew hazy. Sensations became distorted. Each note of music was more pure than the one before. The feel of Jenny in his arms was so sweet, he felt close to tears.

When the set ended, he felt disoriented, and it took him a minute to remember where their table was. Yes, there was her purse, their drinks growing watery.

They danced every set, and when the combo took a break, they danced to recorded music. He would have danced with her all night. It gave him a legitimate reason to have her in his arms.

But finally lights came on and waiters started putting chairs on the tables. They retrieved Jenny's coat from the downstairs coat room.

She pulled her coat more tightly around her body as they hurried across the road to the parking lot. When she got into the car, she scooted over next to him, and he put his arm around her shivering shoulders. They drove like that to the motel.

Stephen took his own small duffel and Jenny's overnight bag from the back seat and followed her up the stairs to the second floor. They stopped in front of 204, and she unlocked it. Stephen took her bag inside and put it on the dresser. "I'll see you in the morning," he said. "Whoever wakes up first can call the other one."

"Kiss me," Jenny said. Her eyes were bright. Her lips full and parted.

He dropped his duffel bag into the chair and met her open arms. "Jenny, Jenny," he said softly, as he held her close. Then she lifted her mouth to him. Her tongue slid boldly into his mouth as she reached for his hand and brought it up to her breast. There was no mistaking her invitation.

"Oh, Jenny, are you sure? Don't do anything you'll be sorry about later."

"That's why I'm doing it," she said. "I'm afraid that if I lose you, I won't have the memory of being with you at least this one time. I know it will only make it worse, but I want the memory, Stephen."

He took her hands in his and stepped back from her. "Today, at Fort Sill, Jenny, I went to see a man who saw my wife and daughter five years ago. It's the first clear lead I've had in all this time."

"And you'll follow it?" she said. Tears were running down her cheeks.

"Yes. I have to because of my daughter. And I have to find out what really happened."

He waited for her response. By all rights, she should turn away from him. "If it helps any," he said, "I'm in love with you."

"But you're still in love with her, too?"

"No. I know that now, but for so long I've thought about nothing but finding them and being a family again. The dream dies hard."

"Do you want to make love to me?" she asked.

"More than I've wanted anything in a long, long time."

With great solemn eyes, she slipped back into his arms.

## Chapter Eight

Jenny was amazed that she felt no reservations. They had fallen away from her like autumn leaves from a tree. She was in love. Her heart sang with it. Her body wanted to celebrate it. She prayed that she could love him for the rest of her life. But if that was not to be, she would at least have memories of what might have been.

They would have a few days, then he would go away from her to search for his past, for his once-beloved wife and daughter. The term "legally dead" had little implication now.

She could not bring herself to hope that he didn't find them. To lose someone you love is a terrible thing, and not to know what happened to that person could only compound the agony. Although Stephen claimed to have been ready to give up on his dream of finding them, any woman in his life who followed Jade would live in her shadow. No, it would be best for Stephen to find his wife and make peace with his feelings about her, even if it meant that Jenny lost him.

Yet she wanted to make love to Stephen, and she wanted to even if this one night in a lifetime was all there was to be. How simple it seemed now after all that agonizing. The fear of losing him, and the pain of knowing he still cared about his wife, continued to re-side inside of her. But life was not without risk. Oddly enough, she thought of Stephen's Aunt Patience who hadn't taken the final risk for love and had lived a life-time of regret.

They stood there in the middle of the generic motel room in Lawton, Oklahoma, clinging to each other, each a little fearful and nervous about taking the next step.

Almost as though he were reading her mind, Stephen said, "Does it matter to you that we're not in some-place beautiful?"

Jenny drew back so she could see his face. "No. I think it's the people and not the place that matters, but now that the decision has been made, I feel over-whelmed with shyness. How do we get from here to there?" she asked, cocking her head toward the bed.

"Would you like me to leave for a while so you can get ready?"

"No. Well, yes, maybe. I don't know." She shrugged helplessly and looked away from him.

He touched her cheek. Jenny turned her face toward his palm and kissed it. His hand went up into her hair. She closed her eyes, relishing the feel of his fingers lux-uriating in the thickness of her hair. He was kissing her again now, his hands holding her face. She parted her lips for him and in doing so felt her entire body open and cry out for him. Of their own accord, her arms slid around his neck, and their bodies fell against each other.

He was solid and manly, and his heart was pounding beneath his uniformed chest. Jenny clutched at his shoulders and back, wanting him closer. The feel of him was both arousing and comforting. It was going to be all right. So good did it feel to be in his arms, so perfectly all right, she wanted to melt into him, to be a part of him.

The clothing that separated them was becoming intolerable. He was pulling at the zipper on the back of her dress. She reached between them to unfasten the brass buttons of his uniform, but she had to stop in order to concentrate better on the sensation of his hand sliding inside the open back of her dress and touching the bare midriff between her bra and her half slip. The feel of his hands on her bare flesh ignited her. She wanted to be naked for him. No, she *needed* to be naked for him.

Jenny wiggled out of her dress, and it fell around her feet. She stepped out of it, kicking it away as she reached behind and undid her bra.

"Oh, my God," Stephen said as her full breasts became bare to him. "Oh, Jenny, you're beautiful."

He fell back on the bed, pulling her down on top of him. His military brass dug into her bare flesh. It was time to get rid of his uniform. Jenny gazed down into his eyes as she straddled his hips and began unbuttoning his jacket. She was glad he was watching her. Her naked torso glowed from his gaze.

"You have too many clothes," she complained.

"We have all night," he said. "You can't imagine how I'm enjoying the sight of you undressing me like that."

His jacket was open. She undid his tie and slid it from around his neck. Then came the buttons on his shirt. She bent forward to bury her face in the hair on his chest.

Jenny moved away from him and pulled off the rest of her clothing, while he extracted himself from his uniform, throwing it across a chair. And suddenly, they were facing each other on opposite sides of the bed. Jenny glanced down at herself to see what he was seeing.

The low light from the lamp was kind, and the swell of desire seemed to lift her breasts.

Stephen's body was lean, his midsection as flat as a young man's, his shoulders and arms well muscled. The hair on his chest was darker than that on his head. He wanted her. Jenny gloried in the visible evidence of that desire.

"I'll never forget this night," she said across the bed.

"I'm so overwhelmed, Jenny, that you have done me this honor. I can honestly say that I've never wanted to make love to a woman more."

"Thank you," Jenny said. "I feel the same about you." And she did. She had never wanted a man more, and she had never wanted to please a man more. The two desires were parts of a whole—to please and be pleased.

Together, they pulled back the covers. "May I leave the lamp on?" Stephen asked.

Jenny nodded. She knelt on her side of the bed. Then somehow, all at once, they were together in the middle of the bed, tangled in their embrace, arms and legs unencumbered by clothing, bare flesh finally touching bare flesh. "Your scar," she cried out gleefully, "I'm touching your scar."

"You wench," Stephen said. "How did you know about that scar?"

"I'll never tell," she claimed.

And they both began to laugh. How wonderful to kiss and laugh at the same time.

"I do love you," he said, looking into her eyes. "I want you in the rest of my life, lovely Jenny."

Jenny lay very still while Stephen touched her eyes, her nose, her lips. Never had she felt so loved. The rest of his life. Yes, she wanted that more than anything else in the world.

They began an exploration of each other's bodies as their kisses became more and more urgent. She couldn't decide what was more wonderful—the touching or being touched. She relished his firm, muscular flesh under her fingers. The maleness of him was intoxicating.

He was groaning, and his body growing ever more tense and ready. So hard he was, bursting with his desire for her. Jenny felt proud.

"Make love to me," she said, bending down so her lips were close to his ear.

And with one movement, he rolled them over. He was above her, his body hovering. Her legs came around his back, making herself open to him. He looked down into her eyes. "I love you, Jenny. God, how I love you."

She answered by reaching around his back and pulling him down into her. It was as though she had waited her entire life for this moment. Nothing had ever felt so perfect, so right, so meant-to-be as Stephen making love to her.

She knew their first time would be hard and fast. They were too full of their need for it to be otherwise. They rose very quickly on a crescendo of white, hot passion, higher, ever higher, and he said her name over and over. She liked that. *Jenny.* He knew who he was making love to. She was Jenny, the one woman, who at this particular night in his life, he wanted above all others.

And when she reached the pinnacle, her body melted around him in warm waves, beginning as a tiny nucleus, then growing wider, ever wider, until he exploded within her and she was engulfed by an ocean of sensation as she yielded completely to the exquisite blending of love.

They clung together for a time, while their breathing quieted and their bodies calmed.

"I knew it would be like that," Stephen said.

"Yes," Jenny agreed. She wanted to ask him if words like destiny and fate were also rolling around in his mind. But words became too much of an effort as she felt their satiated bodies drifting languidly toward sleep.

They slept wrapped up in each other like two puppies. Jenny had no idea how long they slept, but suddenly they were both awake and full of desire.

Their lovemaking was different this time, as prolonged as the previous coming together had been abrupt. On and on they went, moving to the brink, then pulling back, time and again. She hadn't known it was possible to go on for so long. She didn't care if it ever ended. What a delightful game to make it last forever.

And when they finally came together, even that was prolonged, a slow, all encompassing journey to the place of total surrender.

This time, they slept the rest of the night. Jenny didn't even know it was morning until she was awakened by the flash of sunlight as Stephen opened the door and came in carrying a tray, filling the room with the aroma of coffee and bacon. Stephen looked fresh and showered and was dressed in jeans and a plaid shirt.

He put the tray on the dresser and sat down on the side of the bed. "How do you feel?" he asked.

"Happy."

"Are you hungry?"

"Starving."

He pulled the covers aside and kissed her breasts. Jenny smoothed his hair with loving fingers. She wanted him again—just like that. Instant response. Amazing. But the breakfast would get cold, and he was dressed and ready for the day. She sighed. "It's hard to know which part of me is the hungriest."

Stephen laughed. "You're really incredible."

"And you're the most beautiful, most desirable man imaginable—even with your clothes on. Now, please dig my robe out of that bag. I'm feeling pretty wanton, but I don't eat my breakfast stark naked."

Jenny put on the robe and went to use the bathroom while Stephen laid out the meal.

She rubbed the smudged mascara from beneath her eyes, splashed water on her face and ran her fingers through her hair. Her cheeks were rubbed rosy from his whiskers. Her lips looked a bit bruised from all that kissing. Her hair reminded her of Tina Turner. "You look fantastic," she said to her reflection. And she did.

"My gosh, that's enough food to feed an army," she said as she stared at a table laden with bacon, eggs, toast, oatmeal, Danish pastries, juice and coffee.

But she discovered she really was starving. They sat down at the tiny table and began wolfing down the food. "Here, taste this," he said, offering her a bite of Danish.

"Have you tried the bacon?" she asked, holding a piece out for him. "It's ranch-style—thick and crispy and wonderful. This is the best breakfast I've ever had," she said, amazed at her own appetite.

They ate it all, then lingered over coffee to plan their agenda for the day.

Talking about the day made Jenny eager to get on with it. She showered, dressed and put on her makeup. "First, we'll do Fort Sill," she said.

They drove out to the historic Army post and spent the morning visiting the various museums, including one occupying the old guard house that had been used to incarcerate Geronimo.

"Actually, he didn't stay locked up for very long," Jenny explained as they stood in the cellar and stared into a thick-walled cell. "They gave him a little house for his family, and he learned to garden. Sometimes he traveled about with a Wild West show. People would pay to stare at one of the last Indian warriors to surrender... a rather sad end for a legend."

From Fort Sill, they drove out to the Wichita Mountain Wildlife Preserve. They passed a pair of long-horned cattle, then stopped to watch a small herd of buffalo grazing along the road.

"I didn't realize they were so big," Stephen said.

"Yes, it seems incredible that Indians used to hunt them with bows and arrows."

Jenny explained how the creation of the now numerous Wichita Mountain herd had helped save the great beasts from extinction. In the mid 1850s, there were an estimated twenty million buffalo. It took days for the migrating herd to pass. By 1900, there were fewer than six hundred of the animals left.

They stopped at a prairie-dog village and watched the busy little animals dart in and out of their holes. A pair of the little rodents cautiously approached Jenny and Stephen but scampered away when they realized there were no handouts. With Jenny driving, they then took the road that wound around and around Mount Scott until it ended on the mountain's flat top.

"You're right," Stephen said as they stood on the edge of a precipice and stared out at the checkerboard of tilled land, its pattern interrupted by meandering creeks and various-sized ponds and lakes. The land's vast flatness spread out around them for what seemed like hundreds of miles. They could see Fort Sill and Lawton. Jenny pointed to a tiny town at the base of the mountain. "That's where we'll eat," she explained. "I promise you it will be unlike any place you've ever eaten before."

It was cold and windy on top of the mountain, but Jenny led the way down a winding path to a sheltered place between two huge boulders where they stood and enjoyed the view.

"What are those big birds?" Stephen asked, pointing to large, graceful birds flying far below them.

"Red-tailed hawks."

"They really do make lazy circles in the sky, just like in the Rogers and Hammerstein song," he said.

Jenny snuggled against Stephen, and they sat quietly for a time. The world looks so far away, Stephen thought. People should come to high places occasionally if for no other reason than to get a different perspective on the world.

The view was purifying, and Jenny's presence was reassuring. Stephen felt more at peace than he had in a long time. Whatever happened in the future, he wanted to hang on to the feeling. He thought of his father's second wife—plain, sensible Peg, who told him once that he was wasting his life. "Sometimes you have to cut your losses and get on with it," she said. Stephen had argued with her. He had sworn that he would never stop looking for his family until the day he died. He had felt ennobled and full of passion for his cause. But now, he could feel his hold on that impossible dream lessen. He would follow this one last lead to where it took him, and if it was a dead end, he would let go. No more.

Of course, he would never give up hoping that Mindy would someday contact him, that she still might allow him to be a part of her life. But he would search no more. Stephen could almost feel the dream rise out of him and go floating away from the mountain top on a current of air like the hawks far below them. Almost.

But he couldn't quite let go. He knew he would always feel only love for his daughter, but he didn't know how he would feel when he saw Jade again. He no longer loved her, but the memories of the three of them as a family were strong. He had been happy then. Had it all been a lie? What happened to make it end?

Jenny was touching his cheeks. He realized she was wiping away tears.

He wanted to ask her never to leave him. He wanted to cling to her and receive joy and strength for the rest of his life from this generous, loving woman. God, even her body was generous. But he couldn't ask her. Not yet.

JENNY DIDN'T ASK HIM to explain the tears. If he wanted to tell her, he would. Stephen was quiet as they drove back down the mountain to the the strange little town of Medicine Park, built against the base of the mountain by the narrow river. As he looked around, she could sense his curiosity bringing him out of his reverie, but she waited for him to ask.

"Okay teacher, what's the story on this place? I've never seen buildings like this before."

"That's because the area right around here is the only place where they've ever been built. They're called cobblestone houses because they're made of round stones just like streets used to be in colonial days."

"They look like gingerbread houses," he said.

"That's what my boys always said—like something out of 'Hansel and Gretel.'"

"Only as I recall, the witch kept her house in better repair. This place looks like its seen better times."

"Oh, it has," Jenny said. "Back in the 1920s, Medicine Park was a resort town. All these quaint little houses were guest cottages, and apparently the town was quite prosperous and well known. But nobody came during the Depression, and its never amounted to anything since. Half the buildings are deserted. Just wait until you see the hotel."

Jenny parked in front of a derelict frame hotel that looked like something out of an Alfred Hitchcock movie. The upper three floors were boarded up. The broad porch along the front looked ready to collapse. "Come on," she said. "This is where we eat."

"In there?" Stephen said dubiously.

"Sure. Come on. I'll show you a little local color."

They went inside to what was once a large hotel lobby and restaurant. A combination pool hall and restaurant of sorts was still in operation. A picture of Franklin Roosevelt hung over the bar. The seven or eight men at the pool tables looked up when Stephen and Jenny came in. Most of the men were wearing cowboy hats pushed back on their heads, and all were wearing cowboy boots. Several had a cheek bulging with chewing tobacco.

Jenny and Stephen sat at the bar. "Which do you want, hamburger or chicken-fried steak?" Jenny asked.

"We've got fried chicken too, honey," a woman said from the other side of the pass-through into the kitchen. Her gray hair was covered with a brown hair net.

They ordered hamburgers and draft beer. The hamburgers were thick and greasy, served with a thick slice of sweet onion and a generous helping of potato salad.

"This is terrific," Stephen said. "I'd forgotten hamburgers used to taste like this. The ones we get now are kind of pasteurized, aren't they?"

"Listen, I only hang out in classy joints," Jenny said before opening her mouth wide for the next bite of her burger.

She watched Stephen look around the room at the animal heads lining the walls—deer, elk and even bear—at the wagon wheel "chandeliers," the rough wooden floor, the worn upholstered furniture in front of an ancient black-and-white television. "Washington, D.C., it's not," he said.

Jenny looked at the clock on the wall with its picture of a waterfall and the words Pearl Beer in neon lights. It was already past three, and soon they'd be starting back. She wondered about tonight. Would they spend it together? Apparently Stephen was leaving in a few days, but for how long? And then what?

So many things she wanted to say to him dealt with the future. She'd like him to meet her sons and her parents. Someday she'd like to visit him on his turf in the nation's capital. Next time he came to Oklahoma, she'd like to cook for him instead of eating in a restaurant. But would there be a next time? She put her hamburger down, her appetite gone, and sipped her beer instead.

"I seem to have lost you," he said, reaching for her hand.

"What a strange, bittersweet little trip this has been," she said.

"Regrets?"

"No. No regrets."

Stephen paid the modest tab, and they walked a bit up and down the hills of the quaint little town, but Jenny found it depressing. The world had passed by Medicine Park. She wished they hadn't come here.

Stephen drove, on the way back to Oklahoma City. South of Chickasha, they were treated to a spectacular Oklahoma sunset. There were no trees, no hills, no telephone poles to obstruct the view. The oranges and pinks were as vivid as a sunset could possibly be.

"I'll bet you don't get that in Washington, either," Jenny said.

"No. I'd forgotten that sunsets can look so spectacular. It makes me feel reverent, like the Mormon Tabernacle Choir should burst into accompanying music."

"Will you spend the night with me?" Jenny asked as they approached Oklahoma City.

"Unless you want to come to Graystone. I've had some pretty vivid fantasies of you in my bed."

Jenny started laughing.

"Did I miss something?" Stephen asked.

"I'm sure this will come as a complete shock to you, but I've already spent the night in your bed. When my car slid off the driveway in the ice storm, I was stranded and ended up sleeping there."

"Well, that's very interesting," he said. "No wonder I've had such thoughts about you whenever I get in that bed."

"I can top that. I had thoughts about you in that bed before I'd ever laid eyes on you." Her shoulders shook with her laughter. "I can't imagine why I'm telling you this. I must sound pretty foolish, but I had a terrific time in your bed. I toasted you with your really excellent wine and ate your caviar and had pretty respectable fantasies of my own. My sixth sense—Gypsy blood, you know— told me that the man who slept in that bed was a wonderful man who'd do exciting things to my body if he was there with me. Even your aura is sexy."

"Well, while you are playing true confessions, how about telling me how you knew about the scar on my hip."

"My maternal grandmother was born in Hungary, you see, the only daughter of a Gypsy prince. Her name was Sophia, and she was world-class at reading palms, a real Gypsy's Gypsy. But since I have only one-quarter Gypsy blood, I can read palms only when the moon is full or when in the presence of true manhood, and sometimes I have incredible visions—like how you got the nail hole in your rear. I'm having one now. Two people sharing your shower. I wonder who they are."

"I'll get it out of you someday," Stephen promised. "You just wait and see. If I have to hypnotize you in your sleep, someday I *am* going to find out how you knew that I sat on a nail."

Did they have a someday, Jenny wondered, suddenly tired of the game. But no depression was allowed, she promised herself. These days with Stephen might be the only ones in a lifetime, and she refused to waste them being depressed.

"I'm having another vision," she said, pressing her fingers to her temples. "Pizza, beer, a warm fire, music."

"You're not hungry *again*?" he asked.

"Well, it doesn't have to be a large pizza. A medium pepperoni will do, with mushrooms, green peppers and extra cheese."

They stopped at a convenience store for a six-pack of beer, then at Jenny's favorite carry-out pizza restaurant. Stephen ordered a large one. "We'll burn off the calories somehow," he said with a wink.

Jenny selected a spot by the downstairs fireplace for them to eat their meal. She didn't want to spend the evening with Jade's picture staring down at her. And when they went to bed, they'd make love with the lights *off*.

Stephen decided he was in a classical mood and put on Mozart's *Magic Flute*. "Oh, yes, I always eat pizza to Mozart," Jenny said.

But the music was lovely, the fire warm. Sitting on the floor in the elegant living room, eating pizza and drinking beer to classical music didn't seem incongruous at all.

"Will you keep the house?" she asked when they had finished eating. She opened another beer and leaned against the love seat, thinking how beautiful Stephen looked in the glow of the fire.

"I think the time for Graystone has passed," he said, "just like that peculiar little town we visited today. You were the one who said nothing stays the same. If the house were located elsewhere, in a neighborhood of its peers, it might be different, but it is standing in the midst of rows and rows of more ordinary houses. And the truth of the matter is, the time in my life when I would have enjoyed living in a house like this has passed. It's too grand. It would cost too much to maintain. Tell me, Jenny, you compile the history of all these wonderful old homes. Would you ever want to live in one of them?"

"I used to think that I would, but I guess I'm like you. The time when that would have been satisfying to me has passed. Now I wouldn't want the work and responsibility of keeping a place like this. Of course, I wouldn't mind living someplace nicer than my shabby apartment. Maybe when I get the boys out of college, I can move to someplace with a touch more class."

"Will you tell me about your marriage?" Stephen asked.

Jenny was surprised. "Why?" she asked.

"You haven't mentioned him. So many people pepper their conversations with little snide remarks about their ex. I just wonder how you feel about him? Do you wish you weren't divorced?"

"No. It was the worst thing that had ever happened to me at the time, but I can honestly say it was for the best. And I don't make snide remarks about Lewis because there was a whole lot of good about him, about us. I want to remember that along with the bad. I guess if you want to know, I'll tell you about him, but only if you'll tell me about Jade."

And so by the light of the flickering fire, they talked on into the night, sharing themselves. She was lucky in one respect, Jenny decided. She seldom ever thought of Lewis anymore. She didn't need to. Stephen was trapped in his past. She hurt for him—and for herself, because his pain was now her pain.

Stephen's bedroom wasn't dark enough to hide the picture over his mantel. Jenny felt inhibited by it. The woman was more beautiful than she was, and Jade had been his wife and the mother of his only child. Jenny was jealous of her.

Tomorrow night she wanted them to stay in her inelegant bedroom. The bed had a slightly lumpy mattress and cheap pressed-wood headboard. It was the bed she had shared with Lewis, but it held no ghosts for her. It was just a bed.

But in spite of the portrait over the mantel, or maybe in a way because of it, their lovemaking was strong and good, as though they were proving to each other that love could conquer all.

And in the morning, she surprised Stephen by stepping into the shower with him. "See there," she said. "My vision came true. Pass the soap."

They soaped each other, relishing the feel of slippery embraces. They kissed with the warm water cascading over their bodies.

They toweled each other dry before leaping onto the rumpled bed to make themselves sweaty again. Jenny forgot about the painting. She forgot about everything but this man she loved without reservation. She adored him. She would never have enough of him.

Finally they actually managed to leave each other alone long enough to get dressed and go downstairs for breakfast.

They shared kitchen duty, preparing pancakes and sausage. Jenny carried her coffee cup outside with her and sat sipping it in the crisp cold air as Stephen chopped wood. "Observe the bulging biceps," he said as he chopped. "You are in the presence of true manhood."

"My female heart palpitates," Jenny said. She liked watching him. He was strong and manly, and yet like a boy wanting to show off for her.

In the afternoon, they would go to her apartment, and she'd do a bit of showing off herself. They were going to grill fresh salmon on her patio if it wasn't too cold outside. She would fix a wonderful salad and make an apple pie. Barbara would say she was crazy, that modern women bought pies, that she was putting womanhood back twenty years. But if he could chop wood, she could make a pie—from scratch, with fresh apples.

Jenny knew without asking that he was leaving in the morning. Her heart would break if she let it, but life went on, and she'd find a way to be happy without him if he didn't came back to her. She would never be as happy as she could have been with him, however. Of that, she had no doubt.

# Chapter Nine

"A Hershey bar! What's happened to your diet?" Jenny asked as she came into Barbara's classroom. She hadn't seen Barbara at lunch and had gone looking for her. After telling Stephen goodbye early that morning, Jenny felt the need to commiserate with her friend and try to make some sense out of her weekend, but it would appear that Barbara could use a little commiserating of her own.

Holding the candy bar in midair, Barbara looked like a naughty child who had been caught with her hand in a forbidden cookie jar. The telltale wrapper of a previously eaten Hershey was crumpled up on her desk next to an opened can of Dr. Pepper.

"Caught me, didn't you?" Barbara said sheepishly.

"I thought you'd sworn off all things chocolate as being incompatible with a svelte body," Jenny said as she slid into a student desk in the front row.

"Maybe I'm giving up on svelte and going back to matronly where I belong. Chocolate is one of life's greatest and most reliable pleasures."

"You've broken it off with Chuck?" Jenny guessed.

"Not exactly," Barbara said, carefully putting the half-eaten candy bar on her desk. "It seems that Chuck is now somewhat smitten with one of the senior cheerleaders.''

"No," Jenny said in disbelief. "A *student*?"

"Brenda Mae Frasier."

Jenny would have laughed if it weren't for the distressed look on Barbara's face. Brenda Mae Frasier had, during the course of her high school career, gone after practically every male faculty member under the age of forty. She was a buxom, red-haired cheerleader whose tightly sweatered, overendowed chest was legendary throughout the central part of the state, drawing quite a following of young males at high school athletic events. But Brenda Mae ignored mere boys. She had a thing about teachers, it would seem, and her flirtatious behavior was a constant source of ribald teasing at faculty meetings and teachers' lounge coffee klatches. Jenny had always found it rather pathetic the way Brenda Mae would attach herself to a male teacher, hanging around his room between classes and after school, hovering around his car in the teachers' parking lot, writing him suggestive notes, brushing against him when she passed him in the hall.

"I find that hard to believe," Jenny said. "How could Chuck go, in just a few days, from wanting a mother figure to chasing after our resident Lolita. Only last week, he was writing a poem to your 'womanly charms' and cleaning out your garage."

"Don't remind me." Barbara took a swig of her Dr. Pepper. It was not sugar free.

"You're really upset about this, aren't you?" Jenny said, taking in Barbara's haggard appearance. Gone was the eye makeup. Her new haircut looked flat and in need of a shampoo. And there were shadows under her eyes.

"I thought this was what you wanted—for Chuck to find someone closer to his own age and leave you alone."

"Well, I guess I'd gotten more hooked on him than I let on," Barbara said with a huge sigh. "It was so damn flattering to have a younger guy telling me I was still desirable. Intellectually, I guess I knew it had to be just a passing fancy for him, but deep down, I'd started to get used to the idea of having him around permanently, even if he was only eleven years old when my first child was born and he doesn't remember when Kennedy was assassinated, and even if he's never heard of June Allison and thinks the Beach Boys are relics. But, yeah, I was sort of thinking that stranger things have happened. After all, Joan Collins marries younger men."

"I'm sorry," Jenny said. "I had no idea it was more than just a fling for you. I wouldn't have done all that teasing if I thought you were getting serious about the guy. But listen here, Barbara Whinnery, there are lots of other men who will find you desirable and who will recognize you for the lovely grown-up woman that you are—and who remember where they were when Kennedy was shot."

"Jenny, Chuck Ballard was the first man who had asked me out in five years. *Five years.* I'm tired of kidding myself. Someday my prince is not going to come along. I'm forty-three years old, have a tendency to spread and have grave suspicions that the 'freckles' on the back of my hands are age spots." Barbara held her hands in front of her and stared at them glumly. "Chuck was my last chance."

Then with a sigh, she picked up a piece of paper, rose heavily out of her chair and began copying sentences for diagraming on the blackboard.

"You are a beautiful, funny, warm, intelligent human being," Jenny said somewhat impatiently to Barbara's back. "If you don't like the spots on your hands, have a dermatologist take them off. If you don't like spreading hips, stop eating candy bars. And stop being pitiful. It doesn't become you. After all, if Chuck hadn't ended this thing between the two of you, you would have done so yourself eventually. My gosh, Barbara, it wasn't as though you were in love with him. You were just off on an ego trip."

"I suppose so," Barbara said, turning to face Jenny. "But damn it, Jenny, my ego hadn't been on a trip in so long, and now its suffered a crash landing. I'm not sure if it's going to recover."

"What about your idea for putting a singles ad in that little weekly newspaper distributed in restaurants? Before Chuck started hanging around, you'd about convinced yourself you were going to do that. Hey, you forgot to cross the *T* in *advent*."

Barbara turned to cross the *T*. "I was just kidding about that," she said as she wrote sentence number five: *The man who came to dinner, although well dressed and polite, was not as the aging couple had expected him to be.*

"You're in a diabolical mood," Jenny said. "Those sentences will be a nightmare to diagram."

Barbara ignored her comment and kept writing. "*Gazette* singles ads are a joke," she said with a resounding dot on an *I*. "People sit in restaurants and laugh when they read them. That's pretty damned desperate when you have to advertise yourself in a tabloid like a used car."

"The *Gazette* is a perfectly respectable suburban weekly that's had great success with non-X-rated singles ads," Jenny countered with perhaps more conviction than she felt. The ads in the paper were a mixture of funny and sincere. Maybe putting an ad in a newspaper was a bit desperate, but not cheap.

"At least the people who write them aren't just sitting around lamenting their lack of social life," Jenny continued. "They are doing something about it. And I'll bet a lot of those people who make fun of them go right home and either answer an ad or write one of their own. I don't see anything wrong about an ad reading, 'Divorced, middle-aged professional man wishes to meet interesting woman between the ages of thirty-five and forty-five.'"

Barbara countered, "More than likely the ad would say, 'Divorced, middle-aged professional man wishes to meet petite, blonde between the ages of twenty and thirty.'"

"Not all of them. Come on, Barbara, this isn't like you. Nothing ventured, nothing gained. Right? What can it hurt to try?"

"With my luck, my ad would be answered by a homicidal rapist dwarf with body odor." Barbara went over to write the last sentence, then straightened to check over her handiwork.

"All the ads do is provide a means to arrange meetings between interested parties. You can get together at a nice, safe bar or restaurant. No last names given. If you place an ad, the men send an answer to a box number, and you call them if their letter interests you. And if you don't like dwarfs, put in your ad that they need not apply."

"Yeah, but what about the homicidal rapist?" she asked brushing the chalk dust from her palms.

Jenny threw up her hands. "Cripes, Barbara, what do you want me to say—that you're over the hill, that you should retire to the recliner in front of your television and give up? If you want a man in your life, then damn it, take some steps to meet an appropriate one. Join a singles group at a church. Enroll in a dating service. Join a club. Do *something*."

"And if it doesn't work out?" Barbara challenged, seating herself and taking a very deliberate bite from her unfinished candy bar.

"Then at least you've tried."

The sound of lockers banging in the hall announced that the lunch hour was almost over. Jenny picked up her purse and headed for the door.

"Jenny?" Barbara said.

Jenny stopped without turning.

"Thanks. It's nice to have someone who cares enough to get on my case. Can we go get a drink after school? I want to hear about your weekend."

"Okay," Jenny agreed. "Then you can get onto me. I'm really not one to be handing out advice. I don't run my life any better than you do yours."

"I'm glad you're my friend," Barbara said.

Jenny turned and walked back to Barbara's desk. She leaned over and gave her a hug. "I'm glad you're my friend, too."

Jenny wove her way through the mingling students to her own classroom. Funny, she had planned to go and cry on Barbara's shoulder. Instead, she'd turned into an overbearing Ann Landers, but Jenny realized she believed in her own words. If Stephen Carmichael never came back to her, she'd try to fall in love again. She wouldn't just sit around and feel sorry for herself. But it would be damned hard.

She had wanted to go to the airport with Stephen this morning, but he had to turn in the rental car, so they said goodbye at her front door. And there seemed to be nothing to say except goodbye. He didn't tell her when he'd return. He didn't assure her that everything was going to be all right. He didn't even say he'd call or write.

She'd kissed him one last time and sent him off to find his wife, knowing he would be going wherever it was the man at Fort Sill had seen Jade and Mindy, then try to follow a five-year-old trail. And she had a feeling the sighting hadn't been in Des Moines, Iowa.

Jenny went into her classroom and opened her plan book to glance over the outline for her next class. She supposed she should be grateful she had class this hour. If it was her free period, she'd probably go into the teacher's restroom and find an unoccupied stall to cry in.

She felt empty inside. What if Stephen found Jade and realized he still loved her? In spite of all her bravado, Jenny felt like the rest of her life would be meaningless without him in it.

She thought of last night. How long had it been, she wondered, since she'd fussed over a male person who wasn't her offspring. After they'd returned from grocery shopping, Jenny had changed into a loose-fitting shirt and black, tapered pants. She pulled her hair up on her head and took special pains with her makeup. Then she fixed Stephen a drink, and they planned their attack on dinner. The two of them collaborated on its preparation. Stephen had made a curry sauce that was out of this world to go on the grilled salmon. He certainly did know his way around a kitchen, but she'd forced him to sit and watch while she made the apple pie, which was the best she'd ever made. She could have won first prize at the county fair with that pie.

Throughout the weekend, Jenny kept thinking how right it was to be with Stephen, how it seemed only natural that they spend the rest of their lives loving each other, making each other laugh and cooking an endless succession of meals together. Going to the grocery had even been fun and exciting when she was with Stephen.

After dinner, they had coffee and watched an old James Stewart movie on television. Such a simple way to pass an evening, but so perfect when two people liked being together. They finished the evening with some of Jenny's modestly priced brandy and then had gone to make love in her bed. The passion of the two previous nights was replaced by poignancy. It was their last night, and they didn't know for how long.

Her students were filing into the classroom. Their cutting up didn't seem quite so tolerable today, and their physical presence was intrusive and even overwhelming. She didn't want to be here with a roomful of smart-aleck teenagers whom she was actually supposed to teach.

But she had told Stephen she was a good teacher. And she was, though not one of the award-winning sort. She wasn't political enough for that, but she got her own reward during those golden moments when the teaching and the content and the class dynamics were perfect and learning was accomplished. Sometimes she had to put up with a lot to get to those golden moments, but she trusted in their coming. So did her students. So somehow, in a few minutes, she would stand there behind her lectern, and her class would discuss the Spanish American War. If McKinley had been a stronger president, would the war have been avoided? Why had it been such a popular war? Did the nation's new imperialist foreign policy change the course of history?

Jenny would somehow make it interesting. Even the students who refused to prepare for class by doing the outside readings would at least leave class today knowing that there had been such a war, and because of it, their country now owned Puerto Rico and Guam and had once owned the Philippines.

But today, teaching would require Herculean effort. She was tired and dispirited. She squared her shoulders and collected Walkman radios from Bobby Redeagle and Joey Miller to be picked up after class. "Put your shirt back on, Henry," she instructed, "and Lisa, the bubble gum has to go. How many of you saw the story about the upcoming Philippine election on the news this morning?"

When the class was over, she realized she hadn't thought of Stephen more than once or twice over the past fifty minutes, and then only fleetingly. Jenny felt rather proud. Her nights might be wretched, but during the day, she would cope and continue to be a good teacher and do free-lance research on old houses regardless of what happened in her personal life.

When she arrived at Flip's after school, the bartender asked if she was Jenny. "Your friend called and left a message. She's running late. You're not to give up on her."

Jenny sat alone at a booth and sipped on a glass of water. She would wait until Barbara arrived to order a drink. It was the end of the month again, and she could only afford one round, which she would wait to enjoy with her friend.

She noticed that the man at the bar glanced over his shoulder at her a couple of times, but she paid no attention. When she realized he was coming her way, she steeled herself. She was waiting for a friend, she would say. Thank you, but no, she didn't want him to buy her a drink.

"Jenny Bishop," he said. "It *is* you."

Jenny looked at a pleasant, smiling face. "I'm sorry. Do I know you?"

"Well, I had more hair then. And I don't wear size thirty slacks anymore. But it's the same old Randy Cartwright."

"Randy! My goodness, it *is* you." Jenny held out her hand. "How wonderful to see you. Sit down. What are you doing with yourself these days? Last I remember, you'd gone to Alaska to work on the pipeline."

Randy sat down. "Yeah. I lived up there for several years. I'm in Arkansas now. Got a small oil company in Little Rock, but I have some customers here in the city. Say, I heard that you and Lewis had split the blanket. Sorry about it, but I can't say I'm surprised. Lewis was a nice guy, but not the type to settle down. He and I sure had some wild times together back in our carousing days, but I never could understand why Lewis didn't do right by you, Jenny. I sure would have if I'd been him."

"Why, thank you. That's nice of you to say. So your carousing days are over?" Jenny asked.

"Well, you might say that. I'm married and have a couple of great kids. But you know how it is, what you do when you're out of town doesn't count," Randy said with a wink.

"I think that woman over there is trying to get your attention," Jenny said.

Randy glanced over at a young woman who had just come in. "Well, I'd better go. That's my date. It's sure great to see you, Jenny. You're lookin' good, honey, real good.''

Randy gave a cocky little salute and hurried over to his date.

Barbara arrived shortly, apologizing for her lateness. She'd left her parking lights on that morning and had a dead battery. "And guess who jumped my car for me?"

"Chuck?" Jenny guessed.

"Chuck *and* Brenda Mae. He didn't even have the decency to look embarrassed." Barbara pulled a notebook out of her purse and slapped it down on the table between them.

"What's that for?"

"To compose my ad for the *Gazette*. But we can do that later. First I want to know what's going on with you."

"Can we order something first?"

Jenny talked Barbara out of ordering chili nachos. "How about a bowl of popcorn instead? Or a plate of fresh veggies with some yogurt dip?"

They decided on the veggies and a couple of glasses of white wine.

"Okay," Barbara said. "What gives? Did the mysterious Colonel Carmichael ever admit to a wife in the attic?"

"No, he doesn't know where she is. His wife and daughter disappeared seven years ago without a trace. At least there wasn't a trace until Friday afternoon. Can you believe the timing? Some officer at Fort Sill saw the two of them five years ago, and Stephen has gone off to try and track them down."

Barbara let out a low whistle. "No kidding. Well, you knew something weird was going on. How does Stephen feel about this woman? Does he still love her?"

160 A Colonel for Jenny

"He says he loves me, but I worry about how he'll feel if he sees her again. He's thought of little else for a long time now. I think one of the reasons he wants to find her is to put closure on that period of his life—and, of course, he'd want his daughter back in his life. I think that not knowing what happened to them drives him crazy. How was it with you, Barbara, for that time you didn't know if your husband was dead or alive?"

Barbara waited until the waitress had served them before answering. She took a sip of wine, then said, "It was horrible. If Mitch was dead, I wanted to know it. I was always grateful that I got an answer within months instead of years, or never like some of the MIA wives. Strange things happened to some of those women. Even after the MIAs were officially declared dead, even after seventeen, eighteen, twenty years, some of those women still clung to their dream. Chances were one in a million that their husbands might still be alive, but they didn't want to go with the odds. Of course, that's quite noble but not very wise."

"Yes, but I can understand it," Jenny said. "In a sense, hope is all that's keeping those men alive. If you give up hope and let the dream die, then it feels like you're the one killing them."

"A situation like that can do screwy things to a person's reason," Barbara said in between bites of fresh zucchini. "Just for the record, raw zucchini and yogurt are not as good as chili nachos. After Mitch was missing, I started idealizing him and our marriage. One day, I was going on and on about how Mitch had been such a thoughtful, loving husband, and my mother asked who in the hell I was talking about. Mitch was a good guy in his way, but thoughtful he was not. And we had an okay marriage, no better or worse than most."

"But you loved him, didn't you?" Jenny asked.

"Yeah, I loved him—most of the time, but I resented like hell when he volunteered for a second tour of duty in Vietnam and left me alone, pregnant and with two babies. He didn't have to do that, but I think being around two babies drove him up the wall. It drove me up the wall, too, and maybe I'd have done the same thing if I'd been him. I don't know. But anyway, after his plane went down, I found myself idealizing him, romanticizing him, making him out to be bigger than life. Don't get me wrong, he was my man and I wanted him back, but after making a romantic hero out of him, it would have been a shock to rediscover that he was just an ordinary guy who belched when he drank beer."

"I don't think Stephen needs to romanticize Jade to make her bigger than life. I gather she was as exquisite as that painting I told you about, and Stephen admits to a pathological fascination for her from the first moment he laid eyes on her," Jenny said, taking a small sip of her wine, trying to make it last. "If he doesn't find her and his daughter, he'll probably wonder if he should have kept on looking and feel guilty because he gave up on his family. And if he does find them, he might discover how much he still loves Jade. The woman in Oklahoma will become a guilty regret."

"Or maybe he'll see that, gorgeous or not, the woman was a real bitch. Maybe that painting you told me about was an artist's embellishment, and the colonel's forgotten about the wart on her nose. And now, my wineglass is empty and the veggies are gone, but I'm still hungry and thirsty. And I'd better go feed whatever kids are hanging around my house. Why don't you come with me? We still have a singles ad to write for the *Gazette*." Jenny agreed, and Barbara signaled for the their bill.

While they were waiting, Barbara asked, "Jenny, do you know that man at the bar? He keeps looking over here at you. He's paid more attention to you than the woman he's with."

"He's an old friend of my ex's," Jenny explained. "Don't look at him. I don't want to encourage him."

"Gee, why not? He's kind of cute."

"He's married, but he thinks that what men do when they're 'out of town' doesn't count, and he winked when he said it."

Barbara made a face. "On second thought, he's not so cute. In fact, he looks like a jerk."

"Stephen may still be married, too," Jenny said, more to herself than Barbara. "At least, he may have a wife. Oh, hell! I don't know if he is or he isn't. If she turns up alive, how can she be dead? What a mess."

"Stop dramatizing," Barbara scolded. "Stephen's situation is hardly the same as the guy at the bar. He hasn't laid eyes on this Jade person for seven years and doesn't know if she's alive or dead."

"I suppose," Jenny said, counting out her half of the tab. "I hope the waitress doesn't mind a lot of change. The end of the month, you know."

Barbara put a hand on Jenny's arm. "Let's put the shoe on the other foot. What if an unencumbered Stephen had passed through your life at the tail end of your marriage, after Lewis had been gone for a long time and you were tidying up the legalities. In your heart, you knew it was over, but you were in the last throes of indecision. Would you have told Stephen to bug off, or would you have taken the comfort he offered and asked him to wait while you got things straightened out?"

"I suppose I would have asked him to wait," Jenny admitted.

"You're damn right you would," Barbara said. "I think it's difficult to draw a line across lives and declare that on this side of the line one set of rules applies, and on the other side a different set does. The 'line' is usually a big wide swamp that we wander around in for a while, sometimes even straying back where we started for a time, but eventually crawling out on the opposite side, muddied but ready to get on with the journey. This is brilliant rhetoric; you should be taking notes—and sometimes while people are wandering around in the swamp, they find a kindred spirit. I don't think they should pass said kindred spirit by just because they haven't officially reached the other side. In other words, don't be so hard on yourself, kiddo. You have not committed some unspeakable sin by going to bed with a man who hasn't seen his wife in seven years."

"But what if he's still hung up on the past? And how do you know I went to bed with him?" Jenny challenged.

Barbara started laughing. She pointed an accusing finger at Jenny. "I hardly think you would be wallowing around in a moral dilemma over a *kiss*. And the gentleman in question might have been able, through sheer strength of character, to spend a platonic weekend with you, but for you to have stayed away from your handsome man in uniform would have been like locking me up in a room full of Hershey bars for an entire weekend and expecting me not to indulge."

Jenny put her hands up to hot cheeks. She had to laugh too. "But I honestly thought we were going to keep it platonic when I started out."

"So did King Edward and Wallis Simpson."

"You don't know that."

"It's a good guess. I'm on a roll, aren't I? Didn't you think that swamp-relationship analogy was absolutely terrific? Maybe I should write it down. I'm probably wasting myself as a mere teacher of English. I should be writing for posterity. In the footnote of some future high school anthology will be an explanation of how the Swamp Tale came to be. Just think, you'll be a literary footnote all because of me."

"I'm overwhelmed," Jenny said dryly. "It's what I'd always dreamed of. Shall we go?"

"A weekend of Hershey bars," Barbara said longingly. "I sure wouldn't have stopped with just one. I would have had an *orgy*."

"I get your message," Jenny said pointedly as she pushed back her chair. "No comment."

Barbara's daughter was on her way out the front door, portable stereo in one hand, school books in the other. Barbara grabbed her and made her eat a bowl of home-made chicken noodle soup before she headed off to study with her boyfriend.

Then Barbara set the table and poured some jug wine into stemmed glasses.

The soup was good. "I made the noodles from scratch. I haven't done that in years. They were meant to impress the boy biology teacher," Barbara admitted.

"Chuck is too shallow for homemade egg noodles," Jenny said as she ladled out a second bowlful.

They sliced apples and cheese for dessert, then Jenny carried the wine and glasses into the cluttered living room. Barbara pushed an elderly cocker spaniel off the sofa, and the two women curled up at opposite corners. The dog sat in the middle of the floor for a while, glaring at them, then lumbered off down the hallway. "To my bed," Barbara admitted. "But at least, she's a warm body. Okay, it's time to write my singles ad. Shoot,'' she said as she opened her notebook and poised her pencil.

Jenny suggested that Barbara refer to herself as an attractive mother of three seeking a sincere relationship.

"Oh, yeah. Good one, Jenny. That'll bring 'em out in droves. How about, 'High school English teacher seeking to gather her rosebuds while she may,'" she said with a giggle. "Or maybe, 'English teacher looking for a Romeo. No one under forty need apply.'"

They drank the cheap wine and got silly. When Jenny suggested a pun about a dangling participle, Barbara dissolved on the floor. Then she picked herself up, marched into the kitchen for two mugs of coffee. "It's time to get serious. I'm really going to put an ad in that paper. I decided you were exactly right, and I don't have any cause to complain about no men out there when I really haven't searched. I am a victim of my generation. We were taught to sit and wait prettily for a man to happen by. No more. I'm going to send up flares. Maybe I'll even wear track shoes."

Finally they came up with a version that Barbara was reasonably satisfied with, and Jenny headed home to grade papers.

She and Barbara were good for each other, Jenny decided as she drove home. They were there for each other, up or down.

Jenny spent every spare moment over the next week finishing up her report on Graystone. She'd reached the point of diminishing returns on her efforts, but in truth the research could continue indefinitely. Only last week, she'd discovered the identity of a woman photographed with Grace and Patience Ellsworth in front of Graystone. The writing under the picture was in Grace's distinctive backhand and said, "Mrs. Putnam stopped with us during a cross-country flight." Jenny had compared the photograph to some that appeared in the Oklahoma City newspaper in July of 1934. Mrs. Putnam was better known as Amelia Earheart, the first woman to fly across the Atlantic. Jenny knew there were probably other such intriguing pieces of information to be discovered about Graystone, but as in each of her projects she had to draw the line and stop.

It took her several evenings to type a perfect, final version, realizing with every ruined page why she would have made a rotten secretary. But at last, she was ready to take the bound copy to Mr. Jolly and receive her much-needed check. Then she could pay on her Sears bill and get current on the rest of her bills. And she had an interview scheduled for another home research job. It was time to get on to the next job. Past time. Graystone had been fraught with distractions.

Jenny made one more visit to Graystone before turning in her report and handing over the key. She wandered through the house, wanting to feel close to Stephen, but he was right, the house was not really his home. Not yet. It was too impersonal. Only in his bedroom did Jenny get a sense of the man who lived there. A thick terry-cloth robe hung on the back of the bathroom door, and she buried her face in it. It still bore the fragrance of his aftershave.

She stopped on her way out of the room to stare at the portrait of Jade and Mindy. Jade. Such an exotic name. And how it suited the woman. *My rival,* Jenny thought. *Where are you, Jade, and how strong is your hold over the man I love? If you don't love him, please set him free.*

# *Chapter Ten*

Stephen's immediate superior in the Pentagon was Major General Israel Mansfield, a tall, gawky man who reminded Stephen of Abraham Lincoln. For almost twenty years, Mansfield had guided the Ordnance Corps with care and efficiency, something that was probably more feasible in Ordnance because of its relatively small size. But Stephen wondered if General Mansfield couldn't have brought efficiency even to the sprawling Artillery or Infantry.

Those who did not know Mansfield well considered him an inflexible, play-it-by-the-book sort of commanding officer, but after serving under him for twenty years, Stephen knew Mansfield bent the rules on occasion if the reasons were good enough. The two men trusted each other. Stephen had first served under the general in Vietnam and followed him to Washington when he assumed command of the corps. Mansfield and his wife were childless, and in a gruff way, Mansfield treated Stephen as the son he never had.

Stephen was on a sofa at one end of the general's spacious Pentagon office. The paneled room was decorated with handsome Audubon prints, the largest and most outstanding of which was a bald eagle that hung behind the general's desk. Since it was after five, the general opened a cabinet door and poured two Scotch and waters in handsome glasses embossed with the Ordnance insignia in gold. Mansfield seated himself in an old-fashioned Boston rocker, adjusting a cushion behind him, and began rocking slowly back and forth. "Remember President Kennedy and his rocker? He had the right idea," he said. "There's something soothing about rocking, yet I'm not as likely to doze off in a rocker. That can be a problem, you know, when you get to be my age."

"I don't believe that," Stephen said. "You sit in that rocker when you don't want people to know what a tough old warhorse you really are. It tends to make them forget about the two stars on your shoulder until it suits your purposes to go and sit behind your desk and look the part again."

"Well, I'm wearing my genial old-man hat this evening. But believe me, it's fitting better these days. Now, why do you want to go to China, and are we talking Taiwan or mainland?"

"Mainland. I need your help, sir. I'd like a temporary assignment in Peking. I recall hearing that the joint chiefs of staff had expressed some official concern about the armament capability at the embassy there in light of the problem we've had at other embassies. I'd like to offer my services as consultant and go to look the situation over."

"Why would I send a senior officer to do a job that some eager captain could handle with ease?" Mansfield asked, rocking at a slow, even pace.

"Because I need an official reason to go to Peking."

"Your wife?" Mansfield asked over the edge of his glass. "We've been down this road before, Stephen.

Without any evidence, what's the point? China's a big country for wild-goose chases."

Stephen nodded. "My wife and daughter were apparently spotted by one of our intelligence people at a political rally in front of the Great Hall."

"When?"

"Five years ago," Stephen admitted. "But it is the first concrete piece of information I've had in all this time."

"And just how do you plan to follow up on such a lead?" Mansfield wanted to know.

"Through official channels at first. I don't think a man requesting to see his daughter would seem too seditious. I might make some sort of announcement to the foreign press corps about what I'm doing. A little publicity in the world press about an American father searching for his long-lost Chinese daughter might move things along a bit."

"And if the Chinese government claims no such woman and child live in their country, what then?" the general asked, downing the last of his drink. He carried his and Stephen's glasses over to the bar for refills.

"I'd rather not say," Stephen said.

"Then you'll go through unofficial channels unless I miss my guess," Mansfield said from across the room. "Stephen, I doubt if the woman wants you to find her. It seems to me Jade went to a hell of a lot of trouble to see that you didn't."

"Perhaps," Stephen said, accepting his freshened drink and setting it down on the coffee table. "Or maybe she had no choice."

Mansfield resumed his rocking, cradling his drink in his hands. "You know, son, in retrospect, I've found myself wondering if Jade wasn't in this country as part of an intelligence-gathering mission. Looking back, the whole Jade episode seems so peculiar, the way she managed to date you in spite of all her embassy's rules to the contrary and the close reins they kept on their people, and the way she cultivated media attention after your marriage and used her beauty and charm to get close to a lot of people—diplomats, congressmen, government officials, high-ranking military officers, including yours truly. Jade had such an effect on people.''

The general's look grew distant as he remembered. ''I used to enjoy watching the reaction of men and women alike when she came into the room,'' he continued. ''She was so stunningly beautiful that it took your breath away. I'll never forget the first time you brought her out to the house to meet us, and I was absolutely tongue-tied. Beth teased me about it afterward, but she understood. Jade had affected her like that, too. When Jade turned the full force of her beauty and charm in my direction, I could almost feel myself reduced to putty. And Beth wanted to mother her and take her around to all her club meetings and receptions. Jade was like the daughter or the daughter-in-law we never had. But I saw another side of her when I refused to help her get security clearance so she could do classified translations.''

''You never told me she'd asked you for help,'' Stephen said.

''I know. I debated about it and my suspicions, but there was nothing really specific to tell. It was just a look in her eyes for only a split second. Ice, like the eyes of the eagle in that picture on the wall, almost inhuman. I felt as if I had glimpsed into her soul, and she never seemed so beautiful again. Of course, at the time it happened, she recovered instantly and behaved very well, saying that she understood perfectly why I couldn't get involved in such matters. She smiled her very best smile, but it was over between us, and she knew it. I was no longer one of her adoring lackeys, willing to get her invitations to diplomatic gatherings and top-brass receptions. But I didn't tell you about it because she was still your wife and the mother of sweet Mindy. And what could I say, that I thought your daughter's mother was... Was what? Insincere? Strange? Then suddenly she was gone, apparently having accomplished whatever it was she was after—or was recalled because she hadn't."

"Maybe she didn't want to go," Stephen reminded him.

"Look Stephen, I have no proof, and it's just a feeling, son, but I really think she wasn't what she seemed. I don't think she was ever on our side. Her defection was contrived."

"If you're right, that means our marriage was contrived, that I was duped and she never really loved me," Stephen said softly and picked up the drink to down half of it in one swallow. "That's hard for me to accept, sir. You know how much I loved her. Could I have been that gullible, and if so, how can I ever trust my instincts again?"

"When you fall on your ass, you can either sit there or get up and try again."

"You're probably right," Stephen admitted, thinking how the fear was still there that the woman he had loved without qualification had rejected him. "But I still need to see my daughter again. I think deep down inside I was always afraid Jade had left me. Funny how I could have accepted her dying easier than I could accept her leaving me, but I finally came to believe that was what happened. In fact, I'd already had Jade declared dead, but then that intelligence officer identified Jade as a woman he'd seen in Peking five years ago. Until then, I'd only speculated that she'd gone back to China. I didn't really know. I've waited this long to tie up the loose ends, and I figure another month or two won't matter. Then I need to put some sort of closure on this whole bizarre episode and get on with my life. There's a lovely woman in Oklahoma I can't make a commitment to until I do."

Mansfield regarded Stephen a minute, taking in this last bit of information. "It's time," he said. "I wish you'd just court the Oklahoma lady and forget about China. Jade's surely changed her name," the general warned. "It might be impossible to trace her."

"I wasn't going to look for Jade Carmichael," Stephen said. "Her father was a prominent academician. I doubt if he'd change his name, and I might be able to locate her through him."

Mansfield stopped rocking and leaned forward in his chair. "You're pretty determined, aren't you?" he asked.

"Yes, sir, but I need your help. Otherwise, I'd have to resign my commission and use other means to get myself into the country."

"That's blackmail," Mansfield said, getting up to stand at the window with his hands clasped behind him. The windows looked across the river, toward the rolling, grave-covered hills of Arlington National Cemetery. "You know I can't have you resigning your commission. You're more vital to the Ordnance Corps than I am, although I'd never admit such a thing in front of other people."

"When I come back from China, I'd like to start phasing out, sir. I want to become less vital," Stephen said, abandoning the sofa to stand beside the man who was his mentor and best friend. "In a year or two, I'd like to retire and try something else while I'm still young enough to start another career."

"Don't do anything hasty, Stephen. I always thought of you as my natural successor in the corps. In a few more years, you'll be one of the Pentagon's youngest general officers."

"I've always thought that was what I wanted. But I discovered a few things in Oklahoma that I had forgotten existed."

"Such as?"

Stephen felt Mansfield's eyes on his face. "Laughter. Chopping wood. Sunsets. I felt normal."

"So why go to China? Mindy will be one of theirs now. Jade won't risk letting you see her and divide her loyalties. You can go, Stephen, but be honest with yourself about the reason. I think you're going to prove to yourself that you're free of Jade."

Stephen put his hands on the windowsill and closed his eyes momentarily. "Am I crazy?" he asked.

"Yes, but I can understand it," Mansfield said softly. "Jade was no ordinary woman. Can this normal woman in Oklahoma follow in such extraordinary footsteps?"

"When I'm with her, it feels as if I could marry her and never look back. When we're not together, I'm not so sure. I want to be sure, for her sake and mine."

Mansfield nodded. "I suppose you want to go right away."

"Yes, sir. If it can be arranged."

"I'll arrange it on one condition, that you reconsider giving up your career prematurely. You're a brilliant officer, and we'd be hard-pressed to replace you. Your country needs you, son. Maybe the little Oklahoma lady would enjoy being a military wife. Have you asked her?''

Stephen shook his head no.

"You'll seriously reconsider?'' Mansfield asked.

"Yes, sir. I promise.''

The two men shook hands. Then suddenly Stephen was engulfed in a clumsy embrace. He was touched. Generals didn't hug.


"Hi Mom,'' Joe's voice called from the living room. Jenny closed the oven door on her lasagna.

"Hi, guys,'' she called back.

Jenny took off her apron and hurried out to the living room, expecting to greet both of her sons. But there was only Joe with Paula standing self-consciously beside him, clinging to his arm, her glasses still hinged with a safety pin. Paula's red hair was too brilliant against the pallor of her skin. Jenny wondered if the girl was ill.

"Paula, how nice to see you. Joe, you might have told me you were bringing her. Where's your brother?''

"I thought it would be nice if Paula and I came alone,'' Joe said. His voice croaked a bit, like when he was thirteen and it was changing. "Paula and I need to talk to you.''

Jenny looked from one tense young face to the other. *My God,* she thought, *the girl is pregnant.*

The ringing telephone made them all jump. Jenny backed over to the phone. "Hello.''

"Jenny?''

It was Stephen. Jenny closed her eyes and felt her knees go weak. Stephen. Finally.

Talk about rotten timing. Every time the phone had rung for the past two weeks, she had hoped—no, she had prayed—that it would be Stephen. The one time she would have rather had a wrong number, it was him.

"Stephen, how are you?"

"I'm fine. You sound strange. Did I get you at a bad time?"

"Well, actually, I think you did. I believe I'm about to find out that I'm going to be a grandmother."

Joe and Paula glanced at each other, amazement in their expressions. Paula covered her face with her hands, glasses and all, and started to cry. Joe awkwardly put his arms around her.

"You're what?" Stephen asked. "I can't hear you." There was a lot of background noise from his end. He was apparently calling from a public phone.

"My son and his girlfriend are here," Jenny explained, raising her voice. "May I call you back?"

"No, I'm at the airport. I'm going to be leaving the country for a while. I wanted to hear your voice before I go to make sure that you were real and I hadn't imagined you."

"I'd wondered if I was ever going to hear from you again," Jenny admitted, very aware of her son's listening ears. "It's been two weeks."

"I know. I'm sorry. I've thought about you constantly but I wasn't sure you'd want me to call until I had my life straightened out. I'm working on it, Jenny."

"I'm glad. Are you all right?"

"Yeah, sure. And you?"

How was she, Jenny asked herself, staring at her grim-faced son and his distraught girlfriend. Why didn't they sit down, she wondered. They looked so uncomfortable just standing there. Poor kids. It must seem like the end of the world to them. *How am I? Scared. Happy. Sad. In love. Worried sick.*

"I'm fine," she said. "I'm glad you called. I wanted to hear your voice, too."

"Well, I guess I'd better go. It's time for my flight."

"Have a good trip," Jenny said, thinking how stupid that sounded. A good trip, as if he were going on vacation.

"I'm sorry I can't say all the things that are in my heart," Stephen said.

"It's better, I suppose," Jenny said. "I'd rather you waited until you were sure, I think."

"Well, goodbye."

"Goodbye. Take care of yourself."

"You, too."

Jenny hung up the telephone. The only sound in the room was Paula's hiccuping sobs. *I am the adult here,* Jenny reminded herself. *I should say something wise and profound at this point, but all I feel is numb.* Part of Jenny's mind was back on the telephone, hearing the voice of the man she loved, the man she didn't know if she would ever see again. Part of her was caught up in the human drama that was going on in her living room. And yes, part of her even wondered if she'd remembered to turn on the oven. Eventually, she supposed, they would eat dinner.

She took a deep breath, pushed thoughts of Stephen to one side, marched out into the kitchen to check the oven—it was on—and then came back to face Joe and Paula.

"Let's sit down," she said.

Joe and Paula moved like Siamese twins to the sofa and sat down together. Jenny sat on the easy chair with the frayed upholstery, a permanent reminder that they'd once had a cat.

"Tell me what's on your mind," she said.

"We're going to get married," Joe said, unconsciously making his voice lower and more manly. But his sandy hair curled about his ears in a decidedly unmanly way. The scattering of freckles across his nose made him look like a twelve-year-old, but his well-muscled body was that of a man. And he had grown-up hormones, obviously. He'd gotten a girl pregnant. Soon Paula's wonderfully tall, slender body would swell into a pear shape, girlish no longer.

"What about school?" Jenny protested. "You're both just freshmen. And what will you use for money? I can't give you any more than I am right now, Joe. You know that."

"I know," Joe continued in his affected, I'm-a-man-now voice, "but we figured if you and Paula's folks would continue to give us the same amount of money you are now, we can manage. I'll double up on my hours at the Pizza Hut, and Paula can work for a while."

How naive they were, Jenny thought. They had no idea what they were facing with marriage and parenting, with bills they couldn't pay and the eternal laundry. But then no one ever did, not really.

"Are you certain this is what you want to do, son, or are you just being noble and doing the right thing?" Jenny asked. "Because don't think you're doing Paula any favors if you are. No marriage at all would be better for her than one featuring a reluctant bridegroom. What you are proposing is more grim than either of you could possibly realize. I'm not saying it won't work, but it'll be damned hard. Plus the fact that you're throwing away those young, carefree years. And believe me when I say you will someday look back with a measure of regret over that. There are other solutions besides marriage, you know."

"I won't give this baby away," Paula burst forth, finally finding her voice. There were fingerprints all over her glasses.

"We *both* want this baby," Joe announced indignantly.

"Nineteen years old is too damned young to get married. I just can't believe that anyone as bright as you two got yourself into a mess like this," Jenny said. "After all, zoology majors should be well versed in the facts of life."

"Come on, Mom. Everyone slips up once in a while. And you were only eighteen when you got married," Joe challenged.

"Yeah, and look how well that turned out," Jenny said sarcastically. Yet, she would have done it all over again, Jenny realized as she spoke. Her marriage hadn't been all bad, and she had her sons to show for it. She wouldn't have missed being the mother of Joe and Barry for the world.

"Well, Paula and I have decided to get married," Joe said in his big-man voice. "That's what we came to tell you."

"Paula, what do your parents say?" Jenny asked, resorting to her let's-be-reasonable, schoolteacher voice.

Paula looked stricken. "They are so angry. I'm sure they won't even come to the ceremony."

"I doubt that. They're just upset and need time to get used to the idea. After all, you two have done a very foolish thing. Making a baby is not something that should be done accidentally in the back seat of a car, or was it in the pickup truck? But since it happened, I guess we have to figure out a way to make the best of it."

"Don't lecture, Mom. I doubt if Barry and I were the result of a planned pregnancy even if you and Dad were married. And don't tell us we should have waited until after we were married to make love unless you can honestly say that's how you've conducted your own life. Paula and I thought we were being careful, and we made love because we're in love.''

Paula wiped her cheeks with the back of her hand and nodded eagerly. Yes, in love. Her smudged glasses fell down on her nose.

"Now you look here, Joe Bishop," Jenny said indignantly, *"I'm* not a participant in an out-of-wedlock pregnancy. And I'm a whole lot older than you are and more capable of making mature decisions that don't..." Jenny stopped in midsentence. How sanctimonious she sounded. She had twin babies when she was only nineteen years old, and she had thrown caution to the wind with Stephen. She could be pregnant now herself. At least Paula and Joe were committed to each other. Yes, they should have been more careful. Yes, they were too young to be getting married and having a baby. Yes, they were making life very difficult for themselves. But for her to criticize seemed ludicrous—the pot calling the kettle black, as Barbara would have said.

"I want to be called Grandmother," Jenny announced abruptly. "I know that's a mouthful when a child's little, but I've never liked the idea of being called 'Granny' or 'Grandma.'"

Jenny went over and knelt in front of her son and the young woman who would soon be his wife. "Congratulations, my darlings," she said as she hugged them. "It'll be a terrific kid."

Paula started crying again. This time Jenny joined her.

By the time the oven timer went off, they had discussed possible names, where the couple would live, who should perform the ceremony.

"Can we get married here?" Joe asked.

Jenny looked around at her shabby living room. Get married here? What a lackluster way to start a marriage.

"I suppose, if Paula's parents don't change their minds. Maybe I should talk to them myself. And we need to call your grandparents and your father, Joe. Why don't we do that after dinner?"

Paula set the table, and Joe made a salad while Jenny microwaved some broccoli. For dessert she got the remainder of the apple pie she had made for Stephen out of the freezer and put it in the oven to warm.

When they sat down to dinner, Jenny offered thanks for the food and asked a blessing on Joe, Paula and the child that was to be. Joe and Paula joined her in the "amen."

"I still feel compelled to tell you again that it's not going to be easy," Jenny said. "I hurt for you two when I think of all the hard times that are ahead. But if you really love each other, you can have more joy than sorrow and more good times than bad."

After dinner, Joe called his brother to tell him "how Mom had taken the news."

"She's a pretty neat old broad, actually," Joe said. Jenny threw a dish towel at him.

When Jenny's turn came to talk with Barry, she asked, "So what do you think of all this?"

"About like you, I imagine. Someplace between 'oh no' and 'oh wow.' Being an uncle sounds really neat. Having my twin brother be a father sounds positively unreal. I think it's the worst thing in the world for both of them, so why am I sitting here grinning from ear to ear?"

"Well said," Jenny told him. "And Barry, one shock like this is quite enough, if you get my message."

"Not to worry, Mother dear. I'm going to be a household word, remember. Working two shifts at Pizza Hut is not my style. And I want you to know that you're talking to the second lead in an upcoming university production of *Visit to a Small Planet*."

"Oh, Barry, that's terrific. When is it? I can hardly wait. My son, the famous actor."

The next phone call went to Jenny's parents. As Jenny dialed, she felt confident of their response. They would get on separate extensions, as they always did, and both talk at once saying all the right things. And indeed, with her father's failing health, this baby might be his only chance to see one of his great-grandchildren. Strange how things turned out. Jenny would not have recommended this pregnancy in a million years, but it would bring happiness. A baby to be born. Just the word "baby" made her smile.

She handed the phone to Joe and listened while he said, "Hey Gramps and Gran, did you two really like my girl, Paula? Yeah, she *is* a sweet girl. How would you like to have her as a granddaughter-in-law?"

He winked at Paula as he listened to their response.

"Well, I'm glad you approve. Now you'd better sit down for the next bit of news. You're going to get a great-grandkid in about seven and a half months."

Then there was much handing of the receiver back and forth. "No, I can't believe it either," Jenny said.

Joe promised his grandparents he would come see them real soon. "Of course, I'll bring Paula. She's one of the family now. And Gran, would you make the cake for our wedding? I still remember the tiered one you made for Mom and Dad's tenth anniversary. It was really great."

They called Lewis in Colorado but got his answering machine.

"You call him tomorrow, you hear," Jenny instructed Joe. "Both you and Barry. He'll be pleased."

Paula hugged Jenny and started to cry again. "I wish my mom had been nice about this like you."

"Paula, I can promise she will be. When the time comes, your parents will be there at the hospital, as proud as punch. Just give them time."

She walked the two young people out to the newly repaired truck and stood watching in the driveway as they drove away. Shivering in the crisp night air, Jenny turned and walked slowly back up the drive. Pregnant. She shook her head. Well, that'd give her something to take her mind off Stephen Carmichael and the rest of her life.

She stopped to pick up the evening paper and entered her very quiet apartment. She went to the telephone to call Barbara, but the line was busy. Ten minutes later it was still busy.

Jenny felt irrational anger that she couldn't talk to her friend when she needed to, and she felt even angrier at Stephen. Damn him, waiting until he was leaving the country to call her. Suddenly she felt her aloneness very acutely. So much had happened, and she had to digest it all by herself.

She fixed herself a cup of tea, tried Barbara's still-busy number again, kicked off her shoes and curled up on the end of the sofa. She was going to be a grandmother. The knowledge was beginning to sink in. What a strange set of emotions that evoked. She was too young to have to wear that hat. Good grief, she wasn't even forty. Yet another generation was being added to her family, and along with the wonder and joy came a sinking feeling of the years slipping by.

She was going to be a grandmother, yet she herself felt all the same emotions of new love that those two beautiful children felt. She felt the same passion and the same yearnings in her breast. When it came to love and sex, she was no older and no wiser than two nineteen-year-olds. She was just as vulnerable and just as needful of comfort.

Jenny pitied Joe and Paula the poverty and frustrations she knew lay ahead of them. But she envied them their togetherness. Whatever the future held, they would face it with each other.

The phone rang, but for once Jenny's heart did not leap. She'd had her phone call from Stephen for what it was worth. Maybe Barbara's kids let her use the phone for a change.

But it was Stephen's voice.

"Where are you?" Jenny asked.

"In a hotel in Seattle. I just arrived from Washington, and I fly out of here in the morning. Right now, I'm stretched out on the bed thinking how unsatisfactory that telephone call to you was earlier, and how unfair this whole situation is to you."

Jenny sank back on the sofa, holding the telephone base in her lap. "Fair? I tell my sons that fair is what comes to the fairground in the fall. I think you are probably doing the best you can under the circumstances, and I think sometimes we women grow up expecting too much out of the men in our lives. We dream about knights in shining armor sweeping into our lives on white chargers, and carrying us off into a perfect, low-stress happily ever after. But the truth of the matter is when people are our age, they drag around a lot of cumbersome past history and heavy emotional baggage that make 'sweeping' rather difficult.''

"Maybe I can pull a U-Haul behind the white horse to carry all that around in."

Jenny laughed. "Actually, you can put the armor in there too. I'm not sure I'd like to ride double with some man in a metal suit."

"Ah, Jenny, that's better. I like to hear you laugh."

"How long will you be gone?"

"I don't know. See, that *is* unfair."

"I don't like it, Stephen. In fact, I could get angry and make ultimatums. I could weep and cry. As a matter of fact, I have been angry and done some crying. But I won't make ultimatums. I know you'll do what you have to do, and if you don't come back, I will find someone else. I don't want to be alone anymore. But believe me, I sincerely hope that the man in my bed and in my heart for the rest of my life is you. I am truly, sincerely, in love with you."

"Thank you. I feel the same way about you, and I feel damned lucky to have a woman like you feel that way about me. Please, don't start looking for my replacement yet. Okay?"

"Okay."

"Sleep well, pretty lady."

"You too. Goodbye."

Jenny sat with the phone in her lap, her hands resting on the receiver, unwilling to give up her contact with Stephen.

Could she ever find someone else to love after loving him so much? Intellectually, Jenny supposed she could. In her heart, she doubted it.

Why hadn't she told him about Joe and Paula, Jenny asked herself. Was it that he hadn't earned the right yet to share in her family's joys and sorrows? Or was it because a soon-to-be grandmother in plain old Oklahoma didn't sound like much competition against a younger, more beautiful woman in exotic China?

# Chapter Eleven

From his stopover in Tokyo, Stephen flew to Peking aboard a Japanese airliner, since no U.S. military airplanes scheduled flights into Communist China.

With a military passport and diplomatic visa, customs was a formality. Stephen was escorted through by a uniformed official and taken to meet the car and driver sent by the American embassy. The driver was Chinese, and his English was difficult to understand, but Stephen was too tired to bother with conversation anyway. He stared out the window at a surprisingly modern city. Somehow he had expected ancient Chinese pavilions and temples to line the roadway. The biggest difference between Peking and other large cities was the swarm of bicycle riders pedaling up and down the streets. Private cars seemed to be nonexistent.

Stephen checked in with the military attaché at the American embassy, who was obviously puzzled over having a high-ranking Ordnance officer showing up on such short notice with a rather vague assignment. There was no billet for him within the embassy walls, and Stephen was sent to the Huaquio Hotel, a rather utilitarian facility used by the embassy for nonpolitical visitors.

In the hotel restaurant, Stephen was served a late dinner featuring a beef-and-bamboo-shoot entrée in a small bamboo steamer. The vegetable dish was fried eggplant and kidney beans. The food was interesting, but he didn't find it very filling. And he would have preferred Jenny's apple pie instead of the stir-fried mashed walnuts.

Stephen found himself staring at every Chinese woman in the restaurant and in the hotel lobby. There were probably millions of women in Peking, and if Jade were one of them, the possibility of him running into her accidentally on his first night in the city was about as likely as finding a needle in a haystack the size of a mountain.

But he looked nonetheless. He always had. Ever since Jade had disappeared, whenever Stephen glimpsed a small woman with sleek black hair, he had to make sure she wasn't Jade.

The next morning, he spent a half day touring the embassy with the attaché and meeting with the officers in command of the military unit that had responsibility for guarding the embassy compound. Stephen was not impressed with what he saw and heard, and in a way, that eased his conscience a bit. The trip was justified for more than personal reasons, and he could make recommendations for needed changes. The military arsenal at the embassy needed to be increased. Procedures should be changed. In an emergency, the military unit would be hard-pressed to protect the embassy's inhabitants and sovereign territory against terrorists or rioting crowds using the weapons it presently had at its disposal.

After lunch, Stephen went to an office in the Chinese Ministry of Public Security building, explaining to a ministry official through an embassy interpreter that he wanted to locate his wife and daughter. In addition to other information, he gave them the name of Jade's father and a seven-year-old address.

The small, spectacled man wearing a Western pin-striped suit listened impassively to the explanation of the interpreter, who was wearing a shapeless Mao suit of wrinkled khaki. The ministry official indicated his office would investigate the matter and that Stephen should come back in three days.

In three days, Stephen was told by a second small, spectacled man that the mother and daughter Stephen had described did not live in Peking. As for Jade's father, Stephen was told that the man had died six years ago.

"Say that I would like an inquiry about my family to go out on their communications network to every police department in the entire country," Stephen instructed the interpreter.

Stephen listened while a flood of incoherent words passed back and forth between the two men. The interpreter then turned to Stephen and told him he would be notified when and if the police had any results from such an investigation.

That evening, Stephen went walking in the huge Tien An Minh Square where Colonel Cheng had spotted Jade five years before. Located in the center of the city, the vast square was probably the most famous part of Peking, where the relics of the old power structure existed side by side next to the seat of the modern-day Communist government. On the north of the square was the imposing Gate of Heavenly Peace, that gave entry to the Imperial City and to the old Forbidden City within that, which once served as home to the emperors. On the western side of the square was the Great Hall of the

People, an immense columned building that housed the Chinese congress. Stephen recalled seeing news programs with Chairman Mao reviewing parades and presiding over enormous rallies in the square.

There was no rally today, only thousands of pedestrians and cyclists crisscrossing the huge open area. As with other places in the city, the most prevalent sound was the incessant ringing of bicycle bells.

Again, anytime Stephen saw a younger woman dressed other than in a drab Mao suit, he looked at her face. Somehow, he couldn't imagine Jade wearing one of the shapeless, unisex outfits that were so prevalent in the city. He saw many women in Western dress, but even at a distance, Stephen could tell that none had Jade's magnificent hair or her regal bearing. The looking for her made him feel foolish, but old habits die hard. He wondered if he would be searching crowds for Jade when he was an old man with a cane and failing vision.

That night Stephen took a taxi to one of the city's famous roast duck restaurants that Jade used to talk about. As he enjoyed the many-course meal, Stephen found himself thinking how sad it was to be eating such a noteworthy dinner alone and how much he had enjoyed the meals he had shared with Jenny in Oklahoma. He would rather eat a pizza with Jenny than eat this magnificent meal alone.

Over the following week, Stephen worked on a comprehensive plan for rearming the American Embassy building and establishing procedures to be followed in the event of various types of sieges on the embassy compound.

In the late afternoons, Stephen would sightsee, roaming about the Forbidden City and visiting temples, parks, museums. His heart wasn't in it, but he had no idea if he would ever come to Peking again and felt obligated to see as much of the city as he could.

His guide showed him how even the softest whisper spoken close to the wall of the round Temple of the Gods would come back to him from the opposite direction. Without thinking, Stephen whispered, "Jenny." How interesting, he thought. He was in China because of one woman, yet thoughts of another filled even his unconscious mind.

Saturday morning, Stephen rode a train out to the Great Wall. When he stood atop a tower and gazed at the incredible wall snaking its way across the mountain tops, he could understand why the Great Wall was called one of the wonders of the world. Stephen closed his eyes a minute, trying to imagine ancient armies protecting their country from atop the wall, invading marauders attempting to scale the wall, the whistle of arrows, the clanging of swords.

He thought of Jenny who made history come alive for her students, yet never got to visit the places like this where history had been made. Stephen tried to memorize it for her. He would tell her how it looked and felt to be here. Maybe someday he could even bring her here, he thought.

Sunday, he roamed about Bei Hai Lake and Park. The shores of the lake were beautifully landscaped and dotted with temples and pavilions. The unseasonably warm spring day had brought out the residents of the city. The park was full of people doing the traditional Chinese exercise, young people sunning themselves, families strolling, cyclists leisurely riding about. Everyone seemed to be with someone. Stephen felt as conspicuous because he was alone as because he was an Occidental in this decidedly Oriental setting.

Monday morning, Stephen and his embassy interpreter went back to the Ministry of Public Security and waited the entire morning without being allowed to speak with anyone.

In the afternoon a uniformed officer came out to tell the interpreter that the ministry was very sorry, but no evidence had been found that the American colonel's wife and daughter lived anyplace within the People's Republic of China.

Stephen instructed the interpreter to inform the Chinese official that he would come back in two days, and expected to speak with the public security minister in person.

The next day, Stephen began contacting every English-speaking foreign correspondent based in the city and told them the story of his missing wife and child. When the Associated Press correspondent came to interview Stephen in his hotel room, he asked Stephen for a photograph. Stephen pulled out his billfold. There was a studio shot of Jade, which brought an admiring remark from the newsman. There was a first-grade picture of Mindy with a missing front tooth. And there was a picture of the three of them together, which Beth Mansfield had taken. They had been riding horses at the Mansfields' Maryland farm. Stephen remembered sitting on that fence while Beth snapped her pictures and thinking it would be good to have a memento of such a nice day. Beth had given it to him the week after Jade and Mindy disappeared. He had looked at it and wept.

"I LOVE THIS WEATHER," Barbara said, as she stretched out on the blanket and tilted her face to the sun. "Of course, severe weather is predicted for tonight, but this afternoon it's glorious. Turn on the radio, will you, Jen, and find a mellow station—something for the 'mature' listener.''

Jenny obliged, turning on the battery-powered radio that Barbara had borrowed for the afternoon from her kids. She turned the dial until she heard the voice of Barry Manilow. That ought to be mellow enough, she thought. She had planned to spend the afternoon at the Historical Society's microfilmed newspaper archives when Barbara called to lure her out into the spring sunshine.

Jenny's work on her new job, a 1910-vintage house on Northwest 18th, was progressing nicely. She had already turned up some intriguing information about the house from the newspaper morgue. A lover's triangle had resulted in a shooting there in 1917. No one was killed, but the woman in the triangle was the socially prominent daughter of one of the city's wealthy bankers. Her husband and an unknown touring actor had shot at each other on the veranda during a garden party.

Something about the actor's newspaper picture struck a chord with Jenny, and she searched through some microfilmed copies of old magazines at the University of Oklahoma Library. She discovered pictures confirming that the actor and a Hollywood film idol of the twenties and thirties were the same man. The actor had changed his name and grown a mustache, but a careful comparison of the pictures confirmed Jenny's suspicions. The man had become famous playing debonair rogues in countless films and was married for a time to one of the most prominent sex goddesses of the era.

Jenny was certain there would be some publicity in the local press about her discovery. And she planned to submit an article about the long-ago incident to a screen magazine since the legendary actor's films were still shown on late-night television. Her article and photographs about the round stained-glass skylight at Graystone had been accepted by a local home magazine, and she planned to submit another version to a national architectural magazine.

She was busier than she had ever been in her life, with her teaching, the research, the writing and plans for Joe and Paula's wedding, which was to take place at Paula's house the following Sunday.

Yes, there was plenty she should have been doing that afternoon, but the weather was seductive. Spring might not have arrived to stay, but it was certainly giving them a preview. The two women had packed a picnic lunch and gone to Lincoln Park, where they could enjoy the sunshine and stroll about the zoo.

Jenny took a Coke from the cooler and sat cross-legged beside Barbara on the blanket.

"Did you get any letters from your ad yet?" Jenny asked. The singles ad they composed had appeared the previous week in the *Gazette*:

Reasonably attractive, fortyish high school English teacher, widowed with three children, seeks fortyish man with a sense of humor, who likes spectator sports, dancing and movies. Snobs and men whose last date was more than fifteen years his junior need not apply.

"Uh-hmm," Barbara said. "They arrived from the *Gazette* this morning, but I haven't had the courage to read them yet. They're in the side pocket of my purse."

Jenny pulled out the bundle of letters and tore open one of them.

"Well, this gentleman is a school principal looking for someone to teach English and driver's education at a consolidated school in the Panhandle."

"You're kidding," Barbara said, sitting up and taking the letter from Jenny. "My goodness, he doesn't even say if he's married or looking or anything. He just wants a school teacher to *teach*. He says for me to send my resume, college transcripts and three letters of recommendation if I'm interested. A three-bedroom teacherage comes with the job."

Barbara reached for another letter and opened it. Her eyes widened, and she started laughing. "My God. This one's kinky. He's always wanted to make love to a teacher on her desk."

"No!" Jenny said in disbelief, grabbing the letter to see for herself. "Did you see what he wants you to wear while all this is going on?"

"Yeah, he's a real Frederick's of Hollywood freak," Barbara giggled. "Well, on to the next one. The letters are certainly good for laughs, if nothing else," she said, grabbing another letter. "Hey this one's kind of sweet. He's a widowed professor, and his first wife taught English. He says that he always admired her knowledge and love of the language. He is past fifty but jogs every day and is in good health. 'I'd like to share long talks and long walks,' he says."

"Here's a minister who wants a mother for his *four* young children," Jenny said. "And she must be a good cook."

"No, thanks," Barbara said, already smiling over the next letter. "This guy says he's only thirty-two, but he's tired of young, empty-headed women and is ready to date someone more mature. 'I'm a truck driver and on the road a great deal. I'd like to have a loving woman to come home to someday, but right now I'd settle for interesting companionship and a little Western dancing.' That's kind of sweet, don't you think?"

Jenny frowned as she scanned a rather lengthy letter. "This man recently arrived in this country from Greece. He wants a pretty American lady 'to assist poor foreign man to learn better at language of English in order to obtain employment with American business and become rich.' Unless I misunderstand him, this guy already has a wife in Greece but says he is willing 'to make sex for fun.'"

"I want to 'make sex for fun' with a married man," Barbara said, "the only stipulation being that he's married to me."

"That's a good idea," Jenny said, her voice flat.

"Oh, honey, don't get me wrong. Stephen Carmichael is about the most unmarried married man I know."

"Yeah, but isn't it interesting what a difference even a technicality can make? Not many women manage to get themselves mixed up with a man who has a legally dead but probably living wife."

"You okay?" Barbara asked.

"Sure. By this time, numbness had set in. Read another letter."

Barbara pulled another one out of the pile and scanned it. "This man has never gotten over his crush on his high school English teacher. I'm amazed that the teacher part of that ad would create the most interest. But then I hardly expected them to come running because I have three children."

Jenny looked over the last letter and began to read it out loud. "I wonder if it took as much courage for you to write that Gazette ad as it's taking me to write this letter. I don't dance, but I've always wanted to learn. I've been by myself for two years now and have never gotten used to being alone. The evenings are the worst part. There's no one to discuss the events of the day with, no one to watch the evening news with, no one to scratch my back when it itches, no one to laugh and cry with. I'm a librarian and not a very exciting person. My looks are forgettable. I can't remember the punch lines of jokes. I guess the best thing I can say about myself is that I'm honest and sincere. And I'm a pretty good cook.''

Barbara nodded. "*He* goes to the head of the class. The truck driver is second. Third is the widower whose wife taught English. You can throw the rest away.''

"Even the minister who wants a cook to mother his four children?" Jenny said jokingly.

"I've done kids. I'm ready for a new emphasis in my life. I want to nurture a relationship rather than kids. You know, that was fun," she said, indicating the letters. "I'm interested to see what the next batch brings.''

"Are you going to call the librarian?" Jenny asked.

"Maybe I will," Barbara said. "Let's eat now. All this food for thought makes me hungry.''

The two women laid their lunch out on the blanket between them. Barbara had resumed her diet and had included apples instead of Hershey bars. She'd gone back to diet pop, and there were the inevitable carrot and celery sticks.

"Have you talked to Chuck at all?" Jenny asked between bites of her ham-and-cheese sandwich.

"Just a hello when we pass in the hall. It irritates me that he doesn't even act embarrassed or chagrined. You'd think I was just another colleague, but it's all right now. It really is. I wasn't in love with him, I was just in love with the idea of having a younger man court me. And you know, now that I've put a little distance between myself and our affair, I realized the kid was really boring. Maybe that's rationalizing, but so what if it helps. And Chuck *was* boring. He'd go on and on about musical groups I'd never heard of and car stats that I didn't understand. What about your love life? I gather you haven't heard from Stephen?''

"No. Nothing since the en-route phone calls.''

"That's tough, kid,'' Barbara said, patting Jenny's hand.

Jenny fought back the tears that clouded her eyes. She hated feeling sorry for herself. "Let's talk about the wedding,'' she said brightly. "Can you believe all this? My little boy getting married and going to make me a grandmother.''

"Paula's parents have come around, I take it?'' Barbara asked.

"Goodness, yes. Her mother stops every now and then to weep a bit because her baby girl's getting married, but she's gone slightly crazy over putting on a wedding. She makes lists on top of lists, and Paula types them into her computer and does wonderful computer print-outs. Paula's even writing a software program for organizing weddings and setting up households. She's going to put an ad for it in *Bride* magazine. Imagine, getting married by computer.''

Barbara stretched back out on the blanket and covered her eyes with her arm. "What do her folks think of Joe? After all he got their daughter pregnant.''

"It takes two to get pregnant,'' Jenny said dryly, as she stretched out beside Barbara. "I'm sure they wish the kids had waited a couple of years, but it's hard to stay mad over a baby that you already know you'll love.

Joe and Paula are young, but I guess becoming parents at nineteen isn't the end of the world.''

Jenny felt herself getting drowsy in the warm sunshine. Like Barbara, she shaded her eyes with an arm. As always, when she closed her eyes, images of Stephen flitted across her mind. While the sounds of children laughing and calling to one another, the whistle of the tiny zoo train as it circled the lake, the voice of Karen Carpenter singing of true love from the radio all drifted into the background, Jenny imagined what it would be like if Stephen were here with her. They would be on their own blanket, holding hands and dozing in the sun. Barbara and her librarian fiancé would be on a blanket next to them. When they finished resting, the four of them would stroll over to make faces at the monkey in the primate complex, and then they'd check on the newborn brown bear. Later, they'd go to a movie and have pizza and beer afterwards. When they were alone at Graystone, she and Stephen would bathe together in his roomy shower. With big fluffy towels, they would dry each other, then spend the next hour or so making love in his big bed. Jade's picture would be gone from over the fireplace, but there would be one of Mindy on the mantel.

They would go slowly with their lovemaking, caressing each other for ever so long, luxuriating in the feel of each other's clean, moist bodies. The kisses would be soft and tender, the touch of fingers light and teasing.

The sun warmed her from the outside, and her own fantasies warmed her from within. It was amazing how much she thought of lovemaking these days. At one time in her life, Jenny assumed that women her age were no longer sensual, and sexual thoughts no longer crossed their minds. And that certainly a woman on the brink of grandmotherhood would be finished with sex. Relationships at that point became a series of affectionate pats and closed-lip kisses. How silly that notion had been! Jenny was freer in her thinking now than she had been as a younger woman. The inhibitions of youth had fallen away, and she knew how to flow with desire and crest with it. Passion came naturally and was not a condition she had to work toward to achieve. Yes, sex was definitely better at this stage in her life. The man she loved and her own mature body made it so.

Making love with Stephen had been a joy. And oh, how she wanted it again. Surely life would not be so cruel as to show her the delight of loving Stephen and then take it away from her.

"TURN ON THE NEWS," Barbara's voice commanded over the telephone. "Channel Four."

"But I need to walk out the door right this minute or I'll be late to school," Jenny protested, glancing at the clock on top of the television.

"Be late." Barbara ordered. "They said something at the beginning of this *Today* show segment about an American Army officer searching for his wife and daughter in Communist China."

The phone cord trailing after her, Jenny hurried over and turned on the television set. The news portion of the program had begun. Kilauea was erupting in Hawaii. A hijacking was averted over Mexico. The president and first lady were celebrating an anniversary. And Colonel Stephen Carmichael, a Pentagon-based Ordnance officer and much-decorated veteran of the Vietnam War, was in Peking culminating a seven-year-long search for his daughter and Chinese wife.

Jenny listened to the story of Jade's original defection to the West with her family after the Communist takeover of her country and how she had later returned to China with her father as a young woman. Then she had been granted political asylum in this country after marrying Stephen. Jade and Mindy had disappeared from the family's Alexandria, Virginia, apartment without a trace and that "the determined Colonel Carmichael had reason to believe they were now living in Peking," the commentator explained.

"He has vowed to leave no stone unturned in his search and has accused the Chinese government of not cooperating in his effort to locate his family," the newsman read.

Then a picture of the three of them appeared on the screen. They were sitting on a fence, their arms linked—laughing, bright-eyed Mindy; Stephen, handsome and beaming; petite, beautiful Jade. Jade and Stephen were smiling at each other over the head of their daughter.

Jade's long hair was draped over one shoulder. Her head was tilted back, a smile parting her full lips. She had the air of a woman secure in her beauty and in the love of her man.

Jenny had forgotten about the telephone pressed against her ear. "I see what you mean," Barbara's voice said. "She really is lovely. And how terrible it must have been for Stephen, not only to lose them but to never know why. I hope he can find some answers."

"See you at school," Jenny said, and hung up.

She turned off the television and paused in the middle of the living room, trying to think what she had been doing before Barbara called. School. She was going to be late.

But Jenny felt immobilized. Stephen had loved Jade. Of course, she had known that before. He hadn't hidden the fact, and he wouldn't have married Jade if he hadn't loved her. But now Jenny had *seen* that love plainly written on his face in that photograph.

She felt sick. If there had been a medicine to cure her of Stephen, she would have considered taking it. She didn't need pain and agony. But there was no such medicine. She suspected that her condition was incurable.

And life went on.

It was too late to call in sick. And what would she do at home alone except feel sorry for herself.

Jenny picked up her purse. Somehow, she would make it through the day.

# Chapter Twelve

Mindy was knocking on the door of the bedroom in his apartment. She was begging him to open the door, but Stephen couldn't move. He tried and tried, but his limbs were leaden, and he didn't have the strength to lift them off the bed.

"I'm coming," he said. "Don't go away. I'm coming."

Slowly, he fought his way to wakefulness, realizing he wasn't in his apartment but in a hotel room in China. He had been dreaming, but the knocking continued, restrained knocking as though the person at his door did not want to awaken the hotel's other guests.

Stephen put on his robe and staggered to the door. A surprisingly large Chinese man with unkempt hair was standing in the hall. Without a word, he handed Stephen a sealed envelope. There was no writing on it.

Stephen tore open the envelope. It contained one thin sheet of paper. His heart skipped a beat. The handwriting was Jade's distinctive back-slanting style. "Come with this man. Say nothing to anyone." It was not signed.

"Do you speak English?" Stephen asked the man. The question drew no response, not even the blink of an eye. The man was muscled like a weight lifter with an unnaturally thickened upper body and massive neck and shoulders. His forearms bulged under his jacket like hams.

Stephen did not relish the idea of going out into the night with such a man. If it came down to a fight, Stephen knew he wouldn't have a chance, but he had no choice except to go. The man apparently could lead him to Jade. But would he? Stephen looked at the note again.

Such handwriting wouldn't be difficult to imitate. Or even if Jade had written it, there was no telling where he might be taken. The Chinese government had expressed great displeasure to the American ambassador over Stephen's conduct of late. The stories that were appearing about him in newspapers around the world made the Chinese government seem unsympathetic and implied that Stephen's wife and daughter might be in China against their will. It was just a matter of time until the Chinese would formally request that he leave the country, and Stephen knew that American embassy officials would comply. He would have to go. A runaway wife was not worth an international incident.

Stephen would be willing to leave China if he knew that Jade was truly a runaway and if Mindy had not been a native-born American citizen. He knew that if it weren't for Mindy, the embassy would have already sent him away. As it was, they were willing to give him another day or two.

Stephen opened the door wider and indicated the man should come inside, but he stayed where he was. Stephen left the door ajar and hurriedly dressed in the one pair of civilian slacks he had brought and added a knit shirt and windbreaker jacket. He debated about his passport, then left it and his billfold locked in his suitcase. He wished he had a weapon of some sort.

They left the hotel through a side door. Stephen had expected a car to be waiting curbside, but the Chinese man began walking, and Stephen followed.

He tried to memorize the route they were taking but soon gave up. The huge man was leading him through a maze of alleyways, going deeper and deeper into the poorest section of the city. The foul smells that assailed Stephen's nostrils spoke of filth and decay. The houses were little more than shacks and crammed up against one another, with only shoulder-wide passageways in between. The whole area seemed deserted except for an occasional sliver of light at a window, and from one house they passed, a baby cried. There were no streetlights, and their way was illuminated only by a pale quarter moon.

Why would Jade be in such a neighborhood as this, Stephen wondered, growing increasingly nervous. Jade and Mindy would not live in such houses. Jade was an educated woman from an intellectual family. Even if her father really was dead, she would be able to support herself with her incredible linguistic skills.

Finally his guide turned between two houses that seemed indistinguishable from all the others. A twisting path took them past a privy and up a steep hill. At the top of the hill was a cluster of houses, so close together they almost seemed to lean against each other. The rest of the flat hilltop was occupied by a large odoriferous pigsty and a fenced garden.

The Chinese man stopped at the first house and rapped on a door made of bamboo poles. The door swung open on a room illuminated by the flickering light of a kerosene lantern. The man stepped to one side and indicated Stephen was to enter. Stephen approached the door and hesitated, a warning bell going off in his head. Inside, two Chinese men warmed themselves at a charcoal brazier. There was no sign of Jade. Stephen took a step backward. He didn't like the feel of this at all.

Then suddenly pain erupted across the back of his head. He wasn't going anyplace he realized as his knees gave way under him and his vision faded to blackness. As consciousness slipped away, he wondered if they were going to kill him.

A BLUE-JEAN-CLAD PAULA met Jenny at the door. "Don't panic," she said. "I've fixed my hair and got on my makeup. That's two-thirds of the battle. The blushing bride will look more bridelike in plenty of time for the ceremony. Can you believe it? It's my wedding day."

Jenny embraced her soon-to-be daughter-in-law. "Where's the safety pin," she asked pointing to Paula's glasses.

"Mother insisted," Paula explained with a sheepish grin. "She tried to convince me to wear contact lenses for the ceremony, but me and my lenses never saw eye to eye. And everybody would wonder who Joe was marrying if I didn't have on my glasses. So Mother and I compromised, and I got a screw put in the hinge and retired the safety pin."

Jenny thought again how much she liked this lovely young woman with the fantastic skin and the charming sense of humor. If she'd been selecting a bride for Joe herself, she couldn't have done better than Paula.

"You look more like a bride yourself than the mother of the groom," Paula said, standing back to admire Jenny. "That's a great outfit."

"It is rather nice, isn't it? I found it on a sale rack after looking all over for something I could afford." Jenny twirled around so Paula could inspect the smart suit of soft aqua gabardine. The jacket was padded in the shoulders, fitted in the waist, flaring out into a peplum and making her waist look wonderfully small. The smart lines of the suit were softened by a lace jabot at the collar of her blouse. Jenny loved herself in the outfit. When she bought it, she couldn't help but think that such a suit was not only suitable for the mother of the groom, but that one might also use the suit to get married in oneself.

"Doesn't everything look grand?" Paula beamed as she showed Jenny around the downstairs. "It sure doesn't look like the scene for a shotgun wedding, does it?"

"I heard that," the voice of Paula's mother, Phyllis Baxter, called down from the top of the stairs. "I'd appreciate it, Paula, if you'd stop using that term. Your poor old mother is still feeling very sensitive over all this. Hello, Jenny. I'm not ready yet. I need to pull out a few more gray hairs. Can you believe this grandmother business? I'm too young. And I'm too old for weddings with pregnant brides. Paula can show you where to put the food."

"Everything looks wonderful, Phyllis," Jenny called upstairs. "You've done a terrific job in such a short time."

The house did indeed look grand. Jenny was glad the wedding was being held here instead of at her shabby apartment. The Baxters' northwest Oklahoma City home was spacious and attractive. The furniture was not worn, and the carpet looked new. The pictures on the wall weren't framed prints but real watercolors and oils.

And today, the house was filled with flowers and potted palms. Several dozen folding chairs set in rows in the living room and entry hall faced the fireplace, which was flanked by tall candelabra. Huge arrangements of spring flowers burst forth from silver urns on either side of the mantel.

The dining room table had been opened out to its full length and covered with white linen. Another huge floral arrangement dominated its center.

Jenny kissed her parents, who had driven up from Madill early to assemble the four-tier wedding cake that Jenny's mother had made. "Gosh, Mom, you could do that professionally. It's beautiful."

"Your dad helped me," Maxine said. "He's the engineer in charge of this project. And he cleaned up the unbelievable mess I made in the kitchen at home."

Paula helped Jenny carry in from her car trays of finger sandwiches and hors d'oeuvres, Jenny's contribution to the hurriedly planned wedding.

"Come on upstairs and give me moral support while I transform myself into a bride," Paula said.

Jenny followed Paula up to her bedroom. It looked like a typical teenage girl's room. There was the inevitable bulletin board loaded with dried-out corsages and snapshots, and stuffed animals lined the bed and the top of the bookcase. A huge poster of Bruce Springsteen dominated one wall. What a quantum leap Paula was taking—and Joe—from young and carefree to adult and responsible in such a short time.

Paula stripped down to her underwear. "Look at my little round tummy," she said proudly, patting her belly.

"What do you mean round? It's still flatter than mine," Jenny said. "Are you sure you want to get dressed now? It will be at least an hour before all the guests have assembled and the ceremony begins."

"I'm not going to sit up here by myself while everyone arrives. Joe and I are going to mingle. After all, it's *our* wedding."

Phyllis came bustling into the room. Her dress was peach-colored jersey. "I had a terrible time deciding on a dress. I wanted to look like the mother of the bride without appearing matronly, but I think the two conditions are analogous. How come you look so good, Jenny? It's not fair for you to look like someone from the *Dynasty* cast, while I look like one of the *Golden Girls*. I wish my hair fluffed out like that."

"It would if you'd stop combing it down instead of brushing it up," Paula said, handing Jenny a hair brush. "Sit down, Mom, and let Jenny fluff."

Armed with a can of hair spray, Jenny used the brush to put some life into Phyllis's carefully combed hair.

"Hey, that does look better," Phyllis said, taking the hairbrush from Jenny and doing a little fluffing on her own. "Okay. My turn," Paula announced.

Phyllis turned to Jenny. "Can you believe this girl? She refuses to make an entrance. She and Joe plan to greet the guests as they come, then just stroll over to the fireplace when it's time and tell the minister to begin."

Phyllis and Jenny helped Paula into her dress. She had chosen a princess-cut dress of pale pink faille with an ankle-length, gored skirt. The scooped neckline was encrusted with seed pearls, a beautifully simple dress on a lovely bride. Phyllis looked at her daughter and burst into tears. "I'm ruining my makeup," she wailed, "but you look so beautiful, honey. Does Joe have any idea what a terrific girl he's marrying?"

Jenny decided it was time for mother and daughter to have some time alone before the wedding and she went downstairs to see if the bridegroom and his brother had arrived. They hadn't. Jenny introduced herself to the minister and early-arriving guests. Paula's father, Bill Baxter, bustled around serving glasses of wine.

Jenny checked her watch nervously, then went to call home. The boys and Barry's girlfriend, Linda, had been almost ready when Jenny left the apartment. They should have arrived by now.

Paula was downstairs greeting her guests. Barbara waved to Jenny from across the room. Jenny let the phone ring for a long time. Joe, Barry and Linda must be on their way.

Twenty minutes later, Jenny breathed a sigh of relief when her sons came through the front door. Paula flew into Joe's arms. "They were beginning to think you ran out on me."

"Not a chance," Joe said. "We had a zipper problem. The one on the groom's tux pants took a very inopportune time to break. I tried Barry's, but they were too small and I couldn't get them fastened. The rental place was closed."

"What did you do?" Paula asked.

"Well, I used your method of fixing things and fastened the zipper with a safety pin—actually two safety pins. And you can hardly tell. Let's get married so I can put my jeans back on."

"Sounds like a good reason to me."

The guests seated themselves in the chairs. Barry and Linda lit the candelabras. A girlfriend of Paula's played "No Other Love Have I" on the violin. Paula and Joe, holding hands, followed the minister to the front of the room, and Barry and the violin player joined them as attendants.

Paula and Joe had added their own touches to the ceremony, but it was basically the traditional service. They made to each other their promises of love and honor and commitment. Jenny reached for Phyllis's hand. The two women looked at each other and the tears began, but Jenny didn't care. Their children were deserving of tears. The time-honored words themselves filled her with satisfaction. Joe and Paula would be fine. Their voices were firm and true as they exchanged their vows.

Jenny found it amazing how strongly she still believed in marriage. At one time, she had promised herself that she would never marry again. Marriage was too risk-filled a proposition, and while she might live with a man, she wouldn't marry him. But in spite of a failed first marriage, Jenny found that she longed to say the words again. She wanted to pledge her troth to a worthy man and invest her love and energy in making a life with him. Marriage didn't always bring happiness, but that was a failing of the people themselves and not the institution.

CRADLING HIS HEAD on his arm, Stephen lay on his side on a woven straw mat. If he lay very still, he could control the pain inside his head.

He was cold, hungry and thirsty. Stephen had no idea how long he had been unconscious, but he'd been in this small cellar room for three days since becoming aware of his surroundings. The large man would occasionally open the overhead trapdoor and hand him down a dipper of water, and there had been a few bowls of cold noodles.

Stephen did not understand why he was here. He certainly didn't seem to be a political prisoner. This house was definitely not a government prison, and those thugs upstairs were not government officials.

The first day he had been in too much pain to move. He just lay there listening to the footsteps and voices overhead. Yesterday and today, he had forced himself to go over every inch of the small room with its one high window that was little more than a ventilation hole. The only furnishings were a slop bucket with a lid in the corner and the mat he was lying on. He tried to dig a rock out of the wall to use as a weapon, and to discover a way to escape, but he struck out on both counts, and the movement made the pain in his head come back.

Now he just lay there and thought, trying to determine why he was there. What did those men expect to gain from holding an American military officer captive? And what did Jade have to do with this whole scenario? If she hadn't written the note, then someone who was familiar with her handwriting had. Either directly or indirectly, Jade was involved in his abduction.

Stephen knew his captors would be dealt with severely by the law if they were caught, unless of course, they were some sort of unlikely government agents. But the more he thought about it, the more certain he was that they were just common criminals hired to take him prisoner.

But why? Was Jade's privacy that sensitive an issue?

His watch was gone, and the light and darkness from the small window gave Stephen his only sense of the passage of time. He slept a great deal and was trying to sleep now, but it was too cold. The weather had changed. He could hear the wind outside. Stephen curled his body up more tightly. What he wouldn't give for a blanket.

Finally he could feel his body sinking into rejuvenating sleep in spite of the cold and discomfort. He hoped he would wake up and discover this had all been a nightmare, including the still very tender lump on his head.

And when sleep had firmly taken him, it was hard to rouse himself to the voice saying his name. A female voice. "Stephen, wake up. Stephen."

Suddenly, the knowledge of whose voice he was hearing hit him like a sledgehammer.

His eyes flew open.

It was her. Jade. Just like that.

Her face was very close to his. "Stephen, are you all right? I'd like to have the son of a bitch drawn and quartered who did this to you. God, what a mess you've stirred up."

"Jade?" Stephen said tentatively. It was really her. He was not dreaming. How strange. No words of greeting from her. No embrace. Just anger.

With Jade's help, Stephen struggled to a sitting position. He had to close his eyes for a few seconds to control the dizziness and a wave of nausea. He knew his head injury, while still painful, was not serious and that his main problem was dehydration. He'd had so little water since being brought here.

Jade was kneeling in front of him, her hands in the demure pose so typical of Chinese women, but her face was not demure. She was irritated and angry. Her clothing consisted of a shapeless suit of quilted fabric like the Chinese peasants wore, and her hair was stuffed inside a man's billed cap, surely a disguise. Stephen couldn't imagine her wearing such clothing for any other reason.

Her exquisite features were exactly the same, her skin still flawless and smooth as satin, her almond eyes still framed with thick black lashes. Her mouth was wide and full and as sensual as before, her teeth white and perfect. In spite of her unlikely attire, he could see that seven years had not diminished her beauty.

Stephen was very aware how filthy he was. He hadn't shaved in days, and his hair was matted. He smelled disgusting while Jade smelled of gardenias—just as she always had.

So many things he wanted to know, but all he could do was stare. Where in the hell did he begin a conversation with a wife he hadn't seen in seven years?

"Are you all right?" Jade asked again. Her tone was softer now.

"Sure. Terrific," he said sarcastically. "Why I am here?"

She sighed and sat back on her heels. "I paid the large man to bring you to me. He decided to hold you for ransom instead. I've spent the past three days trying to get the money together. After I paid him, he brought me here. When he opened that trapdoor, I thought they'd killed you and thrown you in a hole."

"Where are the men now?"

She shrugged. "Gone."

"Ransom? Why? I don't understand." Stephen rubbed at his temples with his fingertips in an effort to clear his head.

"I guess he figured that if I was going to so much trouble to see you, I would pay a ransom for you," Jade explained. "It is an old Chinese custom. He said he would kill you if I did not pay him. I had no idea where you'd been taken, and I could not go to the police. Obviously I would not have hired him in the first place if I hadn't needed to be surreptitious.''

"I don't understand any of this. Why didn't you just come to me? Why all the clandestine crap?''

"I thought it more prudent to see you secretly and convince you to leave the country. It would be an embarrassment to my family if it became known that I had seen you. This nonsense you have been supplying to the foreign press is very humiliating to me and my family. My father has just now regained the prestige he lost when we left China all those years ago, and I have an important position in the government. And my honorable husband has forbidden me to have anything to do with you.''

"Your *husband*?''

"Yes, my husband. I terminated our marriage when I returned to China and remarried shortly afterwards. I had been betrothed to him before I came to the United States. My husband is a very important man with a sensitive government position, and we have a meaningful life. We have two fine sons, and my husband has legally adopted Mindy. I want you to go away, Stephen. Your presence here has been a great embarrassment.''

Stephen felt the taste of bile rising in his throat. He clenched his fists at his side. Her *husband*. Damn her! All that time he had longed for her, prayed for her, wept for her, she'd given him no thought at all. She hadn't had enough consideration for him to inform him she had ended their marriage.

He had come a long way and taken a long time to find out what a fool he'd been. "You can't take my daughter away from me without my consent. And just for the record, why in the hell didn't you tell me any of this be-

fore now? Didn't I even deserve the courtesy of notify-
ing me that you'd obtained a divorce?''

"I did not want to have any contact with you. I was
afraid you would do something stupid like trying to
come after me, if you knew where I was. I never
dreamed you'd be fool enough to wait around all this
time. Stephen, all you had to do was tell the courts that
I had abandoned you, and they would have granted you
a divorce.''

"I didn't want a divorce. I wanted my family back.''

"You have no family. And you have chosen to forget
the fact that we were not all that happy when we were
together. We played at being happy, but we were not, or
at least I wasn't. You enjoyed having an unusual wife,
but I had no respect for America and things American,
and we were too different in temperament and ideology.
But if you still care anything at all for me and for Mindy,
you will go home. You are making terrible problems for
me. My husband has lost face, and he is very angry.''

"So am I,'' Stephen said, his voice flat. "Why didn't
you just pay that ape you hired to kill me and be done
with it?''

"My God, Stephen, I am not a monster. I don't want
you dead, I just want you to go away and leave me
alone.''

"I won't leave without seeing Mindy.''

"That is out of the question,'' she said with a toss of
her head for emphasis. "Totally.''

"Then I'm not going.''

"You have no choice,'' Jade said. She was getting
impatient. He had forgotten how hard her voice could
be. What else had he forgotten?

"The Chinese government has formally requested
your expulsion from the country,'' she went on. "The

minute you show your face, the American ambassador
will have no choice but to order you to leave."

"Perhaps. But you have forgotten that Mindy is an
American citizen. The ambassador can put on a little
pressure of his own."

"Mindy has formally renounced her United States
citizenship," Jade said with a haughty tilt to her chin.
"She has pledged her allegiance to the People's Republic of China and to her stepfather. Go home, Stephen."

"I want to see my daughter, Jade, and if you don't
arrange it, I'll talk to more reporters. I'll tell them
everything that has happened, and if you think your
reputation has been hurt by the publicity so far, you
haven't seen anything yet. I'll imply that you were a
woman of loose morals. I'll say you were paid to have
sex with American officials in order to gain access to
sensitive information. I'm sure your important husband can keep the story out of the Chinese press, but
with so many foreigners coming into China these days,
surely word of this will leak out. Your husband will lose
more face and get even angrier, won't he? Or if that tack
doesn't work, I'll find some other way to make trouble
for you."

"Maybe I should have had you killed," Jade said angrily. "Maybe I should have just left you here to die in
this stinking cellar."

Stephen grabbed her shoulders. She stiffened under
his hands. How slight she was beneath the padded coat.
"Were you a spy, Jade? Was our whole marriage a
sham?"

She shook off his hands. "What's the point of discussing that now? It's over."

"Did you marry me because you loved me or because you thought it might open doors for you?" He wanted to know it all. He might never have another chance.

"Both, I suppose, but I refuse to talk about it. I must return to my home. I will find someone to direct you back to your hotel."

"Was there any love at all?" Stephen persisted. "Was I that much of a fool?"

Jade sighed deeply. She looked down at her hands in her lap. Her voice was softer. "Yes, there was love, but some things are more important than love."

"Like what?"

"Duty. Fatherland. Go home, Stephen, and leave me alone." She clutched her small hands to her breast. "Don't make any more trouble. Please."

"What about your duty to me? Don't you think you had a duty to let me know where I stood and not leave me in limbo for *seven agonizing years*?"

"I don't have to answer you." Jade was afraid now. Stephen could see it in her eyes. Did she think he would hurt her? She didn't know him at all.

"Do you love your husband?"

"I love being his wife. I have position and respect. And what about you?" Her question was more like a challenge. "Do you love another woman?"

"For years, Jade, I allowed myself to love only you. But now, yes, I love someone else."

"Then go to her, Stephen. Do not try to stay in China illegally. You may find yourself rotting in a political prison or worse."

"I'll go after I see my daughter."

Jade rose. Stephen struggled to get to his feet. He used the wall for support. His head brushed against a beam of the low wooden ceiling.

They faced each other in the fading light of the tiny room. "Mindy is away from Peking with her brothers," Jade said. "Her father sent our children far away to his family's ancestral home when you started all this nonsense."

"Then you'll have to bring her back," Stephen said. "I have a right, Jade. I think even you know that."

She stared up at him, her eyes luminous even in the dim light. "Very well," she said at last. "Then do you promise me that you will leave?"

"Yes, I'll leave then."

"You can't stay here," Jade said. "Those men will try to extort more money from me, and I had a difficult enough time raising their first request. I'll have to take you someplace where you can hide, but we can't risk a taxi. I doubt if you can walk."

"I'll walk."

Jade nodded. "It will be tomorrow evening or the next day before I can get Mindy back here to Peking."

"I want to be clean when I see her."

"Yes, of course. Help me up through the trapdoor. I'll hand you down something to stand on so you can get yourself out of here."

As slight as she was, Stephen struggled to boost her up through the open trapdoor. He had no strength left. He had to find some water to drink, or he was going to pass out.

She handed him down a wooden crate, and he managed to get himself up through the opening. He sat down on the ground floor, his chest heaving. Jade went into the next room and came back with a cup of water and some rice wafers. Once again, she knelt in front of him.

Stephen sipped at the water and nibbled on the wafers. "Is your hair still long?" he asked.

"Yes."

"May I see it?"

Jade hesitated, then pulled the cap off her head. Her hair fell gracefully about her shoulders, framing her face. The heavy fragrance of gardenias heightened. Stephen reached out and touched a blacker-than-black strand with his fingertips. Yes, Jade was still just as beautiful. He could imagine her in a brocade dress with a high mandarin collar, elegant as she stood beside her important husband. But her beauty no longer touched him because the woman herself no longer did. That love could die made him sad. But even as he grieved, his soul opened and swelled for his new love. Jenny.

"Her name is Jenny," he said out loud.

"Who?"

"The woman I love."

## Chapter Thirteen

Jenny didn't need to ask Barbara how her date had gone the previous night. The dreamy expression on her friend's face said it all as she drifted by carrying two Styrofoam cups of steaming coffee. Barbara walked past without even noticing Jenny as she stood visiting with two other teachers in the empty school corridor.

"Barbara! Don't I even get a 'Good morning'?" Jenny called after her.

"Oh, Jenny, I didn't see you standing there. I was just coming down to your room with coffee."

Jenny fell into step beside her. "Just to set the record straight, you were *floating* down to my room. The librarian must have been a success."

"His name's Justin," Barbara said as though that explained something. She stopped for a minute in the middle of the hallway and got the dreamy look back on her face.

"Justin's a nice name, and I take it he was a nice man," Jenny said as she unlocked the door to her classroom. Barbara followed her inside, handed Jenny her coffee and sat down at Jenny's desk.

"Well?" Jenny asked, leaning against a student desk and taking a sip of the coffee. Barbara had forgotten the sweetener. Jenny put it down on the corner of her desk. "I want to hear everything. What's he like? What'd you do? Is he attractive?"

"Attractive?" Barbara said, cocking her head to one side as though recalling the man's appearance. "Well, yes, I think so. He has the sweetest, shyest smile. His ears do stick out a little, but I think that's kind of endearing, don't you? Men don't act like God's gift to women when their ears stick out."

"Well, I hadn't ever thought of that," Jenny said, "but I suppose stuck-out ears are a bit humbling. I had a boyfriend in high school like that. Well, go on. What was Justin like?"

"He loves Emily Dickinson," she said.

Barbara had done minimal makeup this morning. Her hair looked slept in, and the blouse she was wearing could have stood a little touching up with an iron. But she looked prettier than Jenny had seen her in a long time. It was like someone had taken an eraser to the frown lines on her face.

"We all love Emily," Jenny said patiently.

"And Byron. He can recite Byron. And Donne. 'No spring, nor summer beauty hath such grace, as I have seen in one autumnal face.'"

Jenny covered her mouth with her hand to keep from laughing. Barbara didn't seem to notice. "So, what else did you two do besides recite poetry?"

"We took a walk."

"You bought a new dress and had a professional manicure so a man could take you for a walk. And you *like* him?" Jenny asked.

"We're in love," Barbara explained. "He's the dearest, gentlest man I've ever met. He's going to meet my kids this weekend. If he survives that, I'm going to marry him."

Jenny stared at her friend. "*Marry*? My goodness, Barbara, you just met him."

"Oh, we'll go together first," Barbara said with a vague wave of her hand. "I'll make sure he doesn't squeeze the toothpaste from the middle, or whatever it is you're supposed to find out about a man before you marry him."

"A hell of a lot more than that," Jenny said emphatically. "Like how does he stand on kids?" Jenny asked. "He doesn't expect his next wife to have one last baby, does he?"

"He and his first wife had five children, and they're all grown now," Barbara said, staring at her manicure with a critical expression. "He says five is enough."

"I would agree. What happened to his poor wife?"

"She died. I think I'll keep my nails polished. It looks glamorous, don't you think?"

Jenny couldn't help it. The laughter erupted. It was terrible of her, but she couldn't hold it back. She knocked over the coffee as she put her hands around her middle and bent over, growing weak with hysterical laughter because Barbara was in love, after one date with a widowed librarian who recited poetry about autumnal faces, had five kids, ears that stuck out and took his dates on walks.

"That's not funny," Barbara said indignantly.

"I know. Of course it's not," Jenny said wiping the tears from her eyes. "I'm sorry. I'm not laughing because his wife died. I'd probably be dead, too, if I had five kids." And she started laughing again. She was going to make Barbara mad if she didn't stop.

For a moment it looked as though Barbara was considering anger, but finally she started laughing, too. "I really do love him," she insisted, her head bobbing up and down, her shoulders shaking.

"I think it's wonderful," Jenny said, wiping tears from her eyes, "You won't get charged for overdue books and walking is good for the figure."

"And poetry for the soul," Barbara said through her laughter as the first bell began to ring. She rose to go. "I think I'll go enlighten my students about John Donne."

"You teach *American* lit first hour, remember?" Jenny said.

"I guess that's right, although I doubt if any of them would notice if I threw in an English poet. I just feel like Donne today. 'Twice or thrice had I loved thee, before I knew thy face or name.'"

"Go," Jenny ordered, pointing at the door. "I think you're demented."

"Donne also wrote 'As souls unbodied, bodies unclothed must be, to taste whole joys.'"

"If you just went for a walk, I doubt if you tasted any 'whole joys,'" Jenny commented.

"No, but we talked about it," Barbara said over her shoulder with a suggestive little wiggle of her fanny as she walked toward the door.

"Am I to assume that you are officially over Chuck?" Jenny asked.

"Chuck who?"

THE CRACKLING VOICE coming from the public address system informed Jenny that she had a long-distance phone call in the office.

"Be prepared to answer the questions at the end of the chapter when I get back," she told her students as she hurried out the door.

The clamor in the room erupted before she'd even closed the door. Sure, they'd look up the answers to the questions, she thought sarcastically, just like they'd clean the blackboards and dust the erasers while she was gone. But then, it'd been that way when she was in school. Kids would be kids, she supposed.

Please let it be Stephen calling, Jenny thought as she rushed down the hall to the office. Who else would be calling her long distance? Her parents perhaps, but they'd call her at school only if there was an emergency. Jenny hurried faster. Or Joe and Paula could be calling from their honeymoon on Padre Island. That might mean an emergency, too.

Jenny picked up the telephone on the counter and turned her back on the curious gazes of the two office aides. "This is Jenny Bishop." Her voice was breathless.

"Please hold for General Mansfield," a crisply efficient female voice said.

General Mansfield? Who was he? Jenny searched her brain. It did seem as if Stephen had mentioned a general named Mansfield. Jenny took a deep breath and waited.

Shortly a male voice said, "Mrs. Bishop, Israel Mansfield here. I'm Stephen Carmichael's commanding officer at the Pentagon. Before he left the country, he gave me your name and instructions on how to get in touch with you."

"Has something happened to Stephen?" Jenny's hand flew to her breast.

"Then you haven't heard from him?"

"Not since he called from Seattle almost three weeks ago."

"I see. Well, we've been out of touch with Stephen for several days now, and I'm beginning to be concerned. I called on the off-chance that you might have heard from him, and also because I promised Stephen I'd call you if... well, if he ran into any problems. And I think we have a problem."

"Tell me." Jenny's heart pounded, fighting against the fingers of fear that encircled it.

"He's been missing for five days," the general's voice explained. "His belongings, including his passport and billfold, were all found in his hotel room. The Chinese government has formally requested his immediate expulsion from the country, but the American embassy in Peking has been unable to locate him. Frankly, I'm concerned."

"Perhaps he located the woman he was married to," Jenny said, unable to make herself use the word *wife*. "Perhaps she knows where he is."

"Officials at the embassy thought of that, but if the woman lives in the country, the Chinese aren't saying," Mansfield explained. "I'm not sure what's going on, but I'd sure like for our people to find him first. He hasn't made himself very popular with the Chinese."

"I saw the publicity he's been receiving," Jenny said.

"That must be difficult for you. I gather that you were one of the precipitating factors in this trip of Stephen's. He was wanting to wipe the slate clean, so to speak, and get on with his life. I just hope he hasn't gone off half-cocked and made matters worse.''

"You sound like more than just his commanding officer," she said, noting the concern in the man's voice.

"Yes," the general admitted. "My wife and I are very fond of him. Stephen's been rather like a son to us. Well, I'll keep you posted, Mrs. Bishop. I'm sorry if I've alarmed you, but on the other hand, I'm rather alarmed myself."

The general promised to keep her posted and gave Jenny his private telephone number and told her not to hesitate to call him if she heard anything.

Jenny went into the empty teachers' lounge and sat on the vinyl sofa. She had to have a minute to collect herself before she faced the zoo back in her classroom.

Lost in Communist China. It was incomprehensible. Jenny thought of all those millions of people in that endless, alien country. How would anyone ever find him?

A shiver went through Jenny's body. He'd have to find himself. *Please come back to me, Stephen. I love you so much.*

IT SEEMED AS IF they had been walking forever. After being given the water and rice wafers back in the house where he'd been held captive, Stephen felt himself reviving. The walking had actually made him feel stronger, but soon his legs ached incessantly, and his stomach was protesting the sudden input of food and liquid after being empty so long. Surprisingly, however, he was free from his headache for the first time since that goon had hit him.

And his spirits soared. He would soon see his daughter, and he could love Jenny without guilt now. Jade was in his past.

*"We played at being happy,"* Jade had said. Was that all it was? A game. He had always been so proud of his exotically beautiful wife. He had adored his daughter. He had felt an incredible sense of responsibility toward his little family. He had assumed Jade's passive acceptance of their life and the physical side of their marriage was her way of showing love. He had assumed too much, it seemed.

Jenny wasn't passive. She had met him halfway, and he had no doubt that she had wanted him every bit as much as he wanted her.

Stephen wondered if Jade's Chinese divorce was legal in the United States. But legal or not, she wasn't his wife anymore. He could think about her without longing, even without remorse. His remorse was for Mindy, for he had lost his daughter into the bargain, but even that pain could be borne. He thought of the old prayer asking for the strength to change what could be changed and to accept what could not. He could not organize a commando raid and kidnap Mindy, then carry her back to America with him. He wasn't a commando, and Mindy would not want to come. China was her home. Stephen knew he had to accept that, and he had the strength to do that now. His love for Jenny made him strong.

Soon he would go home to Jenny, a free man unfettered by his past.

Home to Jenny. What a sweet thought that was. But where was home? Was it Graystone? Her apartment? His apartment in Washington? Someplace else?

Then with a blinding flash of insight, Stephen suddenly realized where home was. It was wherever Jenny was. Jenny herself was his home.

He wasn't homeless anymore.

Jade was leading him through an endless series of alleyways. She kept having to stop and wait for him.

"Can you not walk any faster?" she asked angrily. "I need to return to my home before I am missed."

Stephen didn't bother to answer her. He kept congratulating himself that he was still on his feet. Finally they were climbing an outside wooden stairway to the second floor over some sort of business establishment. An ancient woman admitted them to a small room lit by a single light bulb dangling from an electrical cord and furnished with a simple wooden table and chairs, a cot, an ornate lacquered chest with rows of photographs along the top and a charcoal brazier in the corner. The walls were decorated with a mirror, a picture of former Chairman Mao and some delicate floral prints. A darkened alcove, apparently a kitchen, could be seen beyond. The room was warm, Stephen realized gratefully.

Jade spoke at great length to the woman in Chinese, then explained to Stephen that the woman had once worked for her family as a servant. The old woman's son had lived there, but he recently had gone to work on a cooperative farm in the interior, and for the present, she lived alone. The old woman had the most wrinkled skin Stephen had ever seen and was missing several teeth. She was dressed in a quilted outfit similar to Jade's, which did not disguise a humped back.

"She is trustworthy for a price," Jade said. "I am sorry that there is no shower or tub, but I have told her you will want lots of hot water. She will wash your clothes for you. And for God's sake, do not go any-place tomorrow. We are in the outskirts of the city, and no Westerners ever come here. The police would hear about you within minutes."

Stephen nodded.

Jade looked directly at him with dark Oriental eyes, her face devoid of any expression. She could have been a carving. Human faces weren't so flawless. But her voice was human.

"You hate me, don't you?" she asked.

"No, I'll never hate you," Stephen said. And he didn't. Maybe he had the right to, but it seemed so futile. He didn't love her either.

"Thank you," she said with a small bow. "I am glad. I will return tomorrow evening with our daughter. You will not try to confuse her, will you?"

"No. She needs to be content with her life. I just want to set the record straight."

Jade left him with his hostess. A little while later, the woman fed him a meal of noodles mixed with mush-rooms and tiny bits of what seemed to be chicken. Stephen was aware of the woman's eyes on him, and he didn't want to appear a barbarian, but he wolfed down his food and wished for more. He could have wept for joy when the woman gave him a cup of wine. He held the cup in both hands and forced himself to sip at it slowly. It burned all the way down, but at last he felt warm. And almost immediately light-headed. This stuff must be a hundred proof, he thought. When he got to his feet, he stumbled a bit. Sleep would be good.

After his meal, the humpbacked old woman indi-cated Stephen was to take off his filthy clothing. Too weary for modesty, Stephen obliged and washed himself, using the basin of hot water she provided, then wrapped himself in a threadbare cotton robe.

The woman opened the door and peered out into the darkness. She indicated Stephen was to follow her quickly, and she led him to a latrine behind the building. She waited outside for Stephen, then hurried him back up the stairs.

Indicating that Stephen was to sleep on the cot, the woman took a pallet out of the chest and laid it in the corner of the room for herself. He supposed he should be gallant and choose the pallet instead of the cot, but the thought of sleeping on a bed overcame the feeling.

The mattress on the cot was stuffed with straw and was hard as a brick, the pillow even harder. But the bedding was clean, and a quilted cover seemed like an incredible luxury. As he closed his eyes, his thoughts turned to Mindy. Tomorrow, at last, he would see her again. She would be fourteen years old, no longer a little girl. How angry it made him, that he had lost those years of his daughter's life.

He wished Jenny could meet Mindy. He wondered if the three of them would ever be together. The present Chinese government would never give him another visa to visit her, but governments change or are overthrown. If that happened, perhaps he could bring Jenny here to visit China's historic places and to meet his daughter. Or perhaps Mindy would be allowed to attend an American university.

Before sleep took him, Stephen let himself think only of Jenny. He smiled to himself. He was back to normal after his ordeal, it seemed. When he returned to America, he wanted to hole up with Jenny for days. He wondered if she could go back to Washington with him. He doubted if he could ever get enough of Jenny, but it would surely be fun trying.

How soon could he marry her, he wondered. Would he have to go back to court and get an American divorce? Whatever it took, he would do it.

DRESSED IN HIS own freshly laundered clothing and newly shaven, Stephen sat stiffly at the table in the small room, waiting. He was getting claustrophobic from all the little rooms where he had lived out these past few days, and he was restless with the waiting. When would Mindy arrive?

His little girl. He was going to see his little girl again. Stephen kept having to wipe his eyes. After all these years, it was overwhelming to think that the time was really at hand. But it would not be the joyous reunion he had always envisioned. There was to be no homecoming. Instead of the rest of her childhood, instead of a lifelong relationship with his daughter and her children on his knee, he knew it was quite possible this one meeting would be the last contact he ever had with Mindy. At best, it would be years before he saw her again.

The old woman sat on the other side of the table reading a newspaper with a small magnifying glass. The sound of the pages turning seemed loud in the quiet room.

Stephen wished he had his watch. He wondered how the Chinese woman knew what time it was since there seemed to be no clock at all in the apartment. Maybe time wasn't important to her anymore. Did time become faster or slower because you couldn't clock it, he wondered.

His skin itched from the strong soap he had used to wash. Nervously, he scratched at the back of his hands. Then he got up for the second time to stare at his face in the mirror. He looked gaunt, and his skin was irritated from the dull razor the woman had provided for him. There had been no shampoo, and the soap had made his hair dry and lifeless. He straightened his shirt and returned to his chair. God, the waiting was excruciating.

Finally he nodded off a bit and was awakened by the sound of footsteps on the stairs. Stephen leaped to his feet and faced the door.

The old woman went to the door, opened it a crack, peered out, then opened it to admit Jade, elegant in Western clothing, and a pretty young woman wearing a school uniform.

Mindy. My god, she was a young woman. Stephen was prepared for her to have grown but not to look so mature. The Oriental influence in her features had grown stronger as her childish plumpness had fallen away, but her predominantly Western blood showed in her wavy, brown hair, and her brown eyes were less hooded than her mother's.

Mindy walked up to Stephen and offered a little bobbing curtsy. "Father, it is good to see you again."

"You used to call me 'Daddy,' Stephen said. "May I embrace you?"

Mindy nodded, and awkwardly, Stephen reached out and put his arms around the young woman who had been a child of seven when he last saw her. He put his face against her hair. She smelled lemony and clean. She was slight like Jade, but was taller than her mother, tall by Chinese standards.

Stephen closed his eyes. He couldn't stop the tears and hoped his daughter would not be embarrassed by them. "Ah, Mindy baby, you'll never know how I've missed you, how sad I've been without you."

When he released her, Mindy looked over at her mother for direction. Jade was standing with the old woman by the lacquered chest. Dressed in a smooth-fitting black sheath, Jade looked like the elegant woman Stephen remembered. She nodded reassuringly at her daughter. Stephen took Mindy's arm and led her to a chair. When they were seated, he wiped his eyes and said, "Do you remember all your English?"

"I study English in my school, and on Tuesday evenings, English is spoken at the dinner table in our home. We speak Russian on Thursday. My brothers are very young, but they also are beginning to learn English and Russian."

"What else do you study?" Stephen asked gently. She was afraid of him. It showed in her eyes. His own daughter. She looked like a captured fawn.

"I study Russian, mathematics, world history, chemistry, piano." She kept looking at her mother's face.

"I don't know what your mother told you, Mindy, but I never wanted you to leave, and I didn't know she was going to take you away. I just came home one day and you both were gone. It made me very sad, and I have searched for you ever since. I wanted you to stay in America and be my daughter forever."

Mindy looked down at her hands.

"Do you remember how you would sometimes hide when I came home from work, and I didn't get my hug until I found you?"

Mindy nodded ever so slightly.

"And do you remember you and your mother and I used to ride our bicycles along the Potomac? And the picnics we had in that park by the apartment building? And the afternoons we spent at the zoo or the Smithsonian? At the Smithsonian, you always wanted to see the writing on the head of the pin. Do you remember what the writing said?"

"The Lord's Prayer," Mindy said in little more than a whisper.

"General and Mrs. Mansfield still have that old fat pony you used to ride. What was his name?"

"Porky."

Stephen was crying again. "And do you remember how you used to come running into the bedroom on Sunday morning and jump on top of me and tell me that I was Porky?"

Mindy nodded. She was crying now, too. She didn't pull her hands away when Stephen reached for them.

"All I ask, Mindy, is that you not forget the life we had together and to remember that I loved you then, and I love you now, and I'll always love you. Nothing can change the fact that I'm your father, and I've gone through all sorts of hell to come here to Peking and tell you that. I want you to know that if you ever come back to America, you'll come into my home as my daughter. Will you remember all this? Will you remember what I've said?"

Mindy bobbed her head up and down. Then her face fell into her hands, and her shoulders shook with silent sobbing.

Stephen fell on his knees beside her chair and took the sobbing girl into his arms. Mindy's arms slid around his neck, and he held her tightly. He sobbed with her. His chest hurt with the sobbing. Why did life have to be so damned sad?

He needed Jenny more than ever now. With Jenny, he could find happiness once again. The hurt over Mindy would always be there, but damn it, the rest of him was going to be happy.

# Chapter Fourteen

Jenny let herself into her apartment and dumped her school things and purse on the coffee table, too tired even to fix her usual cup of tea. She fell back on the sofa and sat there, trancelike, wondering, pondering, even dozing.

Each day it was becoming worse—the getting up and going to school, making it through the day, getting ready for the next day. Jenny was glad the year was almost over. She was tired. These past two weeks had been very difficult for her. The strain of thinking every time the telephone rang, it might be Stephen, the discouragement when it wasn't him, the frustration of not knowing what had happened to him, the uncertainty with which she faced the rest of her life—all had taken their toll. Jenny had not been sleeping well, and she'd lost interest in food. She was getting sick and tired of people asking her if she didn't feel well and found herself snapping an answer back at them.

She had even snapped at her boys on the telephone, reminding them how hard she worked to keep them in college and that they'd better study hard for those exams and make a good showing, and if the truck broke again, they'd just have to walk.

Jenny was still sitting on the sofa when she heard a key in the front door. "Mom," Joe's voice called.

"In here," Jenny said.

Joe, Barry and Paula came trailing into the room. "What are you doing sitting here in the dark?" Barry demanded as he switched on a lamp.

"Where's dinner?" Joe said, peering into the kitchen.

"Oh, my gosh, it's *Wednesday*," Jenny said, getting to her feet. Dinner. She tried to remember what was in the freezer. She couldn't afford to take them out.

"You forgot," Joe wailed. "Even the cherry pie you'd promised. All the time I was slaving away on that chemistry final, I kept reminding myself that in just a few more hours I'd be eating my mom's cherry pie, warm, with ice cream on top."

"Okay, Mom, what gives?" Barry said, his tone sounding like that of a stern parent talking to an errant child.

"Yeah," Joe added, "even Grandad and Grandma have noticed that you're not yourself. You forget to call them, and Grandma says you sound vague when they call you."

"Good grief, do I have to be a cheerleader all the time?" Jenny stood in the middle of the living room, her hands on her hips. She felt the heat rising in her neck. Damn it, all she needed was one more person telling her she 'wasn't herself.' "It's the end of the school year, and that means grading one hundred and twenty exams and figuring one hundred and twenty semester grades. My best friend is probably going to get married and leave me alone in the ranks of the single. I'm facing middle age and grandmotherhood. I pulled out three gray hairs this morning. I'm living on the edge of poverty. The sofa needs recovering. I have a blister on my little toe that is killing me. The car is leaking oil. The new research job I've taken on has led to a dozen dead ends, and the people are demanding their deposit back if I don't come up with a skeleton in the closet pretty soon. So, you will excuse me if I'm not doing my usual joyful Jenny act.''

Then she burst into tears.

Her sons stared at her in open-mouthed wonder. Paula was at her side in an instant, her arm around Jenny, leading her back to the sofa, saying soothing words.

"What the hell . . .'' Barry began.

"Shut up,'' Paula said, pushing her glasses back up on her nose and glaring at her brother-in-law.

"You want to tell us about him?'' Paula asked gently. "It might make you feel better.''

"What are you talking about, Paula?'' Joe asked. "Did I miss something here? I don't recall anything about a *him* in all that tirade. I remember blisters and leaking motor oil, but no *him*.''

"Men are so stupid sometimes,'' Paula said to Jenny. She kept a firm arm around her mother-in-law.

Jenny leaned her head against Paula's shoulder. It was comforting to have physical contact with a caring human being. Barbara was off in Never-Neverland all the time with her librarian. The kids had been busy with finals. She couldn't believe she'd forgotten they were coming tonight when she'd been so lonely and in need of company.

"Do you want them to leave?'' Paula said. "The two of us can fix some sandwiches and just do girl talk.''

"Did I ever tell you I'm glad you married my son?" Jenny said gratefully. "No, let them stay."

"Sit down," Paula ordered.

Joe and Barry looked at each other, shrugged and sat down.

"Did he run out on you?" Paula asked sympathetically.

*"Paula,"* Joe said. "That's my mother, not some sorority sister."

"Are you sure you want them to stay?" Paula asked again.

Jenny nodded. "It's okay."

"Who ran out on you, Mom?" Barry demanded, ready to protect his mother's honor. "If some guy's hurt you, I'll give the son of a bitch what for."

Jenny sat up straight and folded her hands in her lap. "Sit down, Barry. I guess I might as well tell you the whole story. First of all, Stephen Carmichael is not a son of a bitch."

She took a deep breath and began explaining how she had fallen in love with an Army colonel who was sort of married and had gone off to Communist China searching for his long-lost wife and daughter, when he was really in love with Jenny and was now missing in Peking, and she didn't know if he was dead or alive and was worried sick.

"Wow," Barry said when she was finished. "Well, you sure know how to pick 'em, Mom."

"You're really in love with the man, aren't you?" Paula asked.

"Yes, I know it's hard for you kids to realize that people my age fall in love, but I can assure you it happens with the same intensity and pain and joy. And even if I never see Stephen Carmichael again, I refuse to regret it. I wouldn't have missed him for the world, and I feel a whole lot better just sharing all this with you three. Part of my problem has been loneliness."

"You should have talked to us sooner," Paula chastised. "We're family."

"Well, family, I know you are hungry, so come give me a hug, and we'll go look in the freezer. I think there's half a lasagna and a few other leftovers stashed away in there."

Jenny stood and opened her arms first to Joe and then Barry, then the two of them together with Paula joining in. "I love you all so much," Jenny said, her voice catching. "I'm very blessed to have such wonderful kids."

"Ah, Mom," Barry said. "We love you, too. I'm sorry you're having a bad time."

What decent, good kids they were, Jenny thought. No matter what happened with Stephen, it was reassuring to know she'd always have them in her life. And the new baby.

And if Stephen came back and married her, he would inherit the best ready-made family ever.

STEPHEN CAUGHT a military transport out of Tokyo. He tried to call Jenny before the plane took off. He called the school first, but she'd already left. Next, he called her apartment, but there was no answer.

When the plane landed at McCellan Air Force Base outside of Sacramento, an airman was waiting for Stephen. "Sir, are you the Army officer wanting a flight to Oklahoma?" he asked with a smart salute.

Stephen returned the salute. "Yes, I am."

"We're holding a flight to Tinker Field for you."

"Do I have time to make a phone call?"

"They're revving up the engines now, sir. I have a Jeep waiting."

It looked like Jenny was in for a surprise, Stephen thought as he followed the airman to the waiting Jeep. He looked at his watch. Only a few more hours until Oklahoma City.

JENNY WENT into the teachers' lounge for her morning cup of coffee. Mildred Lambert, the girls' physical education teacher, was showing pictures of her new grandbaby, and Jenny lingered a bit. Babies had a whole new fascination for her these days.

She wasn't in a rush to get back to her room, since she'd already put a study outline on the blackboard for her students to use in preparing for their final examination. Today was "Everything You've Always Wanted to Ask About History but Were Afraid to Ask" day. The students could ask any questions about the semester's content and hopefully clear up any misconceptions before the test on Friday.

Barbara came bursting into the room looking bright and crisp in a yellow blouse and a kelly-green skirt.

"Look, I've had my ears pierced," she announced to Jenny, pulling back her hair. "I'm going to wear gold hoop earrings like a Gypsy. I never could stand clip-on earrings. It's a bright new, earringed world for Barbara."

"What does Justin think about pierced ears?" Jenny asked.

"I could have my nose pierced, and he'd think it was adorable," Barbara said. "I can't decide if I'm more in love with him or in love with being loved. Whatever, it's wonderful. Next, I'm going to get my hair tinted. I decided I'm too young for gray hair."

"It seems like only yesterday since you were ready to become fat and matronly," Jenny teased, "but I guess it was at least two weeks ago."

"Say, honey, you've lost weight," Barbara said, scrutinizing Jenny's figure. "Don't pine away, okay. I can't stand for anyone to be unhappy when I feel so full of joy."

"I'm fine," Jenny assured her. "I wouldn't stand in the way of your joy for the world. Go for it. God knows, you deserve it."

Jenny stopped in the office to get her mail before going to her room for first hour. "Oh, there you are, Mrs. Bishop," one of the student office aides said. "Did that man find you?"

"What man?" Jenny asked, sorting through the envelopes and messages.

"The hunk in uniform," the girl said, rolling her eyes. "I told him where your room was."

For an instant, Jenny felt rooted to the spot. The hunk in uniform?

Suddenly she was running, weaving her way through the milling teenagers in the hall. The first bell rang, and locker doors slammed. It had to be him, Jenny thought. It had to be.

"Mrs. Bishop, can I take my test early?"

"Can't talk now, Mark," Jenny said darting around one boy and running into another.

She rounded the corner, and he was standing there outside her room. Students were giving the uniformed Army officer curious looks as they hurried by.

"Stephen," she called.

He turned in her direction. And in an instant, Jenny knew.

She would remember this moment for the rest of her life—the clanging locker doors, the hall full of rushing students, the smell of floor wax, how handsome Stephen was, how her heart felt like it would burst in her chest.

Stephen had come back to her. Whatever had happened in China had not changed the love in his eyes. He was the most beautiful sight she had ever seen in her life.

And he was grinning. He looked like a boy—a happy, excited boy.

She ran the last few steps and threw herself into his arms.

"Jenny, darling Jenny," he said as he engulfed her in his hug, lifting her feet off the floor.

Jenny didn't care that she was a middle-aged history teacher with a hundred pairs of student eyes watching. How could she not kiss him?

The hallway around her came to life. As the second bell rang, students who were going to be late to their classes lingered to offer catcalls and whistles.

"All right," a boy's voice called out. "Let's hear it for the Army."

"Yeah, Army," someone else said.

"Go for it, Mrs. Bishop."

There was pandemonium all around. Students were pouring out of Jenny's classroom to see what was going on, but she had to kiss Stephen again. She took his dear, beautiful face with lipstick smeared all over his mouth and kissed him again and again.

Barbara came to investigate and took charge, dispersing students in her most authoritarian voice. Then she ordered Jenny and Stephen on their way. "I'll manage somehow," she told Jenny. "I'll make your classes write 'I will not talk in class' five hundred times. Go."

"Barbara, this is Stephen Carmichael," Jenny said, suddenly remembering the two had never met.

"No kidding. I thought he was a textbook salesman. Go, forth, my children, and be good to each other. I'll tell them in the office that you had to take one of your emergency days."

Jenny looked at Stephen and grinned. She reached up and wiped at his mouth. How funny it was to see a uniformed colonel with lipstick on his face.

She grabbed his hand, and they raced out of the building. Was it possible to be happier than she was right this minute, she wondered.

Stephen had come home to her.

Life was beautiful.

THEIR NEW LIFE TOGETHER began in the shabby comfort of Jenny's apartment. There was no hurry. They had waited too long, and they had the rest of their lives.

Each caress, each kiss was full of wonder. That the dream had come true was difficult for Jenny to comprehend. Would she wake up and be alone?

But as passion grew, and their bodies became moist with desire, Jenny understood that this indeed was reality. This man was hers for as long as they both would live. Their coming together was such a poignant mingling of reverence and desire and promise. The joy of it!

Stephen was her love—her one, complete and everlasting love.

They clung together, touching, kissing, whispering countless endearments. When they loved again, tenderly this time, it was with tears and pledges of forever.

When at last they could put passion aside and talk, they talked far into the evening—of Stephen's China saga, of their shared future. How good and brave this man was, Jenny thought. And how he must have suffered to leave his daughter behind. More than her own happiness, she wanted to make Stephen happy.

Jenny outlined the features of his face with a fingertip. Such a wonderful face—strong and handsome and sincere. She'd like a son who looked just like him. Or a daughter. And soon. Stephen would like that, Jenny decided, thinking how much he loved Mindy.

"I didn't know such happiness existed," Stephen said, planting dozens of kisses across her forehead.

"It's only just beginning," Jenny promised.

# Epilogue

Timothy Carl Bishop cocked his head to one side while the grown-ups gathered around the table and his mother put a tiny cake with one candle on the tray of his high chair. A larger, decorated cake stood safely out of his reach in the center of the table. A flashbulb popped as his father, Joe, took his picture.

The celebrants were gathered in the dining room of Jenny and Stephen's new home in Norman, Oklahoma. Stephen had been working like a Trojan all week to get the kitchen and hallway painted in time for the party, which was to be a combination birthday party and house warming.

Jenny worried at first that Stephen would regret selling Graystone, but she had to agree with him that the house was too expensive to maintain and too elegant for their informal life-style. "Can you imagine raising a child with silk wallpaper?" he had asked. For by that time, Jenny was proudly pregnant.

Graystone had been purchased by the state historical society and was soon to be a museum celebrating its own and the state's glory years when oil was called black gold and life was gilt-edged.

Jenny had spent the first summer of their marriage with Stephen in Washington, D.C. Then, with General Mansfield's reluctant recommendation, Stephen had managed to get himself reassigned to the Reserve Officers Training Corp unit at the University of Oklahoma, where he taught military theory to college students. He still planned to take early retirement from military service in just two more years and begin a teaching career. Next semester, he was going to take some course work at the university in preparation for that day.

Jenny had given up teaching for the time being and had more research jobs than she had time for, what with remodeling their new home and chasing a crawling infant around. Sometimes she wondered if her body hadn't played a terrible trick on her letting her have one last baby. Beth Ann was exhausting. But Stephen was wonderful with her and did more than his share of the parenting duties. And it was such fun having a little girl after twenty years of mothering boys.

Six-month-old Beth Ann sat in a second high chair next to her one-year-old nephew, Timmy. The flame on the candle caught Timmy's attention, and Paula grabbed his hand just as he was about to touch it.

"Happy birthday to Timmy, happy birthday to you," they all sang happily.

"Blow, Timmy," Stephen said, offering him a demonstration of blowing.

Barry knelt in front of his nephew and made blowing motions. Timmy looked around as his great-grandparents, Carl and Maxine, and Grandmother Phyllis and Grandfather Bill also began making blowing motions. Jenny got the giggles at how foolish they all looked.

Jenny's father had suffered a heart attack only the month before and had the look of a man whose days were numbered. But Carl was grateful, he had told his family, that he had lived long enough to see his daughter happily married and to get to know his first great-grandchild and his last grandchild.

Beth Ann reached for the flame from her adjoining high chair. Barry grabbed her hand. "No, hot," he told his baby half sister. "No, no."

Beth Ann looked up at him with great serious eyes, then with no warning grabbed a fistful of Timmy's cake. Timmy seemed to think that was a good idea, and with Joe snapping stills and Barry taking movies, the moment was recorded for posterity.

Beth Ann held out her handful of chocolate cake to Timmy. He leaned his head forward and started licking at his young aunt's hand like a little puppy dog. Beth Ann stared at him, fascinated.

Jenny stepped back into the circle of her husband's arm, relishing the happy scene that was taking place around her.

The babies were getting chocolate cake and icing all over themselves, each other and the trays of their high chairs. Beautiful, funny, rosy-cheeked babies, who made them all laugh—her daughter and her grandson.

Barry moved in for a close-up of the two babies. He had a mustache now and looked older, more like the actor he was determined to be. His girlfriend, Linda, was smiling from across the table. Barry and Linda had dated off and on over the past two years, but the two young people were still more interested in careers than marriage at this point in their lives.

Joe and Paula were impossibly busy with parenthood, jobs, school. Jenny didn't know how they did it, but somehow they'd arranged work and school in non-overlapping schedules most days so Timmy didn't have to go to the sitter any more often than necessary. The young couple didn't spend as much time together as they would like, but they managed to remain very much in love in spite of occasional squabbles and frequently frayed nerves.

"Your daughter is making a pig of herself," Jenny told Stephen.

"Yeah, but a cute one. I'll put them both in the bathtub in a few minutes."

"That's a good idea," Barry said, turning his camera on Jenny and Stephen. "We can get some shots of them playing in the tub."

"You sound more like a director than an actor," Linda said.

Stephen leaned forward and whispered into Jenny's ear, "Hey, pretty lady, who are you going home with after the party?"

"Why, sir, you sound like you have designs on my body," Jenny whispered back.

"You got it," he said.

"And we're already at home."

"Yeah, isn't it wonderful?"

"You happy?" Jenny said, squeezing his hand.

Stephen nodded. "Yes. I'm a happy man. Thank you, dearest Jenny, for my life."

Beth Ann decided she'd had enough of the cake and held out her arms to her father.

"You look like Tar Baby," he said, as he carefully extracted the gooey child from her high chair.

"Bring your grandkid, Jenny. It's bath time for these two."

THE LETTER FROM MINDY arrived the following day. The postmark revealed it had been several months enroute.

> Dear Father,
> I received your letter informing me of the birth of your child. I rejoice to know I have a sister in America and hope that someday I will have the opportunity to meet her. She is a very fortunate little girl to have you for a father. When Beth Ann is old enough to understand, please tell her of me and tell her that she is often in my thoughts as are you, my Father.
>
> How strange to think that soon you will no longer be in the Army. So many of my memories are of you in a uniform.
>
> My mother sends her regards to you and says I must tell you that I do well in school and make her very proud.
>
> You and your family have my warm wishes for a happy future. I am respectfully your loving daughter,
>
> Mindy

Stephen cried. Jenny cried with him. His sorrow was hers, as were his joys.

Whatever life brought, they would face it together.

# ATTRACTIVE, SPACE SAVING BOOK RACK

Display your most prized novels on this handsome and sturdy book rack. The hand-rubbed walnut finish will blend into your library decor with quiet elegance, providing a practical organizer for your favorite hard-or soft-covered books.

**Only $9.95**

**Approximately 16" x 8" when assembled**

*Assembles in seconds!*

---

To order, rush your name, address and zip code, along with a check or money order for $10.70* ($9.95 plus 75¢ postage and handling) payable to *Harlequin Reader Service*:

Harlequin Reader Service
Book Rack Offer
901 Fuhrmann Blvd.
P.O. Box 1396
Buffalo, NY 14269-1396

BKR-1A

*Offer not available in Canada.*

*New York and Iowa residents add appropriate sales tax.

# Harlequin American Romance

## COMING NEXT MONTH

# *Harlequin American Romance*

## With Barbara Bretton, the password is adventure

Maggie and John discovered that getting involved with Uncle Alistair and PAX meant nonstop action and hijinks. But how could they complain when it also brought them each other?

Catch all the exploits of the men and women of PAX, as Ryder O'Neal, electronics wizard, and Joanna Stratton, master of disguises, join forces to save the royal family—and become one of their own—in #193 *Playing for Time*.

And don't miss the chilling climax when Max Steel's and Kelly Madison's commitment and fortitude are put to the ultimate test in #274 *A Fine Madness*, coming in December 1988.

Join Barbara Bretton's PAX organization . . . and experience the adventure!

---

**HARLEQUIN SUPERROMANCE BRINGS YOU...**

# Lynda Ward

Superromance readers already know that Lynda Ward possesses a unique ability to weave words into heartfelt emotions and exciting drama.

Now, Superromance is proud to bring you Lynda's tour de force: an ambitious saga of three sisters whose lives are torn apart by the conflicts and power struggles that come with being born into a dynasty.

In *Race the Sun*, *Leap the Moon* and *Touch the Stars*, readers will laugh and cry with the Welles sisters as they learn to live and love on their own terms, all the while struggling for the acceptance of Burton Welles, the stern patriarch of the clan.

*Race the Sun*, *Leap the Moon* and *Touch the Stars*...a dramatic trilogy you won't want to miss. Coming to you in July, August and September.

The Welles Family Trilogy